THE BEST OF TEM

Too hot to handle? Maybe a little,
but this 2-in-1 collection of sassy, sexy romances
will have you captivated from page one.

Filled with steamy nights and sizzling days,
these classic stories explore what happens when
a fun, flirty woman meets an irresistible man.
The result of such chemistry is often explosive,
usually unexpected and always unforgettable!
We're sure you'll agree….

These tempting tales prove that sometimes reality
can be even better than your most private fantasies!

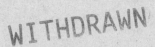

JILL SHALVIS

New York Times and *USA TODAY* bestselling author Jill Shalvis is an award-winning author of over four dozen romance novels. Among her awards are the National Reader's Choice and the prestigious RITA® Award. Visit www.jillshalvis.com for a complete book list and a daily blog chronicling her *I-Love-Lucy* attempts at having it all: the writing, the kids, a life....

New York Times Bestselling Author

JILL SHALVIS

Who's the Boss?

and

Her Perfect Stranger

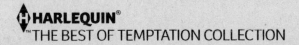

HARLEQUIN®
THE BEST OF TEMPTATION COLLECTION

Recycling programs
for this product may
not exist in your area.

ISBN-13: 978-0-373-60625-2

WHO'S THE BOSS? AND HER PERFECT STRANGER

Copyright © 2014 by Harlequin Books S.A.

The publisher acknowledges the copyright holders
of the individual works as follows:

WHO'S THE BOSS?
Copyright © 1999 by Jill Shalvis

HER PERFECT STRANGER
Copyright © 2002 by Jill Shalvis

Printed in U.S.A.

™ www.Harlequin.com

CONTENTS

WHO'S THE BOSS?

To good bosses everywhere, especially mine—
D. S. Builders.
You're the best.

1

"A JOB," CAITLIN TAYLOR muttered for the hundredth time. She paused from straightening her silk stockings to roll her eyes upward with a wry grimace. "I hope you and God are having a good laugh, Dad. You certainly got the last one on me."

Her heart ached as it had all month, ever since her father had unexpectedly passed away from kidney failure.

It might have hurt a little less, she admitted, if he hadn't given away his fortune to everyone but his own daughter. Instead, he'd left her...a job.

At least he'd done that. In her ice-blue satin lingerie, she faced the full-length mirror. Her reflection wavered as fear gripped her, but she had no illusions. Her naturally wavy blond bob, no matter how she combed it, made her look as if she'd just climbed out of bed. Her overly curvaceous body refused to be tamed by exercise. This morning, her deep brown eyes were heavy from lack of sleep, and already carefully accented with liner and mascara. She looked like a young, beautiful woman with the world at her fingertips.

If only it were true.

Caitlin gave a half laugh and shoved back the unaccustomed fear and panic.

She'd never held a job in her life. Her father had spoiled his only child. In all her twenty-four years, she had only a handful of memories of him, mostly due to his heavy traveling and prominent social schedule. Still, as her only family, he'd made sure her every material need had been met. Fashion had been her first love, and he'd given in to it. Milan, Paris, New York, Los Angeles…she knew these places intimately; they were her playgrounds. She'd gone to designing school in Paris and New York, both on her father's bank account, but the truth was, she wasn't talented enough to make it in that cutthroat world. Since then she hadn't been idle—far from it, for organizing society events was a particular talent of hers, even if it didn't count as a job, or earn her money.

Her father had kept her in style, making sure she had a healthy monthly allowance deposited directly into her account.

That had stopped abruptly with his death, and grief had been forced to take a backseat to survival.

With every credit card her father had ever given her maxed out, less than one month's rent in her bank account and no more allowance, Caitlin faced serious trouble. Enough trouble, she'd finally admitted to herself, that she'd have to swallow her pride and take the poor-paying job she'd been left in her father's will.

"A clerical position," Caitlin said with another humorless laugh that didn't quite cover up her confusion and pain. "And me not knowing the difference between a fax machine and a scanner."

She walked to her brimming wall-length closet and sighed, knowing that by this time next month she would be living in some dismal little apartment. Bye-bye southern-

California beachfront condo. Again, her heart leaped at the betrayal of her father's abrupt desertion. *Why?* she wondered frantically. Why would her father indulge and spoil her all her life, then desert her this way? She didn't understand, but wallowing was getting her nowhere.

With effort, she shrugged into the devil-may-care persona she showed the world. What did one wear for a job that required an eight-o'clock showing? But while she dressed, her thoughts continually drifted back to the burning questions—why had her father pawned her off on some little subsidiary of what had once been a huge engineering conglomerate? A conglomerate split up by his will, all the pieces going to different investors who'd been his close friends.

Friends had rated higher than his own daughter.

Now Caitlin was slated to work for some pencil-laden, calculator-carrying engineer nerd named Joseph Brownley. Because he'd worked with her father for years, she imagined him as old, crusty, tough. Mean.

Shuddering, she slipped into what she hoped looked businesslike enough—a short red crepe de chine suit. The pumps she added gave her an extra three and a half inches, *and* some badly needed self-confidence. She wanted to look sophisticated. Polished. But while she seemed to be able to fool everyone else, she couldn't pull the wool over her own eyes. She looked flighty, ditzy and wild, which sent her back to the bathroom in another attempt to tame her hair with ruthless brush strokes and styling spritz.

She could do this. But for one weak moment, she sank to the bed. Could she? Could she do anything but organize parties for the rich and famous? And how hard would it really be to charge for those services?

Hard, she admitted.

So hard she'd rather do this…work in an office.

But could she really survive on her own?

Swallowing back a sudden sob, Caitlin lifted her chin and forced a bright smile. Her knees trembled as she stood, but she stiffened them and lifted her chin. She had no place in her life for pathetic self-pity or fear, only determination.

The outfit didn't work.

Too showy, she decided with a hasty glance at her slim gold watch. She ripped off the suit to try again, tossing it carelessly aside. No telling what Mr. Brownley thought of tardiness, but if he fired her before she'd even started, she'd really be in trouble. And with her only true working talent being that she could navigate the mazed streets of any garment district blindfolded, who else in his right mind would hire her?

Coming to yet another abrupt halt in front of her mirror, she took a tough, no-holds-barred look at herself. Snug, cropped frost-blue sweater over a long, flowing flowery skirt. Heels, of course—she never went anywhere without heels. But too casual, darn it! She added a muted linen jacket and hoped for the best. As she ran to her car, huffing and puffing from the exertion of the morning, she grumbled about the unearthly hour.

God, she hated mornings.

She thrust her little BMW into gear, leaving her exclusive Newport Beach neighborhood hours before she normally even stirred from her bed. As she hit the packed 405 freeway, she realized her first mistake in allowing only thirty minutes to get from the beach to downtown Irvine. It seemed the entire population of southern California started work at the same time, and given that she was cut off three times before she even hit the first on-ramp, apparently everyone was just as irritable and late as she.

At the interchange, no one would let her over. Frustrated, she tried one of her flirtatious winks and got...a very rude hand gesture.

Did normal people do this every day?

The thought made her shudder. Yes, she was sheltered, but she had friends who worked. *No, she didn't,* she reminded herself. Hadn't she learned that in the past few weeks, as one by one, her so-called friends had ditched her when the terms of her father's will became public?

She was alone, truly alone, for the first time in her entire existence.

And she was going to be very late. No big surprise, of course. Her father had always claimed she'd be late for her own funeral. She'd certainly been late for his, but that had been because the limo she'd counted on all her life had vanished. Repossessed. By the time she'd driven herself, she'd missed the entire service. She knew her father wouldn't have been surprised, but she had a feeling being late *today* was a luxury she couldn't afford.

This little bubble of stress sitting uncomfortably in her belly was new and entirely unwelcome. So was the apprehension about her future, and the lingering, gnawing wound of her father turning his back on her.

She came to a grinding halt in the fast lane, surrounded by thousands of other idling cars. Never one to obsess about anything, she couldn't believe she'd been doing just that all morning.

Shaking her head, she cranked up the music, sat back to wait out the traffic and cleared her mind.

JOE'S FINGERS FLEW over the keyboard. Deep in concentration, he'd been working for hours, but he couldn't stop now. He was so close, so very close, to getting it right.

"Joe."

Vaguely, he heard a female voice calling him, and just as vaguely, he knew it was Darla.

He ignored her.

All those years, he'd had to work on hardware, designing computers for his bread and butter...but no more. Now, with Edmund Taylor's generosity in death—Joe's heart squeezed at the reminder—he could work on his first love. *Software.* And he was inches away from perfecting the system he envisioned revolutionizing every office in the country.

"Joe."

Just another few minutes, he thought, stretching cramped legs that were far too long to be shoved beneath a desk for so many hours. A few more minutes and things might click into place. He could almost hear the big software companies knocking at his door. *Bill Gates, eat your heart out.*

"Joe? Yoo-hoo..."

Without taking his eyes off the keyboard, he growled, waving one hand wildly over his shoulder, his usual sign for *Leave me the hell alone!* With the ease only the hyper-focused can achieve, he sank back into his thoughts. *Just put that command here instead of over there—*

"I'm sorry, Joe."

"No problem," he murmured automatically, not looking up. Why had he chosen to work in the front office, instead of his own down the hall, which would have given him more privacy?

Because he'd been in a rush, that's why. Always in a rush. "Go away."

"Joe," said a now laughing Darla. "Could you *please* look at me?"

With a sigh, he straightened, biting back his impatience. He shoved his fingers through already unruly hair and took his gaze off the screen long enough to glare at the only person who would dare interrupt him. "What? What do you want?"

Darla smiled sweetly. "Lovely to see you, too."

"Great. Nice. Now go away." He'd already turned back to the computer when she spoke again.

"Joe, could you focus those baby blues this way for just another minute? Pretty please?"

"I'm really busy," he said evenly, through his teeth. His fingers itched to get back to the keyboard.

"But—"

"*This*," he announced, "is why I need an assistant. To keep people out."

"You couldn't *keep* an assistant," Darla told him, gesturing to the cluttered office, which admittedly looked as though World War III had gone off in it. Papers were everywhere. So were books, files and an entire city of computer parts. "No one but those other crazy computer programmers you've got back there wants to work for a perfectionist, a workaholic, a technical—"

"*Why* are you here? Just tell me that much," he begged, resting his fingers on the keyboard and eyeing the screen longingly.

"Oh, wipe that frown off your pretty face—I'm not here to bug you for your tax info. Yet."

Darla's insulted scowl worked, and Joe laughed. As the only accountant in their small building, the tall, waiflike Italian beauty had taken on all of the other four businesses in the place, his included. Besides handling most of their bookkeeping, she dished out unwanted advice, unsolicited sisterly affection and more than a few good dirty jokes. "And what could be more important than tax stuff?" he teased, and resigned himself to a break.

"Not much." She grinned, too, making her look much

younger than her thirty years. "But remember that assistant you were just mentioning? I think she's arrived. I saw her roaming around downstairs, scrutinizing the different suites and the business names on the front board as if she had no idea where she's going."

"I didn't hire an assistant."

"You told me Edmund wrote off his investment in this company, making it effectively yours—as long as you guaranteed his pathetically spoiled daughter a job."

"Yeah." Joe rubbed his hand over his chest at the twist of pain. Edmund, gone. Forever.

At the thought of Edmund's daughter, whom he'd never met, his usually receptive heart hardened. "She never even bothered to show up for her own father's funeral." He tried to remember what Edmund had told him about her. A flightly clotheshorse. A party girl. A world traveler— on her daddy's budget, of course.

Nothing particularly flattering.

"Whoever you saw couldn't be her," he stated. "A software company that has yet to prove itself has nothing to offer a socialite."

Darla shrugged. "Maybe not. But Marilyn Monroe's here." She sniffed and gave him a haughty glance that he had no trouble deciphering.

Joe wasn't ashamed to admit he'd had more than his fair share of women flit in and out of his life, and his good friend Darla had hated most of them. But nothing got her goat more than a blond bombshell. "She looks like Marilyn Monroe?" he asked, unable to contain his wide grin when Darla rolled her eyes. "Really?"

"Barbie meets *Baywatch,* actually," she snapped, making him laugh. Darla snorted in disgust. "What is it about that blond, wide-eyed, come-hither look that renders a man so stupid?"

"Ahh…a come-hither look?"

She glowered and straightened, her considerable height accentuating her thinness. "And she's got huge—"

"Darla," he said, still grinning as he cut her off. "She's *not* looking for me—she couldn't be. No way would Edmund's daughter show up." He hadn't read all of Edmund's book-length will, hadn't been able to bring himself to even open the five-inch-thick file that had been sent to him by Edmund's attorney, but he imagined Caitlin Taylor had gotten a very nice chunk of change. She'd have no need for a job.

He glanced at his watch. "And anyway, it's ten o'clock. What kind of an assistant would start work this late?" He happily gave his computer his full attention. "Now go away and let me be."

"Okay…but you asked for it."

Breathing a sigh of relief when she was gone, Joe looked at his screen with anticipation. Now he'd get some work done.

He'd simply kill the next person who interrupted him, he decided, and promptly forgot about everything except what he was doing.

In the back of his mind whirled the vision of his program up and running. And for once, thanks to Edmund, that dream was obtainable.

"Ahem."

Not again! He needed a weapon. Yeah, that was it. A squirt gun, maybe, or a—"Excuse me."

"If the place isn't burning down," he growled, "then I don't—" Out of the corner of his eye, he saw her; words vanished from his brain. She was petite, luscious and one of the most beautiful women he'd ever seen. She smiled and his tongue actually went dry.

"Hi," she said, wiggling her fingers at him.

Trailing behind her, gawking with their collective mouths hanging open, were Vince, Andy and Tim, his three techs. At the moment, they resembled Larry, Curly and Moe. He sent them looks loaded with daggers, and they slunk back, closing the door behind him.

"I'm looking for Mr. Brownley," the exotic creature said in a sweet, musical voice. "I'm Caitlin Taylor."

Caitlin Taylor. Professional socialite. Ditzy, spoiled princess...*his new assistant.*

An imaginary noose settled around his neck. He liked gorgeous women as much as the next guy—maybe even more—but no way could he work with one, especially one with the lifestyle and attitude this one was reputed to have. He couldn't respect someone who didn't know what tough work meant, or the value of a hard-earned dollar, and Joe never worked with anyone he didn't one hundred percent respect. Never.

"This is CompuSoft, Inc., isn't it?" Her voice could arouse the dead, and Joe wasn't, unfortunately, dead. "I checked the suite number downstairs," she said. "You must be the receptionist."

He groaned inwardly and stood up from the front desk. *Never again,* he promised himself. He'd work from the seclusion of his own office from now on.

She flashed another dazzling smile, leveling him with a pair of warm, dreamy brown eyes so deep he felt like swimming. "My father—"

Shit. Her father. His own mentor, beloved friend, father figure. Edmund Taylor had meant everything to him, and Joe had made him a promise. The noose tightened. "Your father told me about you," he managed to say around the month-old lump in his throat.

"He did?" She seemed surprised. "So you know I'll be working here?"

Joe nodded, wondering what to do. He'd never broken a promise and he didn't want to start now, especially not when it came to Edmund, but he had absolutely no use for this woman in his company. None at all.

"Maybe you can tell me something about this place. About the boss," she added with another sweet smile as she moved gracefully into the room. Her skirt flowed around her ankles, clung to her thighs. The light blazer she wore parted in the middle, revealing her sweater, snugged tight over her soft, perfect curves.

In any other situation, Joe knew he'd be flashing his most charming smile and already be deeply into flirt mode. This sort of woman was made for seduction, and while he didn't want to employ one, he loved the interplay.

But playing with her would be pleasure, and this was serious business. *His* business. His pride and joy. Dread filled him at the thought. With this woman around, none of the guys, all of whom drooled at anything in a skirt, would get an ounce of productive work done.

"Is he nice?" she wondered with a slight frown. "Patient?"

"Who?"

A little laugh escaped her. "The boss, silly. You know, Mr. Brownley."

"Uh...nice? No," he said decisively, standing. The top of her head didn't quite meet his chin. She was petite, feminine, beautiful. And he didn't want her here. "He's really...awful. Hard to work for. *Ugly,*" he added desperately.

Caitlin's brow puckered as she considered this. "That really doesn't have anything to do with—"

"You should leave. Now." The idea sprouted from nowhere. He wouldn't be breaking his promise if she left, right? It wouldn't be his fault. "You should go before he sees you."

Caitlin cocked her head to one side and studied him sympathetically. "He makes you nervous, doesn't he?" She inhaled deeply, drawing his attention downward. Dangerously downward, causing his hormones to do a quick, instinctive dance.

"Don't worry," she told him with a confidence he could see was more bravado than anything else. "Maybe now that he has me to help him, he'll be nicer."

Guilt stabbed him. "Uh...yes...well..."

"Things will work out," she soothed, her face open and clear of anything but genuine emotion, which only deepened his guilt. "You'll see. I'll fawn over him a bit. You know, mother him."

Joe had never been mothered, and maybe because of that he tended to have a low opinion of anyone who relied heavily on those family-type affections. "That probably won't help much," he admitted.

"Everyone needs mothering."

"Not everyone." Not Joseph Brownley. He didn't need anyone. Period. Never would. But she seemed so optimistic, while at the same time so touchingly full of nerves, that he lost his desire to continue the farce, even if she were just a gorgeous piece of fluff. "Look—"

"It's all right," she said gently, nodding her head. Wild blond hair flew around her face, cupping her rosy cheeks, framing huge eyes that were surprisingly sharp and self-aware. "I'll be fine."

"No, you don't understand—"

"Yes, I do. You're trying to be kind."

Kind. Joe might have laughed. He'd certainly never been accused of kindness before. "No," he assured her with a tight smile. "I'm not."

"You don't have to tell me how bad of a monster he is." She swallowed hard, making Joe feel like a first-class jerk. "I really can handle it. Just…point me in the right direction." Her voice was a whisper now. "And I'll find out for myself."

Hell. "You already have." Apology softened his voice, and he sighed with regret.

"What do you mean?"

Oh, he was going to have to face this, whether he wanted to or not, but on the other hand, so was she. This was no place for her, and the sooner she realized it, the better for the both of them. "I mean you probably should have left while you had the chance."

Her eyes reflected her confusion, and he didn't blame her. "I'm the monster," he said. "Joe Brownley."

2

"*YOU'RE* JOE BROWNLEY?" Caitlin tripped over her tongue, but she couldn't help it.

She was shocked, to say the least.

"I'm afraid so."

"But..." Good Lord. Well over six feet of rangy, powerful male stared back at her. His ice-blue eyes narrowed, cloudy with thoughts he hid with ease. Although with that square, unforgiving jawline, she could guess he wasn't especially thrilled. His sun-tipped light brown hair curled carelessly over his collar, as if he couldn't be bothered with it. Wide, huge hands rested on his hips, his feet placed firmly apart. He looked utterly poised and self-assured. He wore a plain white T-shirt that bulged over impressive biceps, and faded, snug jeans that fit the man all too well.

He looked like a ruffian. A hood. A gorgeous, *temperamental* hood.

What happened to her old, pencil-laden, calculator-carrying geek? This man was young—early thirties at the most—sharp and, judging by his scowl, tough as nails.

At first he'd seemed sweet and friendly, but no longer. Now he was the complete opposite. And to think she'd been worried about *him,* and his fear of the wrath of the "boss"!

"Oh, dear," she whispered. "This isn't going to work out at all."

Relief flooded his features, softening them. "Really?"

An audible groan came from the other side of the wall. In a flash, Joseph's scowl was back. He reached around her with one long arm and yanked open the door. Three guys—at least two of whom fit her computer-geek image to the last microinch—nearly fell into the room.

They recovered quickly, especially with the glare they received from Joe, and mumbling assorted apologies, slunk back down the hallway.

"Sorry," Joe told Caitlin. "We're short on excitement around here. You were saying this wasn't going to work out?"

She nodded, wondering how a computer nerd could possibly have such a low, husky voice, like fine-aged whiskey. "Yes. I'm sorry. But...well, in my experience, I don't work well with men like you."

He blinked. *"Men like me?"*

A sound came from behind the once again shut door. It sounded like a...snicker. Three snickers.

Joe inhaled deeply and ignored them.

Caitlin pictured the three men once again pressed against the closed door, listening with their ears glued to the wood. She might have smiled, were it not for the frown on Joseph's face.

"What's that supposed to mean?" he wanted to know, straightening his wide shoulders. "That you don't work well with men like me?"

It meant that she was tired of pushing away roaming hands and groping fingers from the kind of man who took her at face value. Tired of being patted on the head as if she were a toy, a pretty, empty shell of a human being.

It had been happening to her ever since puberty, which

had come unfortunately early. In her experience, the kind
of man most likely to treat her that way stood right in front
of her. Cool, collected, knowing, cocky.

"It simply means I'm sorry, Mr. Brownley," she said.
"But this won't work out at all. It's clear that you're a man
who needs no one. Certainly not me." Caitlin turned, got
to the door before she remembered something horrifying.
She needed this job desperately.

Without it, she was headed for the poorhouse. It'd been
so easy for her to forget that little detail, being a woman
completely unused to stress.

Could she find another job?

The idea almost made her laugh. With her qualifica-
tions, she'd be lucky to land the front-counter job at Del
Taco. Her hand stilled on the doorknob, and she grappled
with pride and fear and something even newer...annoy-
ance.

Why hadn't he wanted her?

"Did you forget where you parked your car?" Joe in-
quired politely from behind her.

Great. The sexy thug was a smart-ass to boot. "No."
Plastering her friendliest smile in place, Caitlin turned
back to face the sternest-looking cute guy she'd ever seen.
"I just thought that maybe..." Oh, how she hated to eat
crow. "Maybe I judged you too quickly."

He stared at her for a long moment, his cool eyes giving
nothing of himself away. They both ignored the multiple
sharp intakes of breath from the other side of the door.
"Does this mean you're *not* leaving?" he asked finally.

She winced at the unmistakable regret in his tone.
"That's what it means," she admitted. "Unless I'm fired."

"From what I know of you, you have absolutely no experience in much of anything, except maybe *social* studies."

She stiffened in automatic defense at the disapproval and disgust. "I can do this job."

He sighed heavily. "Dammit. I can't fire you anyway. It's complicated."

From the other side of the door came a joint sigh of relief that made her feel marginally better. At least his employees wanted her to stay. She relaxed marginally with relief. She hadn't failed yet!

I'll show you, Dad. I can do this. But then his words sank in. "You can't fire me? How come?"

His already impossibly hard jaw hardened even more. "Never mind. What do you know about being a secretary?"

"Uh—" What she knew would fit in her back pocket—if she had one. "I can make coffee," she improvised, drawing on the one skill she thought she probably shared with every good secretary.

Joe Brownley closed his eyes and groaned.

"And," she added brilliantly, completely undeterred by his response, "I have a really nice telephone voice!"

Joe was first and foremost a thinker. There was nothing he liked less than to not understand something—and he didn't come close to understanding Edmund's daughter. "Tell me this," he begged. "*Why* do you want this job?"

"Well...that's a long story." A shrug lifted her petite shoulders *and* her not so petite breasts, which were already straining against her sweater. "I doubt you'd understand."

"I'm of average intelligence," he said dryly. "Try me." Curious now, he crossed his arms and leaned back against the door frame. "You're rich as sin, princess. And I know for a fact your father had you in a beachfront condo, and a fancy car."

She laughed shortly, her doe eyes looking a little wild. "So why do you want a job like this?"

"I just do." She licked her lips. "And the will says you'll give it to me."

She was right, and the reminder of it was a slap in the face. Edmund had given Joe everything, *everything,* and in return he'd asked for only one little favor.

It was time to stop griping about it and accept the facts. For better or worse, he was stuck with his new assistant.

At least until she quit.

"Okay, Ms. Taylor," he said wearily, rubbing his temples. "Here's how this is going to work. I'm in the middle of something pretty important and hate to be bothered. I guess I could use someone to handle the phones."

A cheer went up on the other side of the door; Joe hauled it open. Again, the three young men stumbled awkwardly into the room. Immediately, they all straightened, tried to look casual.

Disgusted, Joe said, "These yo-yos are my techs," he told Caitlin. "Huey, Dewey and Louie."

Two of them were identical twins. One of the tall, skinny, dark-haired twenty-odd-year-olds stuck out his hand, a wide grin on his face. "Hi. I'm Andy." He pumped Caitlin's hand so enthusiastically, she feared he might pull her arm right out of the socket, but his expression was so kind, so sincere, she just smiled back, relieved beyond speech by the friendly face.

"I provide tech support to our customers," he said. "As well as keeping Joe here human by dragging him out of here every night."

Human? Could have fooled her.

"I'm Tim," said the other twin. He, too, grinned from ear to ear. "I also help with tech support, but basically Joe couldn't function without me because I have all the charm and personality."

Joe rolled his eyes.

Tim nodded. "It's true." He looked at Caitlin, his eyes shining with good humor. "And you're really great."

"Thank you," said Caitlin smiling, thinking they were pretty great, too.

The third, a medium-built redhead who looked to be in his early thirties, smiled shyly and kept his hands firmly in his pockets when he introduced himself. "I'm Vince. I work in product development with Joe."

"We've been wanting a new secretary," Tim said into the awkward silence. "Really bad. Ever since the last one… uh…left."

Andy nodded emphatically. "Joe scared her off, and—" He broke off at the look on Joseph's face.

Another awkward silence. Tim bit his lip. Andy stared at his feet. Vince watched Caitlin send a curious, cautious glance to Joe. "She, uh…didn't work out," Vince said diplomatically. "It wasn't really anyone's fault exactly."

Joe scoffed. "No need to mince words, Vince. You can tell her the truth."

Whether it was loyalty or simple resistance to Joseph's tone, Vince remained silent, stubbornly buttoning his lip.

"I'll tell her," Tim piped up in a stage whisper that everyone within three miles could have heard. He looked at Caitlin and confided, "Joe scared the last three women off. You don't scare easily, do you?"

"I…" She thought of her bills. Of the creditors. "No."

"Joe's not all that great with women," Tim said.

Vince laughed softly when Joe shook his head, disgusted.

"We begged him to get someone in here to do the filing and answer the phones. And to lighten things up a bit. You know—someone to have fun with. That's all. No offense, you understand," Andy said quickly.

"None taken," Caitlin assured him, delighted with her sweet new workmates.

"But the longest any of them lasted is about three hours," admitted Tim.

Looking into the frowning, incredibly handsome face of Joe Brownley, Caitlin had no problem imagining why. "You don't say."

Vince laughed again, and some of the tension dispersed. "He's all bark, no bite," he assured her, but some of his amusement faded when Joe glared at him.

"Why is everyone talking about me as if I'm not standing right here?"

Vince ignored him. "Sort of like a terrier," he elaborated. "Loud and gruff. Then passive as a kitten."

"Really?" She eyed the very annoyed Joe. The long, lean lines of his body were stiff. His eyes like ice. *Passive* was the *last* word she would have used.

"Back to work, guys," he said stiffly, his wide shoulders tense.

Tim hesitated at the door. "Nice to meet you, Caitlin. I hope you stay."

"Do you really know how to make coffee?" Andy asked plaintively. "Because—"

"Andy," Joe said, his voice careful and quiet. "Don't you have something, *anything,* to do?"

"Yeah, I guess." His shoulders slumped. "It's just that you make really crappy coffee, Joe. And—"

"I'm sure we'll have plenty of time to discuss the damn coffee," Joe grated out, clearly beyond patience. "I'd really, really like to get to work some time today. Would that be all right with everyone here?"

Vince leaned close to Caitlin, confiding, "He's only a bear because he's so close to finishing this project and all this other stuff keeps interrupting him. Phones, paperwork, stuff like that." He flashed a sweet smile. "Don't let him scare you off now, okay?"

He was so kind. So were the twins.

She couldn't remember if or when she'd been shown such simple, untethered friendship. Any friends she'd thought she had were gone. Vanished into thin air because she was no longer a somebody.

But these guys… They'd all looked her in the eyes instead of her chest—another plus in their favor—when they'd talked to her, and while it was obvious they thought she was pretty, they'd treated her with respect.

Caitlin smiled, embarrassed to feel her throat tighten up at reliving their warm, eager greeting. She'd never in her life felt so welcome—the still scowling Joseph Brownley excluded—and a realization hit hard. Everywhere she'd gone, everything she'd done, she'd either been accepted for her looks or for her father's money.

Never for herself alone.

Everyone left and she was standing here with her boss. She knew darn well *he* didn't want her, that he didn't think she could handle this job. But for some reason, he wasn't going to refuse her.

He caught her gaze with his, and his jaw went all hard again. Most of her resolve wavered and what little there was left took a bad beating at his next words.

"Okay, princess, here's how this situation is going to work."

Where had that nice man gone? The one she'd first spoken with, the one she'd thought was going to be her friend? She looked carefully, but couldn't see a trace of him. It was almost as if once he had realized he was stuck with her, he'd purposely turned himself into someone she wouldn't like.

Well, he'd been partially successful, she thought. She *didn't* like him, but she wouldn't run off because of it.

"Last door on the left is my office," Joe said gruffly, stepping into the hallway to point it out. "I hate to be interrupted, so stay out." He looked at her expectantly then, a little hopefully. Maybe she'd still run off if he were boorish enough?

As if she'd read his mind, she laughed at him. *Laughed.* The unexpected sweet sound had Joseph's stomach muscles tensing.

"Are you waiting for me to cower from such a fierce command?" She shook her head, her short blond bob flying. Her flowery fragrance wafted up, assaulting his nostrils, annoying him because she smelled so damn good he found himself straining for another sniff. "Or maybe, better yet, you think I'll run off with my tail between my legs."

Her words put a vivid picture in his mind of what *was* between her legs.

"Should I remind you whose daughter I am?" she asked, breaking into his startling sensual thoughts.

Her father had backed down to no one. "I know whose daughter you are."

"Good. And I don't frighten easily."

Mad at her, at his techs and at himself, he stalked back into the front office.

"Clearly," she muttered, "I'm to follow you."

Why today? he wondered helplessly. Why, when he was so damn close to finishing his program, did he have to deal with this? With a quick glance upward, he grimaced. *Thanks, Edmund. Hope you're getting a kick out of this.*

Caitlin passed him in the hallway. "Maybe I *would* be better off at Del Taco."

He watched as she sashayed prettily into the main office, her hips swinging in tune to his undisciplined hormones. "I'll give you a lift to the nearest one." Then, to soften the words he realized were unkind, he offered the sweetest smile he could.

She shook her head. "Well, I walked right into that one, didn't I?"

Her mouth was pouty, lusciously red, and the most inane thought popped into his head.

She must taste like heaven.

The woman was a blond bombshell, with a complete lack of work ethic, designed to torture him. And yet he couldn't stop thinking about what she'd look like spread across his desk wearing one of those come-hither looks.

"So...how many employees do you have here?" she wondered aloud, interrupting his erotically charged thoughts.

"Besides the three idiots you've already met, just me."

"And now me," Caitlin added.

"I'm doing my best to change that."

Ah, sarcasm. Well, she could understand that. The way he kept his big body so tense, she imagined he was quite uncomfortable. Most men, in her experience, fought unease with a sort of bearish aggression. Her father had been the king of that act, though he'd never used it on her, and she imagined this Mr. Brownley wasn't much different. "I'm sticking, Mr. Brownley."

"So you've said."

Her bravado was quickly taking a beating in the face of his stubbornness. Before she caved in completely, she tried small talk. "I thought CompuSoft was huge. According to my father, this place was the future of progressive software."

Incredibly, Joseph's eyes softened. His attitude vanished. "He said that?"

It was obviously an illusion that he suddenly appeared

so vulnerable. He was about as vulnerable as a starving black bear waking from hibernation. "He was quite proud of this place."

His throat worked. His voice sounded hushed, almost reverent. "I take that as a huge compliment."

Her father never complimented lightly, and just thinking about him hurt when she was tired of hurting. He'd rarely complimented *her.* To combat the thought, she desperately continued her one-sided conversation. "How could you have only the four of you here?"

"This is no longer the huge corporation it was under your father. We've been siphoned off, separated from all his other various businesses. We're on our own, just a few of us designing and supporting software." He gave her that impenetrable stare again. "You didn't get a copy of the will?"

Caitlin noticed that whenever he mentioned her father, he watched her carefully. But she could hear his thick disapproval, and her stomach tightened in response to the unfamiliar stress purling through her.

If he only knew how she'd pored over that darn will, wondering what had happened to her nice, cozy life.

If only he had a clue as to how lost she felt in this new, unsafe world, or how much resentment for her father she harbored deep down in her heart.

"Yes," she managed to answer with her usual cheekiness, refusing to let him get to her. "I got it."

"If the terms were too difficult to comprehend," he said slowly, finally succeeding in stirring her rare temper, "you should have asked someone to explain it to you."

"Contrary to what you must believe about me, I do understand the written word."

"*All* of your father's companies were divested. Compu-

Soft was half-mine to start with, so he simply willed me the other half."

Her father could give this man half a company, just hand it over, and he couldn't leave her a penny. Couldn't leave her anything but a measly job with a man who couldn't abide her. It took every ounce of common courtesy she had not to resent Joe Brownley for this.

Well, okay, that was a big fat lie. She *did* resent him. A lot. "Nice of him."

"Nice?" He missed the sarcasm and let out a short laugh that seemed harsh. "It was incredible. The most generous thing anyone's ever done for me—" He stopped abruptly, stared at her. "I have no idea why I'm telling you this."

She didn't, either. It hurt unbelievably to know her father had thought so little of his own flesh and blood that he'd left this man more than he had his only child. "Where do I start?"

"So you're staying, then?"

"Yes."

He sighed. "Fine. This is the reception desk." He gestured behind him to a wide desk facing the entrance. At least, she assumed it was a desk; all she could see were stacks and stacks of paperwork, files, various computer parts and what looked like an old, forgotten take-out food bag.

"All you have to do is come in on time, which around here is eight o'clock, and answer the occasional phone." He sent her a long look. "Can you do that?"

"Hmm. I think I can manage." She was really going to have to teach him a thing or two about manners. As for the ungodly hour, she'd have to work on it. "Surely you have more needs than just answering your phone."

His light eyes darkened. His mouth curved, making her

blink in surprise. Sullen, the man had been beyond hand-some. Smiling, he was stunningly gorgeous.

"I don't think you want to hear about my needs."

No. No, she didn't, Caitlin decided as her heart took off running. "Probably not."

Slowly, he ran his gaze down the length of her, then back up. When he met her eyes with his, an unmistakable heat radiated from them. Caitlin had been on the receiving end of looks like that ever since she'd grown breasts, so she'd long ago learned to tune them out. Yet now, under Joe Brownley's suddenly hot gaze, as unbelievable as it seemed, she felt herself blush. "Something wrong with my attire?"

"Yeah," he said in that low, disturbingly sexy voice. "In this office, you'll need something a little...more."

She'd known it! Her clothes were all wrong. "More?"

"Shapeless. Like a potato sack."

She laughed. "I wouldn't be caught dead in a potato sack."

"You're distracting."

"Your techs were refreshing and charming. I don't think I'll have a problem here with them."

He turned and started back down the hall, his long legs churning up the distance in just a few strides. "I wasn't talking about the Three Stooges, princess," he called back.

Oh.

Oh.

3

THE BUILDING THAT housed CompuSoft was small for downtown, Caitlin thought. But it was brick and glass and strangely cozy.

There was a small coffee stand on the lobby floor, complete with doughnuts, croissants and mouthwatering pastries. Caitlin couldn't resist stopping there before getting on the elevator, if only to drool.

After all, if she had to suffer mornings, then she needed junk food.

A lovely brunette woman, about Caitlin's age, wearing an apron and a harassed smile came up to her. "Can I help you?"

Caitlin thought of her last dollar drowning in the bottom of her purse. "How much is that chocolate thingie over there, last one on the row?"

"In calories or cents?"

Caitlin laughed. "Either way, I'm sure it's too expensive. Besides, I shouldn't. Oh, man, I really shouldn't." Ruefully, she tapped her curvy hips.

The woman let out a reluctant smile, which softened her entire face. Her green eyes sparkled with life that hadn't been there before. "This is what I tell myself every morning."

Caitlin eyed her spectacular figure—all willowy and slim. "How many do you eat?" she asked doubtfully.

She shrugged. "Depends on how rude the customers are, which varies. The more annoying jerks I serve, the more I eat."

Caitlin sighed and thought of Joe. "I'm afraid if I stopped here every time my boss annoyed me, I'd be busting out of my clothes in a week."

The woman laughed now, and gave Caitlin a much more genuine smile. "You're new here. I'm Amy."

"I'm Caitlin." She dug into her purse to appease her rumbling stomach, and accepted the huge chocolate pastry.

Amy grinned, removed her apron and grabbed a pastry for herself. "Just in case the crowd gets crazy later, I'll take my break now."

They pigged out together.

BY THE TIME he got to his office the next morning, Joe was high on adrenaline, his mind racing ahead, thinking about his software program.

With a little luck, he figured he could make real headway today, if he got in the good ten to twelve hours he needed.

As previously arranged, he had first stopped at one of the local banks to meet with a loan officer, hoping to start the preapproval process. He wanted to be prepared when his program was complete, so he could properly promote and sell it. To do that, he'd need money—a lot of it.

Despite the hassles ahead, he grinned and silently thanked Edmund for the thousandth time. Without the old man's generosity in deeding him CompuSoft, Joe wouldn't even be thinking about this for himself. Edmund had provided the means for Joe to spend the time needed to work on his program. With Edmund's death, that could have all ended for Joe, but it hadn't.

It was a dream come true.

Whether it was just his own bad luck or his unique ability to actually forget absolutely everything but his work, he entered his office and, completely unprepared, stared stupefied at the front desk.

It had been cleaned off, or rather cleared off—everything was on the floor. Amazing piles of important-looking stuff surrounded the base of the desk.

As he took a step into the chaotic room, he tripped and nearly fell flat on his face—over a pair of ruby-red four-inch pumps.

Empty pumps, he noted.

Which would explain the barefoot woman on all fours, facing away from him, affording him the best view he'd seen all morning. Apparently, both Tim and Andy felt the same way, because the two techs, who normally couldn't be budged from their computers, were on the floor, as well, making neat little stacks of God only knew what.

Caitlin's head popped up when he shut the door behind him, and she craned her neck around from where she'd been pulling out more stacks of paperwork from beneath her desk.

Hard as it was to imagine, Joe had completely forgotten about his new secretary.

"Good morning," she said in a sexy, cheerful voice that reminded him he still needed a cup of coffee.

Badly.

Tim and Andy leaped to their feet, faces red.

"Hey, Joe," Andy said quickly, sticking his hands in his jean pockets. "How'd it go at the bank?"

"It wasn't as exciting as it appears to have been here."

Joe lifted a brow as Caitlin stretched her lush, petite body as far as it would reach to get a file that had been shoved beneath the far corner of her desk.

Tim's and Andy's jaws dropped open at the sight, but Joe could hardly blame them. He couldn't remember ever seeing a finer looking rear end.

And he'd seen his fair share.

But his quick surge of lust, coming on the heels of forgetting about his new secretary—whom he hadn't wanted in the first place—only further annoyed him. Already half the morning was gone, and by the looks of things nothing had been accomplished except for a shifting of the mess from the front desk to the floor.

He sighed.

Hadn't he known this would happen if he kept her?

And dammit, hadn't he asked her to wear something to hide that body?

Women, like his work, received his full attention. But they were also simply a diversion—a pleasant one, but temporary nonetheless.

It had to be that way.

He'd grown up in emotional chaos. *Painful* emotional chaos. That's what personal attachments did. Chopped up the heart and spit it back out. Brought nothing but the opportunity for hurt. With hurt came weakness, and he couldn't allow that.

He relied on himself, and that was it. He'd been remarkably relationship free. By choice. And any entanglements he'd enjoyed had been short but sweet.

An involvement with a co-worker couldn't be temporary, couldn't be short and sweet and therefore couldn't be contemplated. No matter how fine the…assets.

To prove it, he purposely turned his gaze away from the incredible sight before him.

Tim and Andy still stood there stupidly, gawking like teenagers. Joe opened his mouth to bark at them, but Vince appeared in the doorway, glasses on his nose, disk in hand.

"Guys," Vince said sternly. "You came out here to check on Caitlin half an hour ago. What's going on—" He broke off at the sight that had rendered both Tim and Andy and then Joe speechless. Carefully, he closed his mouth. Then he glanced at Joe, both amusement and irritation swimming in his gaze.

Joe jerked his head sharply, and Vince nodded. "Tim, Andy, let's hit it."

Joe sighed when they disappeared and wondered exactly how long it would be before the socialite decided she didn't want to play at working anymore.

Hopefully very soon.

"Well, I beat you in," Caitlin announced, obviously expecting a medal.

"You should," he said, watching her wiggle up to her knees in the tightest, shortest, reddest skirt he'd ever seen. How had she gotten into that thing? "It's ten o'clock. What the hell are you doing?"

"Filing." She slapped her hands together to rid them of dust. "This place is a disaster. Don't you ever clean?"

"No, and I knew where everything is...*was*," he protected, trying not to panic.

"It'll be better," she promised him. "You'll see."

He doubted that and was about to tell her so but his phone rang. He watched, fascinated, as Caitlin stood and yanked down the short little jacket that matched her siren-red skirt before scooping up the receiver. "Hello?" Quickly, she covered the mouthpiece and batted her warm brown eyes at Joe. "Should I tell them this is Compu-Soft?" she asked in a loud whisper. "Or is that redundant, do you think, since they called us and they most likely know who it is they dialed?" She bit her full, red bottom lip in indecision.

"Just find out who it is," Joe suggested through his teeth. "That might be a good place to start."

She nodded quite seriously and turned back to the phone. "Yes, who is this, please?" Her brow creased in concentration. Her hair settled around her flushed face. Then she lit up with the most dazzling smile Joe had ever seen. "Oh, isn't that sweet of you," she gushed. "I'm sure he'd love that, yes. Thanks so much." She hung up the phone and dropped back to her knees amid the mess she'd created all over his floor.

Joe found himself once again staring at her very cute wriggling butt. "Caitlin." His voice came out slightly strangled, and he had no idea if it were irritation or something more basic, such as his own software became hardware.

She stopped wriggling and smiled at him. "Yes, Mr. Brownley?"

He knew for a damn fact she was only eight years younger than him and she was calling him mister. "Joe."

"Okay. *Joe.*" She turned back to whatever the hell it was she thought she was doing.

"Who was on the phone?" he demanded.

"Oh. AT&T." She sent him that same dazzling smile, the one that did funny things to his knees. "They're going to send you a one-hundred-dollar credit for switching to their service for a trial period of two weeks. Isn't that sweet of them? Though you probably shouldn't have left them in the first place. I understand from that nice operator I just spoke with they have the best prices in the country."

Joe closed his eyes briefly and reminded himself that though he relied only on himself, rarely allowing another into his life, he *had* loved Edmund. He owed the man, and this woman—this crazy, out-of-control, messy woman—

was his debt. "I'll be in my office," he managed to say finally.

She sent him a vague smile from where she was shuffling papers—*his* papers—around. "No problem."

As he turned to go, he tripped over her pumps, again.

SHE COULD DO THIS, Caitlin told herself. No problem. She'd gone through most of her life figuring things out by herself. She'd dealt with the death of her mother all those years ago. She'd dealt with traveling alone, celebrating holidays alone, generally being completely alone.

She could certainly answer a few phones and straighten up an office, especially since she didn't have much choice.

The bills had to be paid. She'd come home the night before to several messages from credit collectors.

They were getting nasty.

The phones had been blissfully quiet for a while. So had the men, though they were checking on her often, which brought a smile. They were so sweet.

Except for Joe. No one in their right mind would call that powerfully built thug, masquerading as a mild-mannered computer geek, sweet.

She headed down the hallway to the small lunchroom, which held a refrigerator, a microwave, a sink and counter and a small table with chairs.

She glanced at the coffee machine and grimaced. Empty, of course. It would never occur to whoever had taken the last cup to make more. Automatically, her hostess skills leaping to life, she made the coffee. Then, because the room was disgusting, she cleaned it. Maybe, she thought as she scrubbed, she'd been looking at this all wrong. She was an organizer, and these men certainly needed her.

Needed her.

The mere idea stopped her cold. And warmed her heart. No one had ever needed her before.

"How's it going?"

Caitlin, her eyes still misty, smiled at Vince as he came in. "Good." She finished with the sponge on the counter and started sweeping.

"Really?" He didn't look convinced; he looked worried. "I should congratulate you. You made it past the dreaded two-hour mark without quitting."

She thought of her late car payments. Of her rent, which was late, as well. She tried not to think of the stack of bills she'd filed away under her kitchen sink so she wouldn't have to look at them. "Oh, I'm not going to quit," she said with certainty.

"Well, that's a relief. You're like a ray of sunshine around here."

Caitlin glanced quickly at him, trying to decide if that had been a come-on. She'd become a pro at spotting them since she'd gotten curves at the tender age of twelve. But Vince simply smiled kindly. With that shock of deep red hair and Clark Kent–type glasses slipping down his nose, he was really kind of cute.

But Caitlin had decided long ago, the cute ones were *rarely* harmless. "That's me, just a ray of sunshine. I'm so bright you need sunglasses to look at me."

Vince laughed, but didn't make a move to come closer. Unbearably relieved to find someone *genuinely* nice, Caitlin relaxed. "Is it always so…uptight around here?" She graduated back to the sponge and wiped down the table that had an inch of grime on it.

"You mean Joe." Vince shook his head and leaned back against the sink, watching her clean with fascination. "He's just preoccupied. Ignore him. It's the best way." He frowned. "He didn't hurt your feelings, I hope, because he would hate that. He just doesn't have a wide focus. Work is pretty much all he concentrates on, and he really hates it when things get in the way of that."

"Well, someone should mention that work isn't everything in life."

"You handled him well."

"If that was well done, I'd hate to see him when he *isn't* handled properly."

"He's a good guy, Caitlin. Really. He's just under pressure right now. And he just lost Edmund—" He stopped, horrified. Color flooded his face. "I'm sorry. He was your father, so you know exactly how much Joe is hurting."

Yes, she knew and the thought of Joe mourning her father disconcerted and warmed her at the same time.

Joseph's grieving brought an image she hadn't anticipated and didn't know if she was ready to accept. "Which would explain how chipper he's been."

Vince let out a smile. "Well…truth is, he's just about always that way."

"But the rest of you—you and Tim and Andy—you're all so nice and welcoming. How do you do it?"

"Tim and Andy are really great. We've all been friends since…well, forever."

How wonderful those sort of ties must be. There was no one in her past with whom she kept in contact. "Tell me about all of you."

Vince laughed without embarrassment. "We were the proverbial school geeks. You know, the ones girls wouldn't even look at? Luckily, we'll get the last laugh. At our five-year reunion, we realized most of our school buddies are struggling with jobs like bagging groceries. Nothing beats this. Plus we still have hair."

She laughed. "And you're fit. At my reunion, the cheerleaders had gotten fat."

"See?" He grinned. "We're not fat. And we're doing what we love."

They were, Caitlin realized with a spurt of envy. She'd never found her place. She'd never really been satisfied. Maybe that was because she'd never really challenged herself, never held a real job.

That could change, she thought with hope. She could find her place. Maybe even right here.

The phone rang. "Just a sec," she said quickly, and then raced down the hall. "Good morning, CompuSoft— No, wait," she managed to say, breathless from her dash down the hall. "It's almost afternoon, now isn't it?" *Rambling.* A very unattractive trait. "Oh, forget it. Just hello."

She got a dial tone. "Well, hell."

"Nice phone manners."

Caitlin nearly leaped out of her skin at Joe's low, husky voice coming from directly behind her. Careful to roll her eyes *before* she turned to face him, she planted a smile on her lips. "So. You've come out of your cage."

"I smelled coffee—" He broke off abruptly when she suddenly shrugged out of her jacket.

Beneath the splashy red, she wore a sleeveless white silk blouse, pretty enough, and unremarkable but for the body beneath it. The soft material clung to her ripe curves in a way that made his pulse race. "What are you doing?" he demanded, backing up a step.

She laughed at the expression on his face. "Whatever you're thinking, that's not it." She dropped the jacket carelessly into her chair, kicked off her pumps and put her hands on her hips. "For your information, I just cleaned your filthy kitchen and I'm hot. Hence the jacket removal." She sent him a nasty look. "You guys are pigs."

She swung her hand out for emphasis and hit the lamp on the credenza.

Joe grabbed for it—a split second after it crashed to the floor, where it shattered into millions of jagged shards.

"Dammit!" he roared, falling to his knees besides his brand-new, very expensive zip drive. "What's this doing on the floor?"

"I was dusting. Do you have any idea how bad dust is for your computer?"

Strangling her was definitely wrong, he told himself. Carefully, he brushed away some of the lamp glass, but stabbed his thumb on a sharp, jagged piece. Swearing again, he pulled the sliver out of his skin and glared up at the woman who'd single-handedly brought chaos into his life.

Big mistake, looking up.

Kneeling at her feet, he found his face came to a very interesting level on her body. Interesting and erotic as hell. He forced his gaze past her tempting thighs, past the juncture between them, past the rest of her lovely curves and on to her unsettled, melting brown eyes.

"I'm sorry," she whispered, wringing her hands. "It's just that I'm—" Her stomach, inches from his face, growled noisily. "Hungry," she finished lamely. "I'm... very hungry."

Joe closed his eyes. "You're hungry."

"Yes." She nodded emphatically, pressing her hands to her belly.

At that moment, Vince walked in, his gaze widening slightly at Joseph's and Caitlin's suggestive pose. "Did I interrupt something?"

"Just me about to get fired," Caitlin said with a sigh.

Tim and Andy pushed their curious way into the front office, too.

"What's wrong?" Andy asked, after taking note of Joseph's fierce scowl.

"Everything," Joe said, glaring at Caitlin.

"It's really been nice knowing you guys," said Caitlin, smiling shakily at the three techs.

"Wait," Vince said quietly. He looked at Joe. "Wait a minute. Don't do anything rash."

"Yeah, Joe," Tim piped up. "You can't fire her. She made coffee. *Great* coffee."

"And she cleaned," Andy added. "Did you know the tile in the kitchen is *white?*"

Instead of detonating, as Caitlin fully expected, Joe just shook his head.

Then burst out laughing. A full, rich, very pleasant and contagious sound she'd never expected of him. While everyone stared at him, he laughed so hard, he doubled over, hands on his thighs.

Caitlin didn't get the joke. "I'm sorry about the zip drive," she whispered.

Silence. Apparently, for once not even Tim, Andy or Vince had anything positive or hopeful to say.

Instead, they all looked in unison at Joe, their expressions filled with the uneasy worry one gives another before shipping him off to the mental ward.

Joe sniffed, straightened, took a deep breath and said, "Well, shit. I guess it's lunchtime."

"Really, Joe?"

He looked directly at Caitlin, his eyes hooded. "Yeah. What the hell."

Relief and hope surged, made her laugh a little giddily. In that moment, Caitlin forgot that he didn't like silly, untrained women, and that she didn't like hard, know-it-all men who looked too tasty for their own good.

Maybe, just maybe, this would work out after all.

That's when the coffeemaker, still plugged in, burst into flames.

4

LUNCH SHOULD HAVE been simple. After they'd gotten rid of the fire department, the five of them—Vince, Tim, Andy, Joe and Caitlin—all piled into Vince's van.

But Tim and Andy couldn't decide on a place, and Vince kept making the wrong turn when Joe would call out directions. This would have normally greatly amused Caitlin, except for the fact she was pressed up close in the seat next to Joe.

Actually, plastered was more like it.

She found it a bit unsettling to feel the solid power of him against her, to realize how big he really was. And given the rigid way he held himself so as to minimize contact, he was obviously every bit as aware of her as she was of him.

"Wait! *That* way," Tim yelled, and the van swerved as Vince made the turn.

Caitlin could feel the strain in Joseph's body as he tried to remain completely upright and away from her. He didn't quite succeed and at the next quick turn, which came without warning, he had to lift an arm to the back of her seat to brace himself rather than fall directly on her. Still, his jean-clad thigh pressed against her. Their sides were glued together. She was surrounded by him, by his warmth, by his strength.

He smelled like burned coffee.

"Sorry," he said gruffly, and tried to pull back just as the van turned in the opposite direction, landing Caitlin practically in his lap.

"It's okay." She shot him a smile in spite of how her stomach tightened as the bare skin of his sinewy, tanned arm rubbed against her softer, much lighter one.

Their gazes met and Caitlin's smile faded. So did Joseph's. She pulled back, straightened herself. Joe withdrew his arm from around her, but he moved slowly, and she felt his fingers trace lightly over the back of her neck as he did.

She shivered.

Joe frowned at his hand as if he'd lost control of it and if he felt half of what she had begun to feel, then she completely understood.

THEY ENDED UP at one of her favorite restaurants.

Only problem was, everyone in southern California apparently wanted to eat there, too. Her nerves immediately reacted to the thought of waiting for a table in the packed bar, pressed tight against the man she tried to convince herself she disliked.

Caitlin would never be sure how it happened, but somehow she ended up at a cozy table for two—with Joe. The others had gotten a table on the other side of the restaurant, quickly and eagerly abandoning her in their haste for pasta.

Joe, looking slightly pained—and who could blame him? Caitlin wondered wildly—tried valiantly to smile at her.

She couldn't dredge one up in return. "I'm sorry about the coffeemaker."

"The fire chief said it wasn't your fault," he reminded her. "The cord was frayed, just a fire waiting to happen."

"Yes," she said miserably, blocking out the pleasantly noisy crowd around them. "But the zip drive...can't blame that on a frayed cord."

"It's done, Caitlin. Forget it."

She froze, stared at him over her menu. "What?"

"I said, it's done. Forget it."

"No." She shook her head. "Not that. The other."

"What other?"

"You used my name," she breathed, some of her innate good humor returning. "Without that big old frown on your face."

"No, I didn't."

"You did so. Oops, never mind. The frown is back."

They sat in silence. After a moment, Joe asked, "Was there something wrong with me being friendly?"

"No. Not at all. It was kinda...nice. Unexpected, but nice."

"I don't mean to be...unnice."

"I know." And she did. Somehow, she just brought out the worst in him.

He started to lift his water glass, but looked at his hand with a small wince instead.

"Oh, Joe, you're hurt from the glass! I'd forgotten." Grabbing his hand, she studied the base of his thumb. A cut marred the tough skin.

"It's nothing." He tried to pull his hand back, but she held firm as guilt and regret washed over her.

"I know I keep saying this," she told him. "But I'm so sorry." Without thinking, she lifted his hand to her mouth and kissed his palm, directly beneath the injury. "There."

Joe blinked, stunned, as heat and something far more purled low in his gut. Those full red lips lingered on his skin, making him instantly hard. He had to remind himself that he was reacting naturally to the outer package that made up Caitlin. Not the inner one—the airhead, the destroyer of offices. He cleared his throat. "Is that supposed to make it better?"

That quirky, contagious grin of hers crossed her face. "I think so. Or at least, I hope so. I always..." Her smile faded. "I always wanted someone to do that to my hurts. Silly, huh?"

That quick, sharp pang in his chest was heartburn—*not* in any way empathy. He assured himself of this. Promised himself. "No, it's not silly."

"Did it work? Does it feel better?"

Hard to tell, since the ache had settled in his chest, thick and unmovable. Joseph's world had been lived alone. Always alone. He'd learned early he could rely on no one but himself. *No one.* Not the authorities, not his friends and certainly not his parents. Anything he'd needed or wanted, he'd gotten on his own.

Like Caitlin, he'd once dreamed about having someone kiss away his pains. No one, to his recollection, had ever given a damn about him, not until her father had come along and dragged him off the fast track to nowhere. Edmund had saved his sorry hide, had been the first one to care, and now his daughter was staring at him with those huge dark eyes, wanting him to feel better even though it'd been *she* who'd turned his world upside down. "Yeah," he told her. "It worked."

Her beaming smile dazzled him, only this time his reaction was far more than just physical. It went deeper, and he didn't think he liked it.

He didn't want to feel this strange softening toward her. She was everything he couldn't stand. Unmotivated. With a serious lack of ambition. Little common sense.

With Edmund as her father, she'd had the world at her fingertips and what had she done? Thrown parties. Just remembering these things made him suitably irritated all over again, allowing him to forget that he'd almost, *almost*, started to like her.

Purposely, he hardened his face into the expression he knew could terrorize the toughest of souls. That should scare her. Keep him safe.

She smiled at him.

Dammit. How was he supposed to deal with that?

Around them, life continued to the music of clinking glasses and tinkling china. Voices sounded, some low and muted, some not. Laughter. And the smells… In another time and place, his surroundings might have fascinated him; he enjoyed watching people.

Today, he had eyes for only one person, and that bugged him. He stayed tucked behind his menu, pretending to scrutinize the list of entrées he had already memorized. What was happening to him?

It was her clothes—that's what. Her amazing eyes. That infectious laugh. They were all designed to attract a man. Clearly, she enjoyed being looked at.

Knowing this about her helped him control the lust, because if he ever decided he wanted more than a passing fancy with a woman, which he wouldn't, it would be with one who wanted *him.* It would be with a woman who didn't send out signals to anything in pants. A woman who loved him heart and soul—him and only him.

This woman could do none of those things, and telling himself so helped. A little. But nothing could control his lethal curiosity. "Tell me about your father."

She looked startled, then she shrugged. "You knew him better than me, so there's nothing to tell." She set her menu down and before he could continue his line of questioning, she said, "Joe, about your kitchen."

"Don't remind me," he groaned, picking up his glass of water.

"I'll clean it up."

"No," he said quickly, setting down the glass to lift his hands. "I'll do it."

"And your zip drive. I'm so sorry."

"I said forget it."

"Why didn't you fire me?"

He'd wanted to. It had been the first thought that popped into his mind at the time, but he couldn't very well tell her that. He knew he was difficult sometimes, but he never purposely hurt anyone.

"Joe?"

The menu again held his interest for a long moment before he slowly lowered it. "It's best if we drop this now."

"Why?"

The waitress came up to them, and because they both knew what they wanted, she took their menu shields, leaving Joe feeling strangely exposed. Vulnerable.

"Why, Joe?"

Spreading his big hands on the table, he stared at them. "I'll tell you on one condition. No, make that two. First, you don't take this personally, and second, after I tell you, you have to be honest back and tell me why someone with your wealth and means would want this job in the first place."

Humiliating as it would be to disclose her predicament, she had to know. "Deal."

His light blue eyes penetrated hers. "I *can't* fire you. I promised your father I'd give you a job. It's in the will."

The waitress brought their food, and Joe dug in.

Caitlin stared at him helplessly. "I don't understand.

The will doesn't say 'for as long as I want it.' All it says is that you'll *hire* me."

"So much for not taking this personally." He sighed and set down his fork. "Yes, but I promised him."

"When?"

"Before he died. He'd been having health problems."

He'd never told her. She'd never asked. Guilt stabbed at her.

"It seemed to mean a lot to him that you have this job, so I went along with it."

She managed to speak evenly. "You don't strike me as a man who'd go along with anything that didn't suit your purposes, Joe."

"Since that's pretty much true, I suppose there's no use in being insulted." But his jaw was tight as he lifted his glass to his lips. "Let's just call it the repaying of a debt, and in this case, despite any trouble you might cause, I could hire you for the rest of your life and not make a dent in what I owe him."

The image of her father came to mind—powerful, busy, always gone. Much as he'd given her in material things, he'd rarely had time for anything else. It was hard to imagine him inspiring this kind of fierce loyalty. "What is this great thing he did for you?"

"He rescued me." When she just stared at him in surprise, he said, "Twenty years ago, he took a twelve-year-old know-it-all street kid out of an alley where he was about to be killed by a gangbanger for hustling him."

"Were you the twelve-year-old or the gangbanger?"

He grinned, his first, and it was a stunner. "The former."

But Caitlin didn't see the humor. She was horrified, picturing a poor, thin, starving kid fighting off a dangerous thug—no matter she'd thought of Joe as a thug himself earlier that day. "Where were your parents?"

He shrugged broad shoulders. "I never knew my father, and there were six kids. My mother couldn't feed us all. I'd been pretty much on my own for a couple of years."

"Oh, Joe. I'm sorry."

"I turned out all right," he said, lowering his head and shoveling in more food. He smiled suddenly, and the charm of it surprised her. She kept forgetting how good-looking he was, behind all that attitude. "Edmund cleaned me up and hauled me off to a Laker game."

Her jaw dropped. To her knowledge, her father had been too busy for sports. He'd certainly never taken *her* to a game. "He did?"

"Yeah." He smiled at the memory. "They won, too. Then he dumped me in a tough school designed for...troubled kids."

"And for really smart ones, too, I'll bet."

Joseph's head jerked up, his eyes hot and defensive. "Yeah," he said finally, as though it was a hard thing to admit.

Now it made sense, all too well. She knew how attractive a homeless, orphaned, incredibly brilliant *boy* would have been to her father. Especially when all he'd gotten was a weak, not so smart female. Resentment hit, only to be beaten back by shame.

What would have happened to Joe if her father hadn't intervened?

"He came for me every weekend, which at first really ticked me off," Joe admitted. "But he stuck with me until the end." He met her gaze unwaveringly. "He saved my life, princess. I owe him everything, and in return, I'd do anything for him."

Including putting up with a secretary he didn't want. Suddenly feeling a little sick and unbearably lonely even in the middle of a crowded restaurant, Caitlin set down her fork and tried to ignore the tightness in her chest. How pathetic her poor-little-rich-girl story would seem to him. "What happened to your mother?"

He chugged down his water and attacked the basket of bread sticks. "She lives in Vegas. Waitresses occasionally."

"And the others? Your brothers and sisters?"

His blue eyes became shuttered, and she imagined he masked pain and loneliness. "Scattered around." His gaze dropped to the bread he held, which he then polished off in one bite.

She learned far more about Joe by watching his eyes than listening to his words. His eyes were much more expressive than he could possibly know. "Do you ever see them?"

"They're all busy with their own lives. My mother calls me once in a while."

Caitlin swallowed hard, hurting for the boy who'd grown up too fast. Who'd learned to count only on himself. "You support her, don't you?"

He stirred, clearly uncomfortable. "Maybe."

"Why is it so hard to admit you help her?"

"Why is it so hard for you to understand that most people don't like their lives to be an open book?"

She was beginning to realize the man was all bark, no bite. He liked his distance. Too bad she didn't do the distance thing so well.

Joe fell silent as he continued to feed himself with obvious relish, making Caitlin wonder where he put all the food. He certainly didn't have a spare ounce of fat on him. She glanced up, and caught the curious gazes of Vince, Tim and Andy from across the room. The twins grinned at her. Vince's smile was more subdued, worried.

Sweet, she thought. *And chicken.* She stuck her tongue out at them, and they laughed.

Joe polished off his plate and glanced at hers. "Are you going to finish?"

If she drew a deep breath, she'd pop the button on her tight skirt. "No." He continued to gaze longingly at the lasagna left on her plate. Laughing, she pushed it toward him, then watched in amazement as he finished it off.

"To be honest," Joe told her when he'd finally filled himself. "I never thought you'd actually take the job."

Here it comes, she thought. His scorn. And after learning about him and his past, she knew she deserved every bit of it. She took a deep breath. "I need this job."

"Right."

"It's true. I'm deeply in debt, and without the income, meager as it is, I'll be homeless and on the streets just like you once were."

He stared at her. "No way."

"Yes way." She played with her water glass. "Those assets you spoke of that first day, my car and my place, they haven't been paid for. As you know, they're far out of my league with what you're paying me. I'm flat broke."

"What about the will?"

"What about it? I got nothing."

"Then why did Edmund stipulate such a low salary? He was the most generous man I know."

She shrugged, even managed a light smile, but Joe wasn't fooled. Pain blazed from her eyes.

"Maybe he just didn't realize?" he suggested.

"Whether he realized or not doesn't matter," she said. "The sorry truth is, this job is all I have, and I desperately need it. I know you hate it, Joe, and to tell you the truth, so do I. There's just not much choice in the matter at the moment."

Dammit. Dammit all to hell. He didn't want to feel this quick, inexplicable tug of concern, of protectiveness, shame because he'd gotten from Edmund what his own daughter hadn't. "He didn't mean to hurt you." He could bank on that.

"You think so?" She lifted those huge, liquid eyes to his. "Even when I'm a spoiled *princess?* Always had the world at my fingertips? Isn't that what you've thought all along?" She smiled humorlessly at his wince. "But you know what? All I really wanted was his time. How's that for spoiled? He had you, though, and that was all he needed."

Lunch lodged in his throat. "I gather you weren't close."

"Don't pretend that you two didn't talk about me. I know what he thought of my lifestyle."

How to tell her that Edmund had rarely spoken of her at all, and only at the very end? Clearly, he didn't have to tell her; she'd looked at his face and seen the truth.

"I must seem double pathetic now."

"No," he said, leaning close, disturbed by that protectiveness he felt. "Caitlin..."

"Don't apologize for him. It was my fault, too. I didn't see him much because of our respective business schedules. And don't," she said quickly, raising a hand. "Don't make some crack about poor little socialite me. If you're thinking I had it pretty good, you're right. I did. I never had to live on the streets, fighting for my life, and I certainly never went hungry or without clothes. But I also never had what I really wanted, which was someone to tell me they loved me."

Joe hadn't thought, hadn't wondered...all those times he and Edmund spent together, he had never thought to ask about Edmund's daughter, or where she was. "I'm sorry," he murmured, well aware of the inadequacy of those words.

"Don't be sorry for me." She tucked a loose wave of hair behind her ear and gave him a look from beneath lowered lashes that he couldn't quite read. "I'm just glad I still have a job."

He looked at the woman who had cheerfully and without complaint thrown herself wholeheartedly into a job that had been forced on her. She'd genuinely tried hard, even when out of her element. She'd given it her all.

Damn. He pulled his thoughts up short. He'd done it again. Just one bright, open smile and he'd folded. One bat of those long lashes and he was willing to forget that he could hardly tolerate her. Purposefully, he hardened himself. "All I need you to do is answer the phones, Caitlin. *Nothing else. Just* the phones," he said, leaning forward to make his point, grabbing her hand when she ignored him. He thought of how his office looked once she'd started to organize it. "Promise me."

Her voice filled with wounded pride, she countered, "I can do more, far more, if you'd teach me."

The waitress saved him from replying, and he was grateful. She tactfully set down their bill almost in the center of the table, but slightly closer to Joe.

He picked up the slip, reaching for his wallet and scanning the balance at the same time. "Eighteen-fifty," he muttered to himself. "With a tip that's—"

"Two dollars and seventy-eight cents," Caitlin whispered politely, leaning forward discreetly. "But leave three-seventy instead."

"What?"

"Twenty percent." Caitlin was leaning close enough to daze him with that light, sexy scent she wore. "You should leave twenty percent since we got such great service." She opened her purse and he put a hand over hers, halting her.

"Wait a minute." He shook his head to clear it, then gazed back into guileless eyes the color of milk chocolate. "Are you telling me you can multiply in your head like that, instantly?"

Caitlin flashed him a self-conscious smile. "Uh…yes. I'm sorta good with numbers. Big ones." She shrugged. "It's a semi-useless talent."

"Are you kidding?"

"Well, it does come in handy when I'm shopping in Mexico City and trying to figure out the exchange rate."

Again he shook his head, counting out bills.

"Twenty-two dollars and twenty cents," she said helpfully.

"Amazing," he said, dropping the cash in the tray and handing it up to the waiting server.

Caitlin was staring solemnly at him.

"What now? You thinking about calculating the national debt?"

She shook her head. "I've never had to support myself before, Joseph. And I realize I'm spoiled. But that's going to change." She let out a little laugh. "It has to, actually. I don't have any money."

"Maybe a loan," he said desperately. "They have them everywhere now. All the banks…"

"I want to work."

"There are other jobs, other things you could do that would suit you better."

"I'm not a quitter, Joe." Determination and pure grit shimmered off her, and her voice was soft yet strong and even, completely without rancor. "I just need a little time to prove myself. And if you don't have the inclination to give me the time I need, then I'm sure Andy and Tim and Vince will."

She had *that* right, he thought as he glanced at the three cohorts, all staring across the room directly at Caitlin, stars sparkling in their eyes.

Caitlin scooted back from the table and rose with wounded dignity. Every male eye in the place was instantly on her. Every eye but Joe's.

He was lost in thoughts of her determination and grit—two of his favorite qualities. He almost liked her, he realized with some surprise.

How many people could he say that about?

5

CAITLIN GOT UP the next morning and discovered two unpleasant things. One, if she wanted to eat again in the near future, she was going to have to ask Joe how often she got paid. Weekly, she hoped as she stared with dismay into her nearly empty refrigerator thinking that, given a sorry choice of expired cottage cheese or a mustard sandwich on stale bread, payday couldn't be soon enough.

Two, and even more important, her car was gone. Missing. Vanished from the face of the earth.

Just the thought had her hyperventilating. Her BMW, her pride and joy, the one thing her father had given her that she knew he'd bought with her in mind... Well, he hadn't actually paid for it outright, but up until his death, he'd given her the money for the lease and insurance.

She'd already called the police when it occurred to her that she might have missed a few payments.

It wasn't her fault, really. She'd been so busy. First in Paris with a girlfriend for holiday shopping. Then in Mexico at another friend's resort for Christmas. She'd come home in time for New Year's Eve at the Comedy Club.

Then her father had died, and both her so-called friends *and* her money had disappeared.

Well, at least she hadn't been kicked out of her condo yet. That was something, wasn't it?

CAITLIN HAD NEVER in her life had to rely on public transportation. It was every bit the adventure she'd thought it would be and more. And so, of course, she was late.

She dashed through the foyer, waved to Amy, leaped on the elevator and stumbled into the office at ten o'clock to face a not-so-happy-looking Joe Brownley.

"How nice of you to grace us with your presence," he said overly politely.

Usually, nothing flattened her faster than disapproval, but she wasn't in the mood. Not today. She thought about telling him so, but stopped when she realized that, given how he'd grown up, he might not be exactly sympathetic to her losing the BMW she hadn't paid for in the first place.

"I'm sorry I'm a little late—"

"A little?" He let out a short laugh and shook his head. "Princess, there are going to have to be rules in this… this…"

"Relationship?" she suggested sweetly, making him scowl even deeper.

"*Office*. This is *not* a relationship," he said stiffly. "It's a job. You come in at eight like the rest of us. In the *morning*," he added with emphasis.

He wore black jeans today. And a black polo shirt, untucked as usual. It stretched tight across his broad shoulders and snugged his hard, lean chest. With his hands on his hips and that scowl on his handsome face, he looked like a modern-day pirate, capable of pillaging along with the best of them.

She definitely should not have stayed up late reading that fantastic lusty historical romance. The pirate hero had tossed the heroine over his shoulder and stalked with her into his private cabin, where he'd tossed the passionate but virginal redhead on his berth and—"*What* is that?" her pirate demanded, pointing to her outfit.

Caitlin glanced down at herself, but saw nothing wrong with her canary-yellow captain's jacket and matching short full skirt, or her equally yellow high-heeled pumps. She'd needed the extra height this morning to boost her lagging confidence and stomped-on spirits.

She would have preferred an expensive shopping trip to Italy, but beggars couldn't be choosers.

Of course, no one had told her she'd have to walk nearly a mile—*twice*—to catch connecting buses.

Tomorrow, she was wearing her cross trainers.

She'd only gotten on the wrong bus once. Okay, twice, but that second time hadn't been her fault.

"What's wrong with my clothes?" she asked.

"Everything!"

She looked again, just to make sure she'd buttoned all her buttons and didn't have toilet paper stuck to her shoe, but everything was just fine. "What?"

His sigh exploded out of him as he turned away "Nothing."

"It's something."

He whipped around to face her, plowing his fingers through his hair. His raised arms, stretched, tightened, and made her mouth go dry because he was so...

"You said you'd wear...*more,*" he said at last.

She laughed. "No, I never said that. *You* did."

He closed his eyes, a habit she'd noticed he fell back on when frustrated or furious, both seemingly constant elements of his charming personality. "I asked nicely," he said, his voice strained.

"You most definitely did not."

"Please," he said after a moment. "Please, wear more. *Lots* more."

"Is that a rule, too?"

His eyes flashed and she didn't miss the quick humor they revealed. "If I said yes, would you follow it?"

She grinned back. "Probably not. I don't do the authority thing too well."

His gaze became serious. "This isn't going to work."

"It will if you stop bellowing."

He went still. "I haven't yelled at you."

"You raised your voice when I dropped the lamp on your thingie."

"Zip drive," he said through his teeth. "It was a *zip drive*, princess. A very expensive one. And I didn't yell— I nearly cried!"

"You're doing it again."

His shoulders slumped. "I'm sorry. I tend to talk loud when I get— Never mind. Christ! How the hell do you always get me so off track?"

"You were picking on me."

"I was not picking on you." He stopped, drew a deep, ragged breath. "Forget the zip drive, okay? Just answer the phone. Nothing else."

She thought of his disastrous files, which she had started to organize. She could have the office fully operational in no time. "But—"

"No *but*s."

He hadn't fired her.

This man was not nearly as tough as he thought he was, which made her smile. She would fix his office, and he'd see just how valuable she could be.

He'd need her then...and she liked the sound of that.

"Now—" he pointed to the phone "—there are two lines, and the first one—"

"Thank you, Joe," she interrupted softly, laying her hand over his.

He yanked his hand back and scowled. "Pay attention. Our phones are ringing off the hook right now because of the merger. A lot of our customers—"

"Customers?"

"We design and sell software. We also provide the tech support."

"That's what Tim, Andy and Vince do?"

He nodded. "Among other things. Just find out who it is they need to speak to. Put them on Hold, then use the intercom in our offices and we'll pick up." He pointed to another series of buttons, but Caitlin's mind began to wander. She lifted her head and encountered the most expressive light blue eyes she'd ever seen. "Do you wear contacts?" she wondered out loud.

"Caitlin." His nostrils flared. "You're not paying attention."

Paying attention was hard when he was so darn magnificent. He stood there, leaning over her, wearing that fierce expression—his jaw all tight and his sexy mouth hard—and suddenly, she wanted to kiss him.

Bad idea, she decided, and ducked her head. "I'm sorry. I'm listening now."

Vince came out of his office, took one look at Joseph's tense face and changed directions from the kitchen to Caitlin's desk. "Joe," he said quietly, "Tim needs you. He's having trouble with a control panel and wanted me to let you know."

"He'll have to wait a minute." Joe rubbed his temples. "I'm training Caitlin."

Caitlin's stomach tightened uncomfortably with the now familiar feeling of stress. She hated it.

"I'll help her," Vince suggested, tactfully slipping in

between Joe and Caitlin and giving her a shy smile. "After all, I'm the one who trained the last hundred secretaries you scared off. What's one more?"

There was her hero, Caitlin thought. Too bad his smile didn't stop her heart like Joseph's did.

"Good luck," muttered the modern-day pirate as he escaped scot-free.

"Don't worry about him." Vince grinned, which went a long way to relieve Caitlin's tension. "He doesn't have much patience. He's far too focused."

"Well, I hope he focuses somewhere else this morning while I organize this place. It's a disaster."

"Um…maybe you shouldn't."

He was worried and it made her smile. "I can do this. You'll see."

"But Joe—"

"Doesn't know how good I am." She patted his hand. "You'll see," she repeated.

Tim and Andy came through a short time later, looking for fun, as they always did on their break.

Tim toed the controlled mess she had on the office floor, and whistled slowly. "What'd Joe say about this?"

Caitlin had to smile. "After complaining about how late I was, and then my clothes, he sort of ran out of steam. I'm sure he'll get to it the next time he happens by, but I'm hoping to file all this away by then."

Tim looked nervous. "Maybe I should help you," he suggested. "No use riling him up."

He was afraid she'd get herself fired, and it was so sweet she smiled in spite of her own nerves. Besides, she refused to put Joe in a position where his men had divided loyalties. She'd caused enough trouble. "I've got it covered," she assured him.

"What's wrong with your clothes?" Andy wanted to know, looking her over in frank appreciation. "They look plenty good to me."

"He said I needed *more*," Caitlin told him. Both Tim and Andy protested loudly, only to fall completely silent when Joe came into the front office.

He took one look at them hanging around the reception desk, and his jaw went impossibly tight.

Caitlin imagined he'd have quite a headache if he kept it up. "I've got the phone down pat, boss," she said sweetly.

"Terrific." Joe glanced pointedly at the two techs, and they scattered, each offering muttered excuses.

Caitlin's stomach growled, loudly, into the silent office. Joe raised an eyebrow. "Hungry again?"

"My stomach's funny that way. You'd think since I ate so much yesterday, it'd still be satisfied."

He frowned. "You haven't eaten since yesterday?"

That wasn't quite what she'd meant to say, but now that she thought about it, she'd only snacked last night on the last of a stale bag of pretzels. She'd never gotten to dinner.

Then, this morning, she'd skipped breakfast because of her missing car, not to mention an empty fridge. What with bus hopping, she'd been too upset to eat anything, not that she'd had much choice by then.

Joe sighed at her silence, took her arm and pulled her up out of her chair. They headed for the door. "Come on," he said gruffly.

"Where?"

"To feed you, dammit." They were in the hallway, walking at his pace, which was nearly a run for Caitlin in her heels, when her stomach growled again.

Joseph's own stomach tightened as he remembered all too well what hunger felt like. "How did you make it this far without a keeper?" he demanded abruptly.

Under his hand, her arm went rigid. So did the rest of her. "I had one, but he died." She yanked her arm free and met his steady gaze. "Remember?"

Yeah, he remembered. And now she was looking for another keeper. He refused to be it. Horrified that he'd nearly fallen into that position because he'd felt sorry for her, he backed up a step. *Distance.* He desperately needed distance.

"Don't worry, Joe." Her smile was brittle. "Even if I wanted another 'keeper,' you'd be the last man on earth I'd choose."

Heels clicking, hips swaying, attitude popping, she moved away from him, down the hallway.

Out of some sick need to continue sparring with her, he followed her.

The elevator ride was silent and awkward, with her throwing mental daggers and him deflecting them. When the doors opened, she left without a word.

Again he followed.

Outside the office building, she took a deep breath, then jumped a little when she saw him. "Do you miss him?" she asked suddenly.

He didn't have to ask who, and yes, God, how he missed him.

The streets were filled with lunch-hour traffic, both motorists and pedestrians. The crowd was busy, noisy...and impolite. People shoved past them, around them, mumbling and grumbling as they went on with their day.

"Do you?" she asked quietly.

"Yes." He swallowed past the familiar stab of pain. "I miss him a lot."

She nodded and watched the people. The light breeze tossed her short skirt about her incredible thighs. Joseph's unhappy thoughts shifted and he concentrated on her body.

When she crossed her arms tightly over her middle, her full breasts strained against the material of her jacket, making serious thought difficult, if not impossible.

"I do, too," she admitted so quietly he was forced to lean closer. Now her exotic, sexy scent teased him, and he inhaled deeply, torturing himself.

"But I don't understand…why did he do this to me?"

Edmund had served her a direct hit, and Joe felt uncomfortable with her grief and confusion, because he was just as grief stricken and confused.

"You were friends with him," she said. "You were friends, but we aren't."

She was fishing. She needed, yearned…and he ached for her, but he'd never told a lie in his life, not even to save someone's feelings, and he wouldn't start now. "I'm sorry."

She looked at him, accepting his silent admission that no, they were not friends. "I want us to get along."

How to tell her that he didn't? That he "got along" with very few people, and he liked it that way. That the only reason he ever "got along" with a beautiful woman was to "get it on."

"I don't want to be someone you have to babysit."

"That's good. Because I don't babysit," he said.

"You were dragging me off to feed me," she pointed out, ignoring a nasty remark from a harassed-looking woman who had to walk around them on the sidewalk. "I work for you from eight to five, but what I do before or after shouldn't be your concern."

"Then eat, dammit!"

"Yeah, that sort of…um…reminds me…" She bit her lip. "How often do we get paid?"

All his annoyance fled as he stared at her. His stomach suddenly hurt. "Are you *that* out of money?"

She paused. Shrugged. "Sort of, yeah."

Damn. "Today. You'll get paid today."

"I don't want your pity. I just want to know when we get paid around here. Weekly, biweekly, what?"

"Don't," he said harshly, and when she flinched he lightened his tone with effort. "I know what it's like to be hungry, to not eat because there's no food." He rubbed his belly, almost feeling that bone-gnawing hunger from his youth all over again. God, he hated this. A little panicked now, because she made him feel things he didn't want to, he shoved his hand into his pocket and pulled out whatever bills he had in there, slapping them into her palm. "Take this. It's an advance."

Horrified, she glanced downward, then pushed the money back at him. "No. I'm not the local charity case."

"Take it." He shoved the money into her jacket pocket. A mistake. Through the material, he could feel her warm flesh.

"I told you yesterday that I can do this," she said a little shakily as she backed away from him. "I can handle being on my own just fine. I don't think you believe that, but it's true, and I'm going to prove it to you." As she took another step back, she enunciated each word. *"I can take care of myself."*

"Wait," he called out when she turned and took off down the street.

Of course she didn't wait. She never did as he asked.

He could have caught her easily. In those ridiculously high heels, she was hardly moving faster than a quick stroll, but he knew she needed to be alone. She'd resent him intruding now. It would hurt her pride. And he knew all about pride.

Still… He hadn't meant to hurt her feelings, but he just kept doing it. He hated how that made him feel.

Why, Edmund? he wondered for the umpteenth time. *Why have you done this to me?*

Vince came up beside him, watching Caitlin disappear into the crowd. "You have such a touch with women, Joe," he said dryly.

"Hey, most of them like me."

"None of them 'like' you. They *want* you. Some for money, some for that reputed charm of yours, but none of them because they *like* you."

Someone else might have taken offense to Vince's honesty, but Joe always appreciated it. "Look who's talking," he countered. "I don't see you married or anything."

"But you will." Vince stared into the crowd where Caitlin had disappeared. "You will." A muscle twitched in his cheek. "Tell me you didn't fire her."

"We've done fine without a secretary before."

Joe and Vince went way back, but Joe had, in all that time, never seen Vince's temper. He saw it now. The redhead flushed from roots to neck, and his eyes narrowed. "I can't believe you did it," he said furiously. "Fired another one! And she was the nicest, sweetest one we ever had."

"Sweet?" Joe laughed. "Nothing that looks that good is sweet, believe me."

Vince was disgusted. "If I didn't know better, Joe, I'd say she scares you."

"She terrifies me. She's going to destroy our office."

"You know what I mean."

"I didn't fire her, Vince," he said wearily.

Vince relaxed marginally. "But you wanted to."

"Look, I'm stuck with her because of a stupid promise. Yeah, I wanted to."

"No, that's not it—it's not the promise," Vince said as he studied his longtime friend. "I know you better than that. You're running scared." He shook his head in amazement. "And I thought you were fearless."

"I'm not afraid of her."

"Uh-huh. Well, whatever you do, don't hurt her. I like her."

Vince's voice gave away nothing, but the way his eyes were trained on Caitlin's disappearing figure in the crowd did. Not that Joe cared, but Vince clearly *did* like Caitlin. A lot.

He'd probably even ask her out eventually, Joe thought, his gut tightening yet again.

Caitlin would probably say yes.

Dammit. He really hated working with women.

6

FOR ONE ENTIRE AFTERNOON, Caitlin didn't see Joe. He was at meetings with the bank, with customers, with who know whom else.

She was thankful for the respite, which gave her the peace and quiet and nerve to do as she'd threatened. She'd reorganized all the files and now everything was clean, tidy and in its place.

By chance, she'd intercepted the bank statement for the business checking account when it had arrived in the mail. Because numbers had always mysteriously called her, she went ahead and reconciled his statement on her break. She would have and could have easily closed out the month, but picturing Joseph's face, she didn't quite dare.

Vince, Tim and Andy were thrilled with the way the office looked, and how smoothly everything was running. It was amazing how big the place seemed once the floors were clear and it wasn't like walking through a maze just to cross the rooms. Caitlin had no idea how Joe would feel about it, but she could bet he wouldn't offer the joy and easy acceptance she'd gotten from the techs.

However he reacted, he couldn't avoid her forever, or

discount that strange, unaccountable attraction between them that flared up at the most annoying of times.

Every time they looked at each other, there were sparks.

It went deeper than the physical, far deeper, for there existed between them a bond she couldn't deny, and it made her as wary of him as he was of her.

Caitlin was studiously avoiding any serious relationships out of self-preservation. She knew from experience with her father and her fair-weather friends that close relationships brought only pain. Disappointment. Loneliness.

Being on her own was better. Easier.

Either Joe had learned that lesson, too, or he simply didn't like her.

That day he'd given her an advance from his own pocket, she'd come back from her lunch break to find a paycheck on her desk, handwritten by him. The gesture hadn't surprised her. Beneath his rough and tough exterior, she had a feeling he was a big softie.

She laughed at herself. A softie. *Right.*

Well, now she had one paycheck and her pride. It was the latter that allowed her to keep a stiff upper lip in those dark moments when despair threatened, when she cried herself to sleep thinking about her father and the way he'd abandoned her.

She knew all her father's assets were gone, divided among his friends and associates, but she didn't know why. For the first time, she decided she deserved answers. She called his attorney, but because he was out of town for the next week, she had to leave a message.

Feeling marginally better, Caitlin sat on her bed and reviewed her mail. It was a particularly bad mail day, each envelope hiding a big, ugly, nasty bill, all of which were at least second notices.

But the last one really caught her eye—a notice to vacate her condo.

The bank was finally going to sell.

She'd known this moment would come sooner or later, but she'd been hoping for later, *much* later.

Why, she wondered for the thousandth time, hadn't her father paid off her car or her condo? And unfortunately, at the time of his death, he hadn't taken care of any of her credit cards, either, which left her in a position where she couldn't even charge her way out of the mess.

One thing was for certain—she couldn't continue to live as she had. She plopped back on her bed and contemplated her ceiling and came to the only conclusion she could— It was time to sell off everything she had of value, *before* the bank came and claimed it.

Then she could create a whole new life for herself. A lot less luxurious life, but she could handle that. Already, she'd discovered some of the joy of taking care of herself. For one thing, her new friends—Vince, Andy, Tim, even Amy—they were all *real* friends. They wouldn't desert her because she wasn't heir to a fortune. They couldn't care less, they just *liked* her.

Her.

That was a new and welcome surprise.

They liked her for being Caitlin, not for where Caitlin could take them.

It was possible that way down deep, she'd been waiting for this, wishing for the chance to prove to herself she could make it on her own, without any help.

Seemed she was about to get her wish.

DARN IT, BUT she was late again.

"You *had* to stop to talk to that lost homeless lady," Caitlin berated herself as she raced down the street, her

purse flapping behind her. "Had to worry about her instead of yourself and your job and your undoubtedly furious boss."

Huffing and puffing, she dashed into the office building
that housed CompuSoft. Because her lungs were threaten-
ing to explode right out of her chest, she sagged against
the wall in the downstairs reception area, trying to catch
her breath.

"Close to the quarter-century mark," she muttered out
loud, "and already in pathetic shape."

"Caitlin? You okay?"

Holding a hand to her chest, she turned to face a startled Vince, who had one of Amy's scrumptious doughnuts in his hand.

Her mouth started to water. She'd missed breakfast
again.

Amy looked concerned, too, and without a word she
poured Caitlin some water, which Caitlin gratefully took.
"I…will be fine…in just a…sec."

Vince grinned and gave her a slow once-over. "If you're
trying to get in shape, you're too late. You already are."

"Well, I appreciate that," she gasped. "But I'm not…
doing this to myself on purpose, believe me. I hate exercise." Wryly, she glanced down at her running shoes, then
kicked them off. Reaching into her shoulder bag, she pulled
out her high-heeled sandals. She'd been doing this every
morning, changing downstairs while visiting with Amy,
before going to the second floor and facing Joe.

"Why were you running?" Vince held out his arm so
that she could use it to keep her balance while she fas-
tened her sandals.

She grabbed on to him, feeling the bulge of muscle,
the fine silk of his shirt beneath her fingers. Vince, unlike Tim, Andy and even Joe, never wore jeans to work.

He was always dressed impeccably, and today was no different. The deep blue of his shirt and trousers matched his dark sapphire eyes perfectly and toned down the brilliance of his hair.

He waited, his eyes laughing down into hers. "Was that a tough question?"

"I'm sorry," she said quickly, flushing when she realized he thought she'd been staring at him in frank appreciation. She *did* appreciate him, just not in the way he thought.

She appreciated his friendship, because at this point in her life friendship was a new and exciting gift. Somehow, though, she knew Vince wouldn't take it in the flattering light she meant it. "I was running because I'm late. As usual. The bus—"

"Where's your car?"

"It's gone," she said as cheerfully as she could with a lump the size of a regulation football stuck in her throat.

She missed her Beemer!

"You take the bus in from the beach every day?" he asked incredulously. "That's an awful commute, Caitlin."

"It's not so bad." What was awful was the kind and sincere horror in his voice at what she had to go through to get to work. "But the bus never seems to come on time. They say seven-fifteen, but they don't really mean it. Now I finally get the meaning—" she huffed as she worked her second sandal on "—when they say *Californian* time."

Vince laughed as he gently supported her. "Don't worry—I'll tell Joe it was my fault."

"*Your* fault," she repeated. "How on earth could my tardiness be *your* fault—" She broke off as she realized exactly what Joe would think when Vince told him that.

Vince laughed again when she flushed and said, *"Oh."*

"Come on," he said, tugging her to the elevator. "It'll be fun. He's so entertaining when he's furious."

While Caitlin knew darn well Joe didn't want her for himself, she instinctively knew how he would react if one of his techs wanted her. "Just yesterday, when Tim was going to program the clock to swear out loud on the hour, you reminded him how much pressure Joe was under right now."

"So?"

"So why tease him now? He's still under pressure. He might explode."

Vince pushed the button for their floor and grinned down at her. "Yeah. Think how much fun this is going to be."

"Vince—"

He pulled her into the elevator, but just as the door started to close, an elegant, leather-clad foot stopped it.

"Wait!" a female voice cried, and Vince pressed the open-door button.

Caitlin watched as the tall, willowy, incredibly beautiful woman stepped gracefully into the elevator and smiled familiarly at Vince. "Thanks, hon." Her long limbs moved fluidly as she settled herself. Her ankle-length white sheath was striking against her dark skin.

Now, that's a body, Caitlin thought enviously. All lean and toned—no extra curves there! She was just thinking how lovely the waist-length, heavy sable hair was when the woman turned to her...and frowned.

Caitlin recognized that frown, *and* its disapproval.

Joe gave it to her all the time. She stiffened in automatic response.

"This is Darla," Vince told her. "She's the accountant in the building. And Darla, this is Caitlin. Our secretary."

Caitlin smiled, but it wasn't her usual genuine, shining one because she felt suddenly drained.

"Are you enjoying the work?" Darla asked coolly.

"It's interesting."

Darla's expression opened up a bit, surprised. "You mean, he's letting you do something other than answer phones?"

Not that *he* knows, Caitlin thought. "Well...let's just say we're working on it."

"Ah." Darla's mouth curved. "Well, at least you made it past the two-day mark. No one else has."

"What a surprise that is."

Darla did smile then, a genuine one. "I see you're not enamored. That's good. Maybe you have a shot at making it in that office before he eats you alive."

"Enamored?" Because the thought was so ridiculous, Caitlin laughed.

"He's not an easy man," Darla agreed. "As you've obviously noticed."

"I've noticed."

"But he's a good one."

Yes. And also hard, tough, unforgiving and sexy as hell. "He's a good man," she agreed quietly, because it was the truth.

"You know..." Darla tipped her head to study Caitlin carefully. "You're *much* more than Barbie meets *Baywatch.* I'll have to tell Joe I was wrong about you."

"Barbie meets—" Caitlin sputtered, whipped her head to glare at Vince when he burst out laughing at her expression.

The elevator stopped. Darla smiled, and this time it was warm and genuine. "Bye, Caitlin. Good luck today. Or maybe I should wish Joe good luck. I have a feeling he's going to need it."

Caitlin wished she'd left her tennis shoes on, because for the first time in her life she felt like running. She wanted to race directly to Joe and tell him what she thought of him and his accountant.

"Caitlin, wait," Vince called out, trying to keep up with her as she made her way down the hallway.

"I don't think so." She kept going, driven by a need to give Joseph Brownley a piece of her mind. A big piece. A great big huge piece that would knock him flat on his far too gorgeous butt.

Unfortunately for Tim and Andy, they happened to be lurking around her desk when Caitlin stormed in. Twin smiles greeted her, only to die at the murderous expression on her face.

"What's wrong?" Andy asked quickly.

Vince grimaced. "She just met Darla...."

"Tell me," she said evenly, tossing her purse to the floor by her desk and placing her hands on her hips. She blew a strand of hair away from her face. "What did the other secretaries look like?"

In unison, the twins turned to Vince, confused. Vince sighed and shook his head.

"Oh, come on, guys," she encouraged. "*Think.* You remember, the ones who quit?" Her voice held a poisonous mixture of sweet smile and deadly tone. "Were they... pretty?"

"Not like you," Andy said loyally, and Tim shook his head vigorously.

"Darla didn't mean it," Vince said quietly to her, touching her arm, his eyes deep with concern and regret.

"No? But I'll bet Joe did." She dragged in a deep breath, stunned to find herself so upset.

"Caitlin, what's the matter?" Andy asked. "*What* didn't Darla mean?"

All three of them were looking at her in concern. Not one of them was on the verge of laughter. They really cared, Caitlin realized with a burst of surprise and warmth. They cared that she was upset, and they didn't find it funny. It went a long way toward soothing her. "Nothing," she said, forcing a smile. "It wasn't important."

"It was if it hurt you." Tim came closer, peering into her face. "Darla's really pretty great, but she does like a good joke. What did she say?"

Caitlin dropped her gaze from his, feeling a little silly. "Something about Barbie meets *Baywatch*," she muttered.

His eyes widened. He bit his lip, which Caitlin would have sworn was so he couldn't laugh. Next to her, Andy made a suspicious noise, something like a strangled hyena. In a Joe-like move, Vince closed his eyes.

"Oh, stop it," she said, biting back her own smile. "It really wasn't so funny a minute ago."

"You know it's not exactly a put-down," Vince offered in his boss's defense. "Most women would kill to be described that way." His eyes stayed on hers. "And no offense, but you really do look every bit as good as Barbie, or any one of those women on *Baywatch* for that matter."

"Really?" She let her gaze run over his own well-proportioned body. "How would *you* feel to be known as…oh, I don't know. How about Fabio meets G.I. Joe?"

Vince grinned. *"Fabio?"* He flexed his muscles. "Cool."

Caitlin rolled her eyes and gave up. "Oh, never mind." She shooed them all back to their offices and went to the small kitchen. Quietly, efficiently, she started the new coffeemaker, because of course it was empty. She waited impatiently until the coffee began to drip into the pot.

Filling a mug to the top with the steaming brew, she went back into the hall and contemplated the closed door to Mr. Gorgeous Butt's office.

She knocked.

"Go away."

She smiled and walked in.

Joe didn't even waste a scowl on her, but sat hunched over his computer, his fingers whirling away on the keyboard. "Back off or die," he muttered without much heat. "And you're late. Again."

Suddenly he froze. Then he lifted his head and sniffed. "Coffee? *Real* coffee?"

"As opposed to fake?" she asked sweetly, holding the mug just out of his reach. He stood so he could outreach her.

He'd gone all out today, wearing a light blue shirt instead of his usual black. His jeans, faded from wear, fit his long, lean limbs like a glove. When his fingers brushed hers, shocking her with that ever present electricity that ran between them, she gave over the mug.

Clearly unaffected, he sipped gratefully, then let out a huge sigh. "Thanks."

She lifted a brow. "Thanks? *Thanks?* Did you actually thank me? That can't be—you're never polite."

He looked insulted. "I'm plenty polite."

"Really?"

"Of course I am. I'm diplomatic, too."

Caitlin pretended to contemplate this while she walked the length of his office. Turning back to him, she asked, "Is it *polite* to discuss your employees with friends? Is it *diplomatic* to laugh at them, about them, behind their back?"

"What are you talking about?"

"Is it considered politically correct to resort to name-calling, especially before you even really know that employee?"

"What the hell are you talking about?"

"Does 'Barbie meets *Baywatch*' mean anything to you?"

His mouth opened a bit. "Oh," he said, his face unreadable. "You've…met Darla."

She waited for more, but he said nothing else. "That's *all* you have to say?"

He shrugged. "If it matters, you don't look like a model in the least to me."

"Gee, thanks," she said, feeling inexplicably flattened. The first man in the universe who didn't think she was pretty, and this depressed her?

She was an idiot.

"You have too much…" He waved his hand wildly, gesturing to her body, under the mistaken impression she wanted a detailed analysis of her body type. "Everything. Yeah, that's it. You have far too much *everything.*"

"Hmm." The warning in her voice might have deterred another man, a normal man, but then again, Joe was anything but *normal.*

"And your hair isn't like Barbie's at all," he offered. "It's short, for one thing."

"I see."

"As for *Baywatch*…" He shrugged. "I've never seen the show, but it's supposedly got those tight red bathing suits, and I can't see you in one of those, either."

"You can't? Too much 'everything' to fit into one of them, huh?"

"Come on, princess, I can't be telling you anything you don't already know."

"I'm not a princess." Each word was enunciated, and spoken very quietly. "If I were, do you think I'd be working for pennies for you?"

Suddenly wary, he looked at her, as if just realizing she wasn't taking this in quite the same lighthearted tone he'd meant it. "Caitlin—"

"Set down your coffee, Joe," she said evenly.

He did. "Why?"

"Because I'm going to act like a princess and have a

temper tantrum. I don't want you to burn yourself." She swiped at the neat stack of papers on his desk, knocking them to the floor. She reached for another stack, getting into the spirit.

Laughing, he grabbed her hand and held it tight in a fist that might as well have been steel. "What was that for? Wait!"

But she simply switched tactics and tried to evade him. "Don't...patronize me," she demanded. "Don't talk about me behind my back, and *don't*..." She let out a huff of steam when he grabbed her, roaring with laughter.

Seeing red, she fought him. "Let me go!" she demanded, puffing and gasping for air as she fought.

With surprising speed and agile strength, he managed to wrap both arms around her and haul her close, pressing her now useless limbs against his own.

At the contact, she went utterly still.

So did Joe.

In the silence, their rough breathing sounded abnormally loud.

And arousing.

"Are we fighting," he wondered in a suddenly low, husky voice, all traces of humor gone as he stared down into her uplifted face, "or are we playing?"

"I...I don't know."

7

"I THOUGHT WE were fighting." Caitlin stared at Joe with her huge, glowing eyes. She wiggled a bit, pressing all those terrific curves to him and causing interesting things to happen to his insides. And outsides. "But now...I've lost track."

Joe had, too. His heart was pounding, his body responding to the tight, erotic hold he had on her. She stared at his mouth, only inches from hers. Then hers opened slightly and he nearly moaned.

"Joe."

"This is crazy," he muttered.

"Yeah. Insane." But she tipped her torso up to his, and her round breasts pressed into his chest.

He was lost.

"Stop me," he begged, dipping his head down so he could slide his lips over her jaw. He nipped at the corner of her delicious mouth. "Stop me, Caitlin."

She skimmed her hands beneath his shirt to streak across his bare back, and caught the lobe of his ear between her teeth. His eyes crossed with lust, and the ball of heat he'd been stoking in his gut for days kindled.

"I...don't think I want to stop you." She sounded breathless. Confused. Aroused.

"So we're both crazy. Hell." And he kissed her.

Her fingers dug into his shoulders as the ball of heat erupted into fire. The soft, needy whimper that escaped her undid him, and he dragged her closer, lifting her up against him so that he could get better access to those lips and what lay beyond them. Under his fingers, her skin felt so soft, so warm, so inviting, he became dizzy with it.

So did Caitlin.

Passion.

Desire. She hadn't realized just one kiss could provoke it. Demand it. He surrounded her with his strength, his hunger. This was what she'd been missing. *This.* And she wanted more.

Joe stroked his fingers down her neck, discovered the pulse drumming at the base of her throat. Unable to resist, he bent his head to explore it with his mouth. She tasted like heaven, all sweet, melting irresistibility. Bringing his mouth back to hers, he swallowed her gasp as he trailed his fingers across the soft, slick silk of her snug-fitting blouse. He cupped her breasts, running his thumbs over their tight peaks. Gasping, she arched her body into his.

He had to see her eyes, had to know if she felt half of what he did. He was breathless when he lifted his head to look into her face. At the sudden loss of his warm lips, Caitlin protested wordlessly by fisting her hands in his hair and capturing his mouth again.

He understood, for he also feared he might never get enough. And he'd seen the cloudy desire in her eyes, mirroring his own. Her mouth opened to his, hot and hungry, and the room was filled with their sounds of pleasure...

Then the sound of the office door opening.

Caitlin jerked in his arms. Still holding her, Joe lifted his head, prepared to bite someone's—anyone's—head off.

But whoever had opened the door had already retreated, leaving a conspicuously empty doorway.

Joe forced himself to look into Caitlin's eyes, prepared for the regret and the recriminations he deserved, but there were none.

Arms still looped around his neck, she smiled at him. A full, dazzling, vivid smile that did funny things to his heart and made his throat tighten uncomfortably.

There was an excellent explanation for what was happening, he assured himself—*insanity*. It was all he could come up with to account for holding this wild, unstable, unpredictable, irritating-as-hell woman in his arms. For kissing her until they'd both lost their senses.

"I don't suppose," she said softly, threading her fingers through his hair, making him want to purr with satisfaction at just her light touch, "you'd like to try that again."

"Caitlin." It wasn't possible. They shouldn't have indulged in the first place. Slowly, with some regret, he reached up and unhooked her arms from around his neck.

"I guess not," she said, still sounding cheerful, and she backed up a step, which allowed him to see into those incredible brown eyes.

They were filled with hurt. Silently calling himself every name he could think of, he reached for her, but she danced back. "No." She shook her head and scooted around his chair, holding it between them like a shield. "No pity embraces, okay? You kissed me, you're regretting it, let's just let it go at that."

"I don't pity you," he said gruffly. "You're far too maddening for that."

"Another compliment." She pressed a hand to her chest

and batted her lashes at him. "You really must stop—it'll
go to my head."

"This is a business," he said carefully. "And I don't mix
business with pleasure."

"Well, you've got a funny way of showing it, but don't
worry, boss, I won't forget who signs the paychecks." Caitlin swallowed her hurt. "And if it makes you feel any better,
I can not like you very much and still enjoy kissing you."

"I meant," he said tightly, his probing gaze pinning her
to the spot, "that this…this—"

"Yes? This what, Joe? Relationship? No, that would be
too much, wouldn't it."

"What do you want from me?"

His expression wasn't grim or angry; those she could
have easily resisted. He seemed…genuinely baffled. And
scared.

That stopped her as nothing else could have. He was
nervous and unsettled. The big, restless, ill-tempered, bull-
headed man was backpedaling as fast as he could because
she terrified him. "That's the funny thing here, Joe. I don't
want *anything* from you."

"Women always do."

"Is that right?" She studied him thoughtfully. "Yeah, I
can see that might be a problem. Gorgeous, smart…and
such a charming bedside manner. How ever do you fight
them all off?"

When he took another step toward her, scowling, her
heart raced, but not from fear. Damn him, he'd done the
impossible. He'd made her want him and now he was regretting it. She could really hate him for that. But she knew
if he so much as touched her, she'd fling herself into those
very capable arms.

She backed to the door, grabbed the jamb for balance

and sent him a smile, though it wavered. "You know what? Never mind this whole thing. I've got work."

"Wait." He paused, drew a ragged breath. "I'm sorry," he said in that unbearably sexy voice that was now filled with tenderness and affection—two emotions she would never have expected of him.

She turned away. "I'm not."

"Caitlin." She stopped, but didn't face him, and when she heard his words, she was glad for it.

"This won't happen again. It can't."

"Okay."

"I mean it." His stern voice reminded her that she didn't like stern men who didn't see past her exterior to the woman beneath.

"Fine." Now, pride fierce and hot, she looked at him. "Remember that the next time you grab me close, Joe, okay? *Keep your lips to yourself.*"

THE CROWNING GLORY came late the next afternoon. Caitlin made the mistake of thinking about Joseph's kiss while working the new coffeemaker. She got herself so hot and bothered, she didn't pay attention to the strange crackling, sizzling sound coming from the outlet on the wall where the machine was plugged in.

The cord caught fire.

She figured the ensuing explosion was Joseph's final straw.

He came storming into the kitchen, eyes wild, hair standing up on end from where he'd plowed his fingers through it. "Again?" he yelled. "You're incredible! How does this happen to you? To *me?*" Unplugging the scorched, blown-up unit from the wall, he hissed at the heat. Now that there was coffee from ceiling to floor, there were no more flames.

Just that scorched-coffee smell.

With one swift look at the calamity around him, he went straight to her.

Caitlin couldn't bring herself to look at him, but he lifted her chin with his fingers. "You okay?" he asked, his voice low and serious.

She nodded, sure she'd never felt so stupid in all her life.

"You're sure?" He turned her face from side to side, inspecting her thoroughly. She nodded again.

"Good." He drew a deep breath and glanced at the mess around them. "Then I can yell at you and not feel bad."

"Maybe I'm not so okay after all," she decided, but he didn't find her humorous in the least.

Tim, Andy and Vince appeared in the doorway, eyes wide, faces grim.

"In fact," she said urgently, "I'm critically injured. Probably going to die."

"She's kidding," Joe told them. "I'll handle this." To underscore his point, he shut the door in their faces. The room suddenly shrank.

"I can't work like this," he said, far too quietly. "If I don't get some peace soon, Caitlin, I'll blow up. Just like the coffeemaker."

What could she say—she had no idea what she'd done wrong, other than be born. Man, he had such great, wide shoulders—perfect for setting her head down on. They were so strong, so durable. She could lean there and cry it all out—her fears for her future…how she was beginning to feel for him…that she didn't want to be alone anymore. She thought maybe he could feel the same way about her if he tried really hard and overlooked all the little things that drove him crazy.…

"I'm sorry. I really do know how to make coffee, honest."

"I'm so close to finishing this program. I'm so damn close, and you keep distracting me, driving me insane. Do you do it on purpose?"

"No, it's just a special talent of mine." But she thought it only fair he take half the blame for the coffeemaker thing. It had been *his* lips, *his* touch, *his everything* that had distracted her in the first place; otherwise she would have noticed the fire.

He paced the small kitchen, his sneakers making squishy noises in the coffee. He looked huge. Powerful. Very dangerous. "I thought I could do this—I swear I did. Dammit, I wanted to for Edmund."

Her heart lodged in her throat. "What are you saying?"

"That I can't do this anymore. I just can't." With a sound of disbelief, he gestured around him. "Look at this, Caitlin. Did you know we've been here for years and never once has that damn thing exploded? You've done it twice now." In disgust, he lifted a foot, and it came loose from the linoleum with a loud pop. "We've never even had to mop before you came here."

"I don't think that's necessarily something to be proud of. A good cleaning never hurt anything, Joe."

"Well it's gotten two cleanings in four days! There are more important things to be doing, dammit!"

"And I'd be happy to be doing them, but you don't trust me!"

"Trust you! You can't even work a coffeemaker!"

"All right, fine!" she yelled back, her hands on her hips. "But we all make mistakes. You don't see me flinging yours in *your* face."

"Because I haven't made any," he shouted, matching her tone as they stood nose to nose raging at each other.

"You make me so—"

The doorway to the kitchen was suddenly filled with curious, frantic techs.

"Get out!" Joe reached over and slammed the door.

"That wasn't nice." Caitlin lifted her chin. "They're probably just wondering what you're hollering about."

"They're used to it, believe me," Joe assured her. He let out a slow breath. "And you're changing the subject. I make you so…what? So mad?"

So horny. The thought came unbidden, but it didn't quite apply here. "Yes! Mad and irritated and frustrated and anxiety ridden."

"Is that all?"

"You also infuriate me."

"That's the same as mad."

"It's mad multiplied."

"My point exactly." He nodded, quite calm now. "We drive each other crazy, so—"

"I never said you drove me crazy."

He sighed and closed his eyes, looking so defeated, she wanted to hug him. *Hug him?*

Maybe *she* was crazy.

"You're skirting around the real issue."

"Of course I am," she snapped. "You're trying to fire me and pretend it has nothing to do with what happened earlier in your office. Which is a crock!"

A knock came at the door, followed by Tim's hesitant voice. "Guys? Everything all right in there?"

"It would be if you would go back to your office and do your job!" Joe roared at the closed door.

"There's no need to yell at him—he's just being sweet," Caitlin proclaimed, nearly yelling herself. She never raised her voice, so it was startling to realize how good it felt. So exhilarating. So freeing. "And no need to shout at me, either. It's yourself you're so mad at."

Joe let out a short laugh and glanced around him at the coffee mess. "How in the hell do you figure that?"

"*You* kissed *me*," she reminded him, jabbing a finger to his chest. "And you liked it, Joe."

"Joe? Caitlin?" This time it was Andy, and the knob turned. Bravely, he pushed open the door. "You're going to bring the place down. What's going on?"

"Nothing!" they shouted in unison.

"If you're trying to fire her," Vince said flatly, peeking around Andy. "Forget it. We took a vote. She stays."

"It's *my* vote that counts," Joe said. He'd made a living out of calling the shots; retreat didn't come naturally. He met Caitlin's fathomless dark eyes and couldn't, for the life of him, look away.

Time stopped and inexplicably he couldn't remember why he was so mad.

As if she sensed that, her lips curved softly.

His heart tipped. Just tipped right over and broke a little. Yeah, he wanted her, but even worse, he *needed* her. Not an easy admission, even to himself. Never losing eye contact, he said, "Fine. Dammit. She stays. You're all crazy."

It threw him to see her smile fully now. "What's so damn amusing?" he demanded.

"*You are*." She said this sweetly and full of such warmth and affection that for a minute he couldn't breathe, much less speak. "You think you're so tough," she added softly. Moving close, she reached up and cupped his cheek.

At the unexpected contact, he flinched. "I *am* tough."

She shook her head, still smiling. Her eyes glowed. "You're a big softie, Joe Brownley."

Vince laughed from the doorway. "Yeah. A big softie. Ask him for a raise, Caitlin. Let's see just how soft."

Joe shifted uncomfortably. He wasn't soft at all, but hard

as a rock at just her touch. "Get out of here, guys. Caitlin and I have things to discuss."

"Things?" Andy lifted a brow curiously. "What things?"

"Yeah, what things?" Tim wanted to know, ignoring the order to leave. They leaned against the doorjamb, comfortable. Completely uncowed by Joseph's glare.

So much for tough. "Get out," he repeated firmly, keeping his gaze on Caitlin.

He didn't hear anyone budge. Not until Caitlin turned to them with that endearing smile, the one that could make a grown man beg, and said in her light, gentle voice, "It's all right. We'll try to keep it down."

Joe watched, stunned, as Tim and Andy smiled back at Caitlin dopily, completely entranced, and then did as she asked. Vince left, too, silently.

When they were alone, he said, "That's amazing. The way you twist everyone around that little pinkie of yours."

"What things do we have to discuss, Joe?"

"Rules, princess. Rules."

"Ah." She nodded. "Those rules again."

He ran his gaze over her lush, curvy body, and his fingers itched to explore. "Apparently, you've forgotten them."

"Gee, I guess we're back to the topic of my clothes."

They both looked at her choice for the day—narrow denim skirt unbuttoned from ankle to well above the knee, topped with a tight, siren-red, ribbed cotton top.

He cleared his throat. "I told you we were conservative around here."

"No, you said I should wear *more*. Well, my skirt goes practically to the floor." She lifted her foot and wiggled her bright red sandal, exposing a terrific looking leg to midthigh. "I'm trying to fit in with the norm around here."

"Which is?"

"Casual." Caitlin lifted her gaze up to his and found his

beautiful eyes filled with equal parts heat and annoyance. *Perfect.* Now their moods matched. "What do you think?"

He curled an arm around her waist, still annoyed. Still hot. He dragged her closer. "I think you're courting disaster."

"Am I?" she whispered, their lips nearly touching as she strained against him on tiptoe. Gently, she framed his face, marveling at herself. Never in her life had she made a move on a man; now she couldn't seem to stop. "This isn't a disaster. This is the rescue."

"Rescue?" His voice, thick and sexy, nearly had her dissolving in a boneless heap.

"Yeah." She kissed the corner of his mouth, loving the feel of his warm and solid body against hers. "You're something. All those hard muscles and that bad attitude. But you can't fool me, Joe. You care. You feel. And you need this." Her lips trailed over his clenched, slightly stubbled jaw, and she lingered, suddenly overwhelmed by how he made her feel. She closed her eyes and kept going, expecting him to shove her away any second, but he didn't. Instead, he tilted his head, letting her have her way. "You need me," she whispered.

"You're pressing your luck, Caitlin." He didn't sound very steady or very tough at the moment.

"I don't think so."

Now he did move away, capturing her busy little hands in his. "You don't know me." In a gesture that tore at her, he lifted their joined hands to his lips. "You don't know the real me. All I care about, all I feel, is a passion for my work. There's not room for anything else."

"Or *anyone* else?"

"I don't want anyone in my life." He stared at her hands resting in his. "I really don't."

It was hard to reconcile this man with the abrupt, gruff

one that she usually saw. Both were passionate, fierce, intelligent. But this Joe...*this* one she could really like. She told him so.

He let her hands go. "I don't want you to like me."

"You can control your computers, Joe," she said softly. "But you can't control me."

"I *can* control this," he contradicted her. "I can and I will. Because it would be a mistake, Caitlin. We would be a huge mistake. You'd get hurt, and I..."

"Yes?" she wondered with patience. "You'd what? You'd maybe get hurt, too? Well, isn't that what life's all about?"

"Dammit, we're not talking about me. We're talking about you, and how you'd feel when it was over. Afterward."

Now she laughed, though without a lot of humor. "I never said I wanted you, Joe."

"You do."

She let out a genuine chuckle. "Okay, maybe I do. But don't panic—it's just physical. Pure and simple. I'd be crazy to want more with you."

But she *was* crazy, she thought. And she did want more, much more. She sidled up close, batted her lashes at him flirtatiously. "Come on, Joe. Let's play."

"No. No way." He nearly ran to the door.

Just before he shut it, she called out, "So can I have the raise?"

8

CAITLIN SPENT THE WEEKEND in a strange state of awareness.
Friday night, she went dancing with Amy, where they met
Tim and Andy and had a great time.

Caitlin realized how much more these friends meant to
her than any others she'd ever had.

Things had changed for her, she decided. They'd
changed with her father's death, with her new job. Once
she'd lived her life casually, without thought to past or future,
but no longer.

For the first time, she had people in her life who cared
about the *real* Caitlin, not the spoiled rich one.

Everything else—her financial woes, her worries of
what would happen to her future—paled in comparison
to that.

Somehow, in the past few months, priorities had shifted.

Now when she looked in the mirror, she no longer saw
a pampered woman, but one who lived, laughed, cared....

One who loved.

BY MONDAY CAITLIN was already out of money—again—
and very tired of taking the bus.

To cheer herself up, she'd spent the last of her pocket

change on doughnuts from Amy's stand. And while this endeared her greatly to Tim and Andy, she didn't imagine the scale in her bathroom was going to be so kind.

As she went into the small office kitchen, she glanced down at herself and rolled her eyes. Even wearing one of those bras that promised to control and contain—whatever the heck that meant—she still spilled out of whatever she wore. The flowered print dress she had on today dipped a little low in front, emphasizing the problem. And was it her fault her hips strained against the soft cotton? Nope, she decided, taking another bite of a huge chocolate-buttermilk roll. She might as well face it; she was never going to be a waif.

She studied her image in the front of the steel-door refrigerator. Wild blond bob. Red lips. Big eyes.

"You're beautiful, you know."

Jumping a little, she faced Vince. He shot her a little smile and gestured to the door she'd been using as a mirror. "You don't have to check," he said. "You are."

"I'd rather be known for my brains."

She said this with such disgust, he laughed. Then he sobered, stuck his hands into his trouser pockets and came closer. "I saw you and Joe on Friday. You know...in his office."

So *Vince* had interrupted their kiss!

"I don't want to see you get hurt," he said carefully. He squared his shoulders. He didn't have a single wrinkle. He was a man who appreciated fine clothes, a man with expensive tastes, a man after her own heart...and she didn't feel anything but a sisterly sort of affection.

What was wrong with her?

"I don't think it's a good idea for you to get involved with him."

Her brain, protesting the early hour, went on full alert. "Vince, he's your boss and your friend."

"I know. And I care about him very much." Vince met her gaze, and she knew he was genuinely sad. "But I care about you, too. Joseph's not easy on women, Caitlin. They come in and out of his life in a heartbeat. He rarely looks back."

Her unease grew. "We shouldn't be discussing this. It's not right."

"I care about you."

"But I'm a big girl," she said gently. She reached for his hand and squeezed. "You don't have to worry about me."

Everything about him was tense, even as he let out a little laugh. "I can't seem to help that."

"Well, seeing as there's little between me and your friend, except resentment and bad air, you don't have much to worry about."

"What I saw between the two of you was a lot more than bad air, Caitlin."

The kiss again. Well, it *had* been quite a kiss. Quite a very good kiss. The mother of all kisses. But it had meant nothing to Joe, which was what Vince was trying so gallantly to make sure she understood.

What she really understood was that Joe didn't *want* it to mean anything. That he wasn't comfortable with the intimacy, and she could understand that, as well. Neither was she.

What, she wondered, would Joe say if he knew she'd never experienced any sort of intimacy at all? It wasn't something she'd set out purposely to do, but she'd never found the right man. Somehow, it had been easy to resist the fast, rich, slick kind of guy her so-called friends had all hung out with. So now, despite her travels and exciting lifestyle, she was the oldest virgin in the Western Hemisphere. "I'm not going to get my heart broken over one kiss," she said, more weakly than she would have liked.

"I'm not doing a good job of warning you off him, am I?" Vince asked wryly.

"It's not your fault. I just never seem to learn what's good for me."

"I could be good for you," he said seriously.

"Oh, Vince."

He shook his head. "I'm sorry. I didn't mean to say that so soon." Softly, he touched her cheek, then walked away.

It didn't take long to get distracted. She took a call from the mortgage company for the condo her father hadn't left her. The by-the-book loan officer on the line was not impressed by her employment.

"Look, Ms. Taylor," he said in a voice bordering on nasty. "I do realize you have a job now, and apparently, you should be commended for that."

While Caitlin took his not so polite disdain, Joe walked by. He wore the customary faded jeans and T-shirt and was every bit as aloof and dangerously sexy as her dreams had assured her. With his heavily lidded eyes, that perpetual frown on his beautiful, scowling mouth and the rugged, muscled yet lean body, he looked every bit the hoodlum she imagined most mothers warned their daughters from.

But Caitlin didn't have a mother, and she doubted she would have listened to a mother's advice, anyway.

"Ms. Taylor," the mortgage officer said in her ear, "you can't expect this company to believe that you'll be able to make the payments, given your current salary. Not to mention how far behind you are already. I'm sorry, but the lock-out will take place on Friday evening, unless you come up with something else."

Lock out.

As in a huge padlock on her front door. She would have

no place to go. "You're going to put me out on the street because you don't like my job?"

Joe, already across the office and halfway out the door, froze. Mortified, Caitlin lowered her voice and her head. "You can't do this," she told the jerk on the line. "You can't. My father—"

"Is dead," the man said bluntly. "And hasn't provided any means for paying the mortgage. You have no experience, no credits to your name and no viable means of providing us what is due, Ms. Taylor. You can't possibly blame us for this situation."

"What can I do to prove myself?" she asked, more than a little desperately. What had happened to her great life? To security? To a full stomach?

"Marry a rich man," he advised. "Quickly."

Floored, she hung up the phone and stared at it. She'd mistakenly thought her life was starting to be under control. But it wasn't even close, she realized, and dropped her head down to her desk.

What could she do?

Hand still on the office door, Joe stared at Caitlin's bowed head. Her full hair fell forward, exposing her pale, soft neck. She seemed small, vulnerable. Dammit, no. *No,* he told himself firmly.

You aren't going to worry about her.

But he let go of the door. Of their own accord, his feet took him to her desk. *Not his problem, absolutely not. Run, don't walk, to the nearest exit.* He perched a hip on the corner of her desk. *This has nothing, absolutely nothing, to do with his promise to Edmund. He'd gone over and above the call of duty so far. Anyone would think so.*

Anyone.

Instead of running, he heard himself say, "Caitlin? What's the matter?"

She jerked upright, flashed him a smile minus her usual megawattage and said with false cheer, "Nothing. Everything's perfect. Absolutely perfect."

"You're out of money."

"Nothing new."

"You're going to lose your place."

Her shoulders sagged. Her smile faded, and in its place came a disturbing helplessness. "It's not mine anyway."

So many emotions attacked him then, he couldn't think straight enough to sort them out from each other. But leading the way was guilt—guilt because Edmund had taken care of *him,* a punk kid with no future, yet he'd ignored his own daughter.

Despite how Joe felt about her, and how he *didn't* want to feel about her, she didn't deserve this. Anger bubbled. Anger at Edmund, anger for Caitlin and anger for himself at being left to deal with the mess.

He was distinctly uncomfortable cleaning up the messes other people made of their lives. He'd done it for his mother. He'd done it for his siblings. He'd done it for countless "friends" over the years who'd assumed that because of what he did for a living, he had an overabundance of money.

He didn't want to do it anymore. "I can help."

"No." Abruptly, Caitlin got up. "I need to walk," she said, slipping off her high-heeled sandals, replacing them with running shoes. Joe watched, fascinated and mesmerized, as her dress gaped and revealed soft, full, plump breasts rebelling against their constraints.

He was a jerk, he thought, staring down her dress when she was undergoing a crisis. He told himself this quite firmly. But he didn't—couldn't—stop looking.

When she grabbed her purse, he stopped her, pulled her back. Their thighs touched, but it no longer startled him to feel that inexplicable heat in his body. "Caitlin."

"No," she said quickly, trying to pull back. For once, her eyes didn't give her away. "No pity, remember?"

"I already told you," he said, lying only a little. "You're too prickly to feel sorry for."

"*I'm* prickly?" She laughed a little. "Right."

"Let me help," he said rashly, having no idea why the words popped out. "I want to."

"Why?"

Because already I can't stop thinking about you, and if I have to be worried on top of being distracted all to hell, I'll never get any peace. "Because you need it, dammit. Because your life is out of control, and you need help. I can supply that help. It's that simple."

She stared at him for a long moment, and he could have sworn she was waiting for something, something more. Her lovely dark eyes searched his, but he was still befuddled by the view she'd just given him, and by touching her, and he didn't know what else she could possibly want.

Finally, she turned away, but not before he saw her expression fall a little. "Thanks, but you've helped me enough. More than enough. Be back after lunch." She ran out the door.

He watched her go, remorse and lust gnawing equally at his gut.

CAITLIN FOUND HERSELF in the lobby, aimless.

"Hey, there."

She mustered a smile for Amy, who leaned over her food stand with a friendly smile that faded quickly enough at the expression on Caitlin's face.

"Uh-oh, you've got *the face* on." Silently, Amy turned and grabbed a plate.

"What face?"

Amy bustled a moment, then turned with a heaping

serving of cinnamon crumb cake. "The kind that is crying out for food. Preferably junk food, the more fattening the better."

Caitlin had to laugh. "Yeah, it's been that kinda day."

"Hmm, no kidding. Tell me."

"You tell me first," Caitlin urged, needing to hear about someone and something other than herself and her own troubles.

"Okay. My first customer of the day hits on me every morning despite the fact that I am madly in lust with the UPS guy. The UPS guy, who by the way is the most fab man on the planet, doesn't know I exist. My supplies were late and so was my alimony check, which means I am now late making my rent."

Caitlin hummed her complete understanding and nodded, encouraging Amy to continue because suddenly her own problems didn't seem so major.

"And if I'm late on my rent, it goes on my credit, and if I get bad credit, I can't buy a new car at the end of the year like I promised myself." She shrugged. "That about sums it up for today," Amy said. "Now you."

"Okay, my boss thinks I'm a helpless idiot. His best friend is falling for me and I don't want to hurt him. And…I think I'm falling for my boss."

"The one that thinks you're a helpless idiot."

"Yeah." She could have complained about the condo and the car. Or about her serious and frightening lack of money, but strangely enough, that stuff didn't matter as much.

"I like being my own boss," Amy said into their companionable silence. "And you couldn't hurt anyone if you tried, Caitlin. You're too kind."

"I— That's a very generous thing to say." Caitlin's throat tightened at the look of utter sincerity on Amy's face. "But you don't really know me."

"I think I do."

Hot tea came next, and Caitlin found herself being pampered by nothing but the best crumb cake she'd ever sampled and an even better friendship.

"You know," she mumbled around a huge, heavenly biteful, "I've been everywhere in this world. I've eaten at the most amazing places." She smiled at Amy's curious face. "But nothing has tasted as good as this."

"Well, I haven't been anywhere, other than Los Angeles, but that doesn't really count 'cause it's just in the next county over, you know?" Amy laughed completely unselfconsciously. "But I still know a good person when I meet one, Caitlin. Don't let them get you down. Life's too good, too short."

Caitlin stilled as the simple truth sunk in. "It is, isn't it?"

"You could get another job and drop all the problems in one shot."

Another truth, one that just a few days ago she would have thought an impossibility. But now she knew better. She knew she was smart enough to learn how to do whatever she wanted. "You know...you're right."

And she thought about it for the rest of the day. Imagined herself in another job, being appreciated, rewarded. Cared about.

Without Joe.

The tightness in her chest deepened and became an ache.

She was in bigger trouble than she ever imagined if the thought of being without Joe Brownley could so unsettle her.

CAITLIN DRAGGED HER FEET as she carried CompuSoft's bookkeeping to Darla's office, but it had to be done. Joe had told her. She had explained it wasn't necessary as she'd already reconciled his checkbook and had arranged his accounts receivables and payables.

He'd laughed. "And I'm the Pope."

She'd been disgusted, then furious at his assumption that she'd been joking, but now all she felt was hurt.

Amy's suggestion bounced around in her head.

Another job.

The prospect didn't seem quite so daunting anymore.

She found Darla in her office, laughing over something Tim had said. The phone rang, distracting her, for which Caitlin was thankful. She needed a moment to collect herself.

Tim smiled shyly as Darla dealt with her call, which went a long way toward boosting Caitlin's spirits. "You look really pretty today, Caitlin."

"Thanks." She forced a smile in return because Tim was probably the sweetest, most unassuming man she'd ever met. "Just tell Darla everything's there." *And done.* As she dropped the package on the desk, her gaze ran over a complicated spreadsheet opened there.

Darla hung up the phone and nodded politely to Caitlin, her eyes filled with curiosity. "Thanks. How's it going?"

"Perfect." But she was distracted. She pointed to the spreadsheet and spoke without thinking. "Did you know that this column is added up wrong? You've got the tens and hundreds column transposed."

Darla's dark gaze widened, then narrowed. "So that's why I didn't balance— How in the world did you figure that out so fast?"

"I just added them up." Caitlin held her breath at the look of bewildered shock on the woman's face. "Adding is a basic function you know. Even blondes can do it."

"This is more than just adding two plus two." Stunned, Darla stared at Tim. "Did you know she could do that?"

"No." Tim looked at Caitlin, *not* as though she were a freak as she expected, but with affection. "Cool. You're blond, beautiful *and* smart. Marry me?"

Darla snorted and shoved him out of the way. She opened the package Caitlin had brought. Her surprise was clear as she spread out the papers, realizing most of the work was complete. "This isn't Joseph's messy scrawl."

"No, it isn't."

Darla looked up. "Is it right?"

"You've seen me add."

Darla smiled slow and warm. "You know, *nothing* irritates me more than when someone sticks their nose in the air over the clinch cover on one of my favorite romance books. Do you know what I mean?"

"That I shouldn't make fun of your choice of reading material?"

Darla grasped Caitlin's hand, sent her a small, regretful smile. "I judged *you* by your cover, Caitlin. And I'm sorry for that. I hope you can forgive me."

There was no sign of the aloof woman Caitlin had first met on the elevator. Even that long, lean, perfect body of Darla's suddenly seemed less intimidating. "I did the same," Caitlin admitted, smiling in return. "Just forget it."

"I never forget a fellow number lover," Darla vowed. "When you get tired of Mr. Gorgeous Grump, come here. I'll hire you on the spot."

"I'm tired of Mr. Gorgeous Grump."

Darla laughed. "Well, then we've got a lot to talk about. You want to think about another job?"

"I already have."

Darla nodded approvingly. "Then let's do it."

THE PHONE RANG, and Joe automatically lifted the receiver, but his greeting died as Caitlin's mortgage officer introduced himself.

"You just missed Ms. Taylor," Joe said coolly. "But

I'm her...attorney. How much does she owe and where do I send it?"

He took the information, silently calling himself every sort of fool. So he had this bizarre sense of protectiveness, so what?

If you had to become a bleeding heart, you idiot, you could have gotten a puppy. It would have been far cheaper.

Vince came in. "Where's the Huntley contract?"

"I had that one out last week. It should be...hell." With dread, he looked down at the desk that was now Caitlin's. It was cleared off. So was the floor, he realized with growing horror. "I had it here. I used to have lot of files here. Oh, God." Sick, he looked up. "I don't see any files here, Vince."

Vince bit his lip.

"Tell me she didn't file," he urged. "Please. Tell me she's just been sitting here answering phones, blowing up coffee machines and looking pretty."

"Well..."

With one short, concise oath, Joe stood. "Where?" he said quietly, and Vince pointed to the series of filing cabinets against the wall. "She told me the other day she'd been doing a little at a time. She, uh...revamped your system for you."

"Oh, great." Knowing Caitlin, things could be anywhere. Individual contracts could have been grouped and filed away under *N* for "Nasty-Looking Documents." Detailed software instructions, which tended to look like maps, could have been filed under anything from *D* for "Directions," to *L* for "Looks like Latin to me."

"I'm going to have to kill her."

Vince sighed and moved toward the files. "No. Then I'd have to kill you. Too messy, Joe."

Unreasonable jealousy reared up and smacked him, hard. She'd made instant friends with these guys. Real friends. They were already as loyal to her as they were to him, maybe more. Joe had never in his life made an instant friend, and he was afraid that said something about him. Something he didn't like.

She was just a woman, he reminded himself. One woman. And while he knew it was a rotten, unfair generalization, he'd found that most women were manipulators. That had always been fine with him, since he'd never wanted one for more than the usual quick fling.

But now things were different. He didn't want a quick fling with Caitlin. All he wanted was his work. Oh, man, he couldn't lie to himself. He *did* want a quick, hard fling, and that really got him. This was his *work*, dammit. Work and pleasure did not mix!

Tim and Andy came in, and when they found out what Caitlin had done, they quickly offered to help.

"Keep in mind," Andy said, flipping through the first drawer, "if you fire her now, we'll go back to answering our own phones, and you'll get even less done. Think of your program, Joe. The one you're almost done with. Our future, man. Just remember."

"Yeah, our future." Joseph's mouth tightened. Since Caitlin had joined them, he'd accomplished little toward that goal. What made it worse, he couldn't put all the blame at her feet.

For some reason, when he sat at his computer, he now spent a good amount of time just staring at it, seeing a certain brown-eyed, sweet-smiling, drop-dead-gorgeous blonde. Thinking. Wishing. Hoping. And it annoyed him.

The files were…perfect. *A*s were in the *A*s. *B*s in the *B*s. And so on. The Huntley file was with the *H*s. It was a miracle.

And he was a jerk.

"She did a good job," Vince noted casually.

"But…I told her to answer phones." Baffled now, he looked around. He hardly recognized his surroundings; everything looked so good, so clean. So…uncluttered.

"She's done much more than just answer phones," Vince said, somewhat accusingly. "She's *made* this place, Joe. You should tell her. Thank her."

That Vince was right didn't help, but how to explain what he'd known all along? Caitlin could drive him off the brink. She was sexy, and yes, dammit, smarter than he wanted to admit.

This, he told himself harshly, was what happened when he went against his better judgment. He hadn't wanted to work with her. Had tried to find a way out of it. But short of breaking his promise to a man who'd meant everything to him, he hadn't found a way.

"Here's the general ledger that Darla called about. It's right here, in the accounting stuff, just where it should be."

Joe groaned, knowing the ledger that Darla had been asking for was two weeks overdue, and one thing Darla wasn't, was patient. He'd had it on the front desk, but apparently his efficient secretary had taken care of it for him.

He would have to face Darla, too.

The phone rang again, this time from a slimy used-car salesman Joe wouldn't have turned his back on. When he realized that Caitlin had called this guy, looking for a used car she could afford, his stomach actually cramped. She'd lost her car.

Dammit, Edmund. *Why?*

He hung up on the sales-scum, then promptly took another call. It was the building electrician. The wiring in his kitchen was faulty.

Faulty.

Joe grit his teeth as he listened to the man explain how

the entire kitchen could have gone up in flames instead of just blowing up the coffeemaker.

It hadn't been Caitlin's fault—neither time.

He was rotten to the core.

BY THE END of the week, Joe was losing it. Really losing it. For days, he'd been making a new career out of staring at his computer. Sometimes, for variety, he swore at it.

But the final straw came on Friday.

Caitlin didn't show.

He was in his office with Darla when Vince informed him that Caitlin wasn't coming in.

"Good, maybe I'll get something done for a change," Joe said with bright relief for Darla's and Vince's benefit. Meanwhile, his insides sank. A weekend was coming up. Now he wouldn't catch a glimpse of her for three days. Not one look at those huge, haunting brown eyes. Not one peek at her full red mouth that he knew damn well was more addicting than any drug. Not to mention her other notable…parts.

Worse, he'd have no one to spar with. Oh, he could pick on any of the techs. Or Darla. All of them could be counted on to give as good as they got. Except Tim, who usually just pouted.

But no one gave him what Caitlin did. A run for his money. A kick start to a whirl of emotional adrenaline he hadn't experienced in far too long, which itself was good enough reason to stay clear of her. He didn't need to feel that attachment. Didn't want to.

Nope. In fact, he should be ecstatic that she wasn't coming in, and his temper stirred when he realized he wasn't even close. "Is she sick?"

"No." Vince moved to the door. "She's moving tomorrow and needs to do some stuff."

"What?"

"She didn't tell you?"

To the amusement of both Darla and Vince, Joseph yanked up the phone and called her. "Why didn't you tell me you were moving?" he demanded when he got her on the line.

"What does that matter?" came her surprisingly weary voice. "But I'm sorry about today. I'll be there Monday."

She hung up on him.

The nerve. No one had ever— "Vince," he barked as his poor tech was trying to escape. "She's moving? By herself?"

"Yeah."

He'd paid the mortgage, dammit!

"I told her I'd come tonight to help her pack. She didn't want me to, but I'm going anyway." He hesitated. "Actually, she sounded poorly. I think I'll just go now."

Joe swore again. Darla lifted her brows and glanced at him. The knowing light in her eyes was hard to take.

"Fine," he said stiffly to Vince. No problem, he was fine with it.

Vince left and Darla smiled. "Okay," she drawled. "Where were we? The expenses, I believe." She lifted her pencil and smiled at him.

"Yeah. The expenses." He tried to concentrate. He didn't want to think about the woman who'd set his world upside down with one sweet smile and a little chaos. Because then he'd have to admit that Caitlin's presence wasn't so much an intrusion as a breath of fresh air. That having her around didn't disrupt him nearly as much as his feelings for her.

"We agreed that you were going to capitalize—"

And his feelings for her were driving him crazy. "I just can't."

"Okay." Darla shrugged. "I'll talk you into the capitalization thing later." She tapped the spreadsheet. "About the revenue."

"No."

"No?"

"I can't." His head dropped with a loud thunk to his desk. "This is out of control."

"Not you," she said with amusement. "Not the king of all control. Smooth, unruffled computer whiz Joe Brownley, paving the way for the offices of the future..."

"Darla?" His voice was muffled against the wood of his desk.

"Hmm?"

"Shut up."

"I'd love to, darling," she said smoothly, sympathetically rubbing his back, "but I need your tax info."

"Take it," he begged. "I need some peace."

"Yeah?" She pondered this as she worked on the knots of his shoulders. "Been rough, huh?"

"Worse."

"Then I guess now is not the time to tell you that Caitlin did most of the grunt work on this accounting."

He lifted his head. "What?"

"She's a little math wizard, Joe."

"She's a..." He closed his eyes. "I'm such an ass."

"Undoubtedly," she agreed. "But stop sweating the small stuff." She tugged him back up. "And get to the meat of it." She tapped the paperwork in front of them. "Tax time, buddy."

But all he could think was that Caitlin had sounded so sad. So alone. And she'd done his accounting while he'd ribbed her intelligence, mocked her at every turn.

"Let's get a move on." Darla looked at him, her eyes sparkling with humor. "Unless, of course, there's something else—or *somewhere* else—you need to be?"

Vince is probably nearly there. "Just get on with it," he urged, needing to be sidetracked. Vince was perfect for her. Perfect.

"Okay." Darla shoved some papers beneath his nose. "I need you to…"

Nice, sweet, caring Vince, he thought sarcastically. Caitlin needed someone and the superterrific, infallible, all-around-perfect man Vince was going to be it.

Darla sighed, loudly. "Joe, you're not paying attention to me. I think I should be insulted."

"I'm sorry," he muttered, rubbing his face. "I didn't mean to hurt your feelings."

"You didn't." Her voice was kind. Amused, but kind. "But stop mooning over her. It's unattractive."

"I'm not mooning."

"Sure about that?"

"Yeah." Vince would probably offer consolation, maybe a hug, and that would lead to a kiss. Dammit! Joe knew how incredibly Caitlin kissed, so he could only surmise where *that* would lead, and— His heart stopped, ice-cold at the thought. "No!"

Darla smothered a smile and shot him an innocent look. "Is that no, you don't want to expense your equipment out all in one period?" She tucked her tongue in her cheek. "Or no, you don't want Vince to get a piece of my assistant?"

In one smooth, angry motion, he rose and moved to the door. "She's *my* assistant, dammit. You can't have her."

Darla let her smile loose. "Joe, sweetie? Give her a kiss for me, would ya?"

"Bite me," he retorted, and slammed the door.

9

CAITLIN DIDN'T KNOW if she could handle the humiliation, but at this point, she was almost beyond caring.

"Nice," Chastity murmured, sugar dripping from her voice. She held her wrist up to the light, where the tennis bracelet glittered with three carats of white diamonds. "How much did you say, darling?"

Caitlin glanced at the bracelet and tried to harden her heart at selling off the only piece of jewelry she'd ever gotten from her father. "It's part of the set," she managed to say. "You have the list."

"Yes." Chastity gave her a cool glance, then reappraised the other items spread out over Caitlin's dining-room table. "You're still giving me all the furniture at the price we agreed on?"

It was far, far, less than what everything was worth, Caitlin knew. But despite the fact she'd just gotten a call from the mortgage company, and now knew Joe had bought her some time, she still couldn't afford the place, which only made her all the more desperate. Chastity, snob that she was, was prepared to give her a check today because she ran the private charity auction house that would come to cart Caitlin's stuff away. That the two women used to run in the same circle only added to Caitlin's humiliation.

But what could she do? She needed fifteen hundred to cover the check she'd just written for first, last and security deposit on her new apartment. *Shack* would have been a more accurate term, but it would put a roof over her head, and at the low monthly rent, she could just afford it. The proceeds from the sale of the jewelry would help cover the cost of a new—and very used—car.

She'd also finally figured out that she wanted to go back to college and get a degree, in something involving numbers. She could do it at night, work for Darla during the day—soon as she quit working for Joe—and she'd be fine. Just fine.

Right. And pigs could fly.

In spite of everything, though, a little burst of pride zipped through her. She'd be supporting herself, and it felt so good she almost could have hugged Chastity. Almost.

The knock at the door took her by surprise. So did the sight of Vince standing there.

"Hi," she said, panic welling. *Not this.* She could handle having to sell everything. Having to move. But she couldn't take having a friend watch. "Why aren't you at work?"

"I wanted to help pack."

"No! I mean…I'm fine. I told you on the phone. I'm just fine."

Chastity came up behind Caitlin, and eyed Vince with open curiosity. Caitlin moved to try to cover Chastity's view and prayed the woman would keep her mouth shut.

"You sounded…funny at work," he said in a low voice, keeping his eyes on Caitlin's instead of on the tall, model-beautiful woman behind her. She could have kissed him for that alone, but desperation moved in.

"As you can see, I'm really doing okay." She managed a smile that only made him frown harder.

"Are you sure?"

"Yes, I'm sorry, I don't mean to be rude, but I'm really busy. I'll see you—" She started to close the door, but he blocked her.

"I want to come help you move tomorrow," he said firmly, lifting his gaze for the first time and eyeing Chastity with mistrust.

"Hello, there," Chastity purred, and Vince nodded before looking at Caitlin again.

"I'll come early, okay?"

"Fine." She pressed on the door, knowing it would be faster to agree than argue. His help would be welcome, and so would his support.

"Wait." Vince pulled an envelope from his back pocket. "I brought your paycheck. I thought you could use it."

She took it without much enthusiasm, knowing it wouldn't make a dent. "Thank you. See you tomorrow, Vince." Before he could protest, she shut the door on his tense, worried face.

And felt like a jerk.

"Was that your boyfriend?" Chastity asked slyly. "He's awfully cute for a redhead. All that warm concern and those burning green eyes."

"He's not in your tax bracket," Caitlin said dully, and Chastity laughed.

Caitlin opened her check and did a double take. Joe had given her a raise. A big one. Her heart squeezed painfully. More pity? she wondered. Or something deeper?

"Is Vince part of CompuSoft?"

Lifting her gaze from the surprising amount of money in her hand, she asked, "What do you know about Compu-Soft?"

"There's lots of buzz about the company's future."
Chastity's eyebrows rose. "And of course, its owner, Joe
Brownley."

Caitlin went still, her raise momentarily forgotten. "You
know him?"

"I met him once. At one of your father's fantastic
parties. I think you were in Paris at the time. Or maybe
it was Milan. I can't remember. He's really something."

"My father?"

"Keep up, darling." Chastity again admired the bracelet
on her sleek, tanned wrist. "Joe Brownley. He had every
woman at that party drooling. And to think, now you work
for him."

"Drooling?"

Chastity shook her head. "You sound like a parrot."
She sank to the leather couch and ran her fingers lovingly
along the back. "I just might keep this one for myself—you
have such good taste." She sighed in pleasure and leaned
back. "What was I saying? Ah, yes. Joe. A tough-talking,
amazing-looking bad boy if I ever saw one. I love them like
that, all nasty attitude and an insatiable sexual appetite."

Joe and Chastity. Weak, Caitlin made herself ask, "Did
you two…"

"No, I'm sorry to say. But it wasn't for lack of trying
on my part, let me tell you. The way that man fills out a
pair of jeans could make a grown woman beg for mercy."

"Could we just get on with this?" It hurt. Not losing
her things—they'd never really been hers to begin with.
Not having to move; since she'd truly begun to crave her
own place filled with her own stuff, purchased with her
own money.

What hurt was something else entirely, something horrifying.

She missed Joe. Missed his smart-ass comments, his

from-the-gut laugh that always jump-started her own. Missed his sardonic grin and his piercing light blue eyes. His deep understanding of life and its intricacies. One day without him, and she ached.

She was in trouble.

"I'll take everything," Chastity said, brandishing her checkbook. "All of it."

The doorbell spoiled the relief. "Who now?" Caitlin muttered as Chastity excused herself for a minute, needing to use the telephone.

Caitlin made her way past the open boxes she'd already started to pack. At the front door, she hesitated, putting a hand on her inexplicably rapidly beating heart. Then she pulled on the knob, only to have her heart stop completely.

Joe had his arms braced against opposite sides of the jamb. His head had dropped between his shoulders, so that when she opened the door, she could have leaned forward an inch and kissed him.

He lifted his face and pierced her heart with his gaze. He didn't move, didn't smile, just looked at her.

Her entire body responded, going weak and strong at the same time. Every sense became heightened so that she felt his look as she would a touch. When she spoke, her voice wavered. "You paid the mortgage on this place until the end of the month. Then you gave me a raise."

"Ask me in, Caitlin."

That would be a disaster. She lifted her paycheck and waved it under his nose. "Why, Joe?"

"Ask me in and I'll tell you."

"Was it guilt? Or pity?"

"All right," he said evenly, pushing past her to step into the foyer. "I won't wait to be asked."

"Joe—"

"Where's Vince?"

She narrowed her eyes at his low, deceptively soft voice. "How did you know he was here?"

"Where is he?" His jaw tightened as he tried to peer around her. "Upstairs?"

"Up— Of course not!" She put her hands on her hips. "I don't want you here. I—"

He gripped her waist and hauled her to him. She felt as though she'd stepped off a cliff into thin air, as if she were falling in slow motion, slipping, gliding in weightlessness. Her heart beat hard and high in her chest. "Back off." She grabbed handfuls of his hair, meaning to push him away, but somehow ending up pulling him closer instead.

She shook. So did he, she could feel his muscles ripple against her. Their eyes locked, her breath came even quicker. "Joe—"

He claimed her mouth with his. She opened to him, hot and hungry. Hands still clasped in his hair, she changed the angle of the kiss and dived deeper, swallowing his incoherent masculine murmur of pleasure.

She wanted him, not just to hold, not just for a few stolen kisses and not just for comfort, though she wanted that, as well. She wanted him in a way that she'd never wanted anyone before. *Crazy,* she told herself. *Insane.* She couldn't afford to be thinking about this, about him. Not with her world falling apart. But she kept kissing him. Kept holding him.

He lifted his mouth from hers, but kept her close. "If you let Vince do that…"

Slowly, the words computed past her own dazed brain. "You came here because you thought I could…with Vince…that we…" With a sound of pure frustration, she pushed him away. "How could you even think it?"

Bitterly disappointed, she tried to move past him.

Joe caught her around the waist and placed her between

the wall and his muscled body. There was no doubt that he was angry when he kissed her this time, but he kept at it, nibbling and possessing until the temper evaporated into hot, delicious passion and she was kissing him back with everything she had.

When he finally released her, her body throbbed and tingled. It only marginally satisfied her to see his chest heave with his own unsteady breathing.

With a surprisingly gentle touch, he tucked her wayward hair behind her ear. "I'm sorry. You confuse me."

"It makes two of us," she assured him. "I didn't even let Vince in, Joe. And he didn't *force* his way in, either."

"I never claimed to be a gentleman, princess."

She stared at him, painfully aware of her body's response to his presence. She vibrated with it. "I still can't believe what you thought, or how much I care what you thought." She slapped her paycheck to his chest. "Keep your pity."

"Pity had nothing to do with it. You earned it. Why didn't you tell me you could do more than answer phones?"

"I *did* tell you!"

Chastity came into the room, and oblivious to the thick tension, she announced, "Here's a check, darling. I'm paying for everything. *Everything.* So don't even think about cheating me when the men come tomorrow with the truck— *Oh.*" At the sight of Joe, she dropped her businesslike tone and switched to sex kitten in the blink of an eye. "Isn't this interesting?"

Caitlin dropped her head back on her shoulders and stared heavenward. *Haven't I learned enough humility?*

"So nice to meet you again," Chastity said sweetly, holding out her hand to Joe. "I hear so much about you these days."

"You can't believe any of it," Joe assured her. "Unless it's all good."

Caitlin rolled her eyes. Chastity practically preened. "Very little of what's said about you is good, Joe. Mostly... *outrageous.*"

"Outrageous, huh? Haven't lost my touch, then." His eyes sharpened slightly. "What brings you here, Chastity?"

"Oh, we go way back," Caitlin said quickly. "Don't we, Chastity?"

"Old friends?" Joe smiled and nodded, as though he understood perfectly. What he really understood was that Caitlin seemed desperate to break up this conversation. "That's nice. Funny how Caitlin would pick today to socialize, seeing how she's moving tomorrow."

"And since I'm so busy," Caitlin interrupted, trying to pull him to the door, "you'd better get back to work and let me get to it. Thanks for coming—"

"Looks like you have a lot left to do," he said smoothly, evading her hands. "Maybe I should help you pack."

"Didn't Caitlin tell you?" Chastity laughed, managing to make the sound bubbly and full of pity at the same time. "I'm saving her pretty little hide, so to speak. I'm taking most of her things—on generous donation, of course—and using them for a charity auction next week."

Joe looked at Caitlin. She stared at something fascinating on the floor. She seemed pale, dispirited, and Joe felt sick.

Chastity glanced at her narrow gold Rolex. "Oops, gotta run! I'll be back in the morning with a truck and a couple of hunks to load everything." She scribbled something down on a scrap piece of paper, and as she walked past Joe, she stuffed it into the front pocket of his jeans, damn near fondling him in the process. He took it out and wasn't surprised to see her phone number and address. "Wait a minute."

"No," Caitlin leaped to action and rushed up behind Chastity to open the door for her. "She can't wait—she's in a hurry. So are you. Scoot now, Chastity, I'll see you."

He could fix this, Joe thought with a surge of unfamiliar panic. Otherwise, she'd lose everything, and he knew how it felt to own nothing. "Caitlin—"

"Leave it alone," she whispered frantically behind Chastity's back. *"Please,"* she added so bleakly, he swallowed his protests and let her show Chastity out.

When the woman was gone, Caitlin turned to him, her face tight and drawn. "I want you to go now."

How long had it been since he'd felt so helpless? It had been a mistake to kiss her, to touch her again. She made him feel things he shouldn't. Made him want things he didn't want to want. There'd been plenty of times in his life he could have had a shot at a future with someone and he'd chosen not to. It was too late for him now, far too late. He wanted to be alone.

And maybe if he kept repeating it to himself, he'd believe it. He'd believe he didn't want this woman in his life, *really* in his life. "Caitlin."

She held up a hand. "I need to be alone," she said quietly, dignity humming. "I *want* to be alone."

"I can't leave you. Not like this." He moved close, but at the last minute, stopped short. What right did he have to hold her? To offer comfort? He wasn't a long-term bet, and she deserved no less. Clasping his hands behind his back to keep them off her, he drew a deep breath. "Have you eaten?"

She gaped at him. Then laughed. "That sounded suspiciously like a question from a man who cared. But that couldn't be, because you would never let yourself do something as foolish as that, would you, Joe?"

"I'm trying to help you." He refused to rise to the bait, though his temper stirred. "I'm trying to offer support."

"Why?"

"Because we're friends."

"No." Sadly, she shook her head. "Friends trust one another, Joe. And you have a real problem with that. You can't let go enough to trust me."

"I care about you," he stated gruffly. "And I'm tired of you throwing it back in my face."

She looked at him, startled. "I'm sorry for that," she said softly. "I know it's not easy for you to care, and I have no right to make you feel as if it's not welcome. It is." She took the few remaining steps between them. Gently, she touched his chest, resting one hand lightly over his steadily beating heart. Watching her fingers, she whispered, "I care about you also, Joe. Far too much."

Beneath her hand, his heart beat faster. "I don't want you to," he said so low she nearly missed it.

For a moment, she stood there, head bowed. Then she raised a wet gaze to his. "I know. But that's just the way it is." Reaching behind him, she opened the front door, inviting him to leave her alone.

10

HE WAS TOUCHING HER, finally touching her. He ran his fingers down the length of her body, making her shiver with delight, anticipation. When he kissed her, slow, deep, lazy kisses that made her weak with pleasure and dizzy with desire, she moaned and begged him for more.

He pushed the blanket down, away from her, and the moonlight glowed over their bodies. His was perfect, hard and rippled and pulsing with life. She'd always felt hers was too soft, too…much, but he whispered how beautiful she was, how good she tasted, and at the needy heat in his eyes, she believed him.

For the first time in her life, she felt truly beautiful. Desirable.

As he kissed her again, he touched her—her face, her throat, her back, her legs, then back up again, stopping at the part of her burning for him.

As he lifted his head, Joseph's light eyes held hers. "I want you," he whispered thickly. "So much." His fingers skimmed over her, lightly, teasing, until she arched up against his hand.

"I want you, too." She clasped her hands around him, holding him close. "I love you, Joe. So much."

He stilled. "No," his low, shaky voice came. "You don't know me."

"I know enough."

His eyes burned brightly. "I'm…not an easy man." His voice was strangled with emotion. "And God knows I don't deserve you, but Caitlin, don't leave me. Don't ever give up on me."

She started to shake her head, but his fingers worked their magic, and her entire body started to shake. "Joe!" she called out, on the very edge and teetering crazily.…

SHE WOKE UP, twisted in her sheets, damp with perspiration and breathing as if she'd just run a marathon.

A dream. Just a dream. The most real, most perfect dream she'd ever had.

She was alone in her moonlit bed, which was scattered with moving boxes. On an empty shelf sat a porcelain kitty, filled with rose petals. It had been her first purchase for this place, and she hadn't wanted to pack it because then it would be real.

She was leaving.

She lay in her bed, *by herself,* breathless, shaking, alone. Alone and…hot. Very hot.

She had fallen in love with Joe.

She hadn't meant to, but it had happened and now she was really in trouble because he'd never allow himself to love her back. She could give and give until she was exhausted, and still, Joe would never give it back.

Trembling in unfulfilled passion, Caitlin did the only thing she could. She dropped her face to her pillow and burst into tears.

SATURDAY MORNING DAWNED bright and early. Too early, Caitlin thought with a moan and flipped over, burrowing under the covers.

Her body still tingled, still felt a little neglected, a little needy. That dream had really shaken her, and if she'd had the energy, she might have drowned her sorrows in an ice-cold shower.

When the knock came at the door, she jerked upright with panic as she remembered. It was her moving day. A day of fresh beginnings.

Yeah, right. More like the day she stepped down in the world, from beachfront condo to seedy apartment. Well, it could be worse. She could be pushing a shopping cart and muttering to herself at Venice Beach.

She had to remain positive. She was on her own, supporting herself, a first for her. Unmistakable pride boosted her spirits, as did a healthy amount of fear. Life in the real world, complete with real worries and doubts and insecurities about survival.

A day of change.

The knock came again, not so patiently this time, and with a little laugh, Caitlin leaped out of bed. Vince had kept his promise to come help, to bring the twins and Amy. The thought of having friends around cheered her considerably.

And if a little part of her wished it were Joe, she shoved that thought from her mind as she pulled on a denim mini-skirt and a tank top. Joe had no place in her life.

No place at all, she thought as she wrenched open the front door a minute later and faced…the man of her dreams.

He wore his black jeans with a black polo shirt that was actually tucked in today. His scowl matched the clothing, forcibly reminding her of that modern-day pirate again. And now that she knew he even *kissed* like a renegade, her knees went a little weak at the sight of him. He seemed

so big, so tall. She wished she'd put on her platform sandals for some desperately needed height and confidence.

"Joe." Was that her voice, all breathless and excited? She
cleared her throat and tried again. "What are you doing
here?"

Joe wished to hell he knew. What he *did* know was that
he'd never felt so lonely as he had last night. For the first
time in his life, he'd felt a deep, burning need to be with
someone who cared about him.

To allay that need, he'd looked elsewhere, but had found
no one. There'd only been one other person he'd let into his
life, but Edmund was gone now. In an attempt to bring the
man back fresh into his head, Joe had finally gone through
his thick copy of the will. What he'd discovered at the back
of the file had stunned him—a personal note from the
dead. From Edmund, the note was in his pocket right now.

Joe,
If you're reading this, it's over for me. To be honest,
it's been over for a while now. I invested too heavily
these past years, and the price is high. All my assets
will go to my investors—except CompuSoft, which
was always yours in heart anyway.

Make sure you give Caitlin that job we talked
about. It'll be all she has—there's nothing left to
give her. She will have to learn to take care of herself now, and there's nobody in the world who can
do that better than you.

Teach her, Joe. I know you'll resent this intrusion,
but I also know you'll help show her what I couldn't.
Please, for my sake, don't tell her how stupid I've
been. Let me have that at least, but help her.

She'll need you.
Best always, Edmund.

Sick to the depths of his soul, Joe had lain awake all night. Edmund had faced financial disaster, and he hadn't known. Caitlin had been suffering because of it, and he hadn't paid attention. She'd even proved herself over and over, and he had closed his eyes to it.

All those times he'd been so rough. So cruel. She'd given everything she had in the first adverse situation of her life, fighting like a trooper to survive, and he'd done little but groan about the trouble she'd been. Edmund would have been ashamed of him, and Joe had never felt so disgusted in all his life.

"Joe?" Caitlin was looking at him expectantly. "Why are you here?"

"You're letting that Chastity woman take everything, every possession you have, rather than accept my help," he said in a very controlled, very soft voice. "I hate that, Caitlin."

"Do you?"

Gently, he pushed his way in, his mood darkening when he saw the scores of boxes lining the place.

"Why didn't you didn't let me help you?"

"Maybe I wanted to do it myself."

He looked so startled at that, Caitlin had to laugh. "What's the matter? Didn't think the spoiled brat would be able to do it?"

"No," he said with brutal honesty, meeting her steady gaze. "I didn't. But that was before I knew you. I'm beginning to realize you're capable of just about anything."

"I am." Unable to stand there looking at him and not remember her dream, that delicious, perfect dream where he'd touched her with those big, warm hands and sent her to heaven, she turned away.

"Is that what you're wearing to move in?"

She glanced down at herself. Her ribbed, shocking-pink tank top was appliquéd with a huge happy face on the chest. She felt comfortable. Definitely fashionable. But just not quite tall enough… "Yes, it is, but just a sec," she exclaimed, and ran up the stairs.

"Sorry, Chastity," she murmured, and reached into one of the ten huge boxes of shoes she'd agreed to sell. "You'll have to do without these."

After she had the clear, high plastic platform sandals on, she felt better. Much better. She left her room, grabbing the porcelain kitty filled with rose petals, deciding on the spot she wasn't giving that up, either.

At the top of the stairs, she smiled down to an impatiently waiting Joe. She thought she was hot stuff now. Really, really untouchable.

As she reached the second stair, the heel of her right shoe caught. Without warning, she bounced down the stairs on her butt. Rose petals rained down as they spilled out of her porcelain kitty.

When she hit bottom, Joe was right there, on his knees, face grim. "You okay?" Rose petals shimmered in his hair, on his shoulders. "Caitlin! Answer me, dammit."

The only thing hurting at the moment was her pride. Well, and maybe the rug burn she'd just gotten on her tender backside. "I'll live."

He looked so ridiculous with that fierce expression as rose petals fell off his nose, but she didn't dare laugh. She nearly choked holding it in, then she exploded.

He scowled at her laughter. "Are you sure you're not hurt? I know you couldn't have broken that hard head of yours, but…"

She kept laughing, unable to stop.

His frown faded; he bit his lip. Then he started laughing, too.

"You're unbelievable," he said when he could talk. "Take those damn heels off before you kill me."

"Kill *you?*" she gasped, wiping her tears of mirth.

"Yeah." His voice had gone deep and husky.

She followed his gaze.

Her skirt was hiked up indecently high, exposing a long length of thigh and even a peek at her panties.

She shoved the skirt down, face suddenly hot.

Just like his eyes. "They match," he said unevenly.

Puzzled, she glanced down at the black-and-yellow happy face sewn on the front of her can't-miss-me pink tank top. She thought nothing could embarrass her more than her pratfall down the stairs, but she'd been wrong. Her brilliant pink panties also had happy faces on them, and remembering her graceless slide down the stairs with her skirt up around her ears, she imagined Joe had gotten quite a view of them.

Revenge was simple enough.

When Vince, Tim and Andy showed up, she put them all to work along with Chastity and the men she'd brought.

"This is perfect," Caitlin said casually several hours later.

Tim, Andy and Joe moved by, each staggering under the weight of a huge box. Joe stopped, breath huffing, muscles straining in all sorts of interesting ways. "What's perfect? That we're doing all the work, or that you're the boss for a change?"

She grinned, her revenge complete. "Both!"

LATER VINCE PULLED her aside. "You really okay?"

"Hey, I've got four studs at my beck and call." She took in his designer sweats, and compared them to the jeans of the other men. She had to laugh. "Well, three studs and one really finely dressed man. I can't think of one reason why I shouldn't be just peachy fine."

"Because you're losing everything," he said gently, running his hand up her arm.

"Thanks for the reminder." Why wasn't his touch causing goose bumps? Making her shiver with desire? He was perfect. Any normal woman would have told her so.

But she wasn't normal.

"Are you sure about this, Caitlin?" Vince asked, clearly concerned. "Are you sure you didn't pick too hastily?"

It took her a minute to realize he was talking about her choice of apartment, not the man she'd fallen for.

"I looked up your new address on the map last night, and I don't think it's such a great neighborhood."

Caitlin knew it wasn't, but she hadn't had much to work with. And she was doing her darnedest not to obsess or dwell, since she hated to do either. But it was getting increasingly difficult to stay cheery with Vince reminding her of everything she'd been trying not to think about. "Well, at least my car won't get stolen."

"Why?" He looked blank and she sighed.

"Because I already got it repossessed. Remember?"

He frowned, for a moment reminding her of another man. The man who was at this moment grappling with a large box, for her, sweat making his skin glisten, exertion making his arms bulge.

Her darn knees went weak and she wasn't even wearing those platforms; Joe had tossed them with great ceremony into the Dumpster.

"Caitlin?" Vince looked at her. "You could come with me. Take your time and find something better."

"I don't think so," Joe said lightly in a voice of steel as he came back inside.

Tim, clearly sensing the sudden tension, clapped his hands and announced cheerfully, "Well, we've got everything you want to bring, Caitlin. I vote we stop for a pizza on the way to the new apartment."

"A vegetarian one," Andy said. "With anchovies."

Tim groaned loudly. "Pepperoni and sausage."

Vince ignored them and stared at Joe. "Have you seen her new place? If you have, you can't possibly believe she'll be safe there."

"But she'll be safe with you?"

Caitlin quickly stepped in between the two. "Okay," she said with a huge, tremulous smile. "Pizza it is. But I'm sorry, Andy. Anchovies make me puke. You can have them on the side."

"I can't believe you said that," Vince said to Joe.

"Why not? You've been drooling after her for weeks now. Falling all over yourself like a love-sick fool."

Vince shook his head in disgust. "And what is it you've been doing, Joe? Because it sure as hell hasn't been working on our program."

"Oh, knock it off, both of you!" Caitlin tried to appeal to their common sense, but the testosterone-fueled men weren't listening. "If you don't, I'm going to get really tough and make you kiss and make up."

In tune to Andy's and Tim's snickers, she pushed each of them out the door toward Vince's van, where everything was loaded. Fast as she could, she told three quick dirty jokes in a row, leaving Tim and Andy in stitches. Even Vince cracked a smile as he hopped into the driver's seat.

But Joe stayed solemn and quiet.

Until they got to her new apartment—which they discovered had been given away only two hours before. Caitlin's deposit check had bounced.

CAITLIN HAD BEEN TRYING—really she had. But she'd lost every ounce of cheer when over an hour later, she dragged herself back into her condo.

"I'm so sorry," Andy said quietly, taking her hand.

"It's not your fault he didn't have another apartment

available," she said wearily. "Don't worry, guys. I'll come up with something."

Joe nodded at the twins, and they reluctantly left.

Vince hovered stubbornly at the door. "I want you to come with me. You're practically homeless."

"No, I'm not. Thanks to Joe here, I can live in this empty place until the end of the month if I want to."

Vince and Joe stared at each other.

"Not that again." She rubbed her head, perilously close to tears. "I can't handle it right now, guys. I'd like to be alone."

Joe's heart cracked at the utterly forlorn expression on her face. He couldn't stand it. "Come with me."

Caitlin's eyes widened. So did his own as he realized what he'd just said, but he wouldn't take it back, not with Vince waiting, watching. Wanting.

"You can come to my place if you'd rather," Vince said quietly.

"Vince—"

"You can stay with me as long as you like."

Immeasurable sorrow filled her eyes as she turned to Joseph's head tech. "I'm sorry, Vince. I just…can't."

Vince's confused gaze searched hers a long moment.

"Don't hate me," Caitlin whispered, squeezing his hand. "I know it sounds stupid and cliché, but I really, really need your friendship."

"I'll always be your friend, Caitlin. Always. But I'll probably also always be hoping you change your mind." With a curt jerk of his head toward Joe, he asked, "Do you have any idea what you're getting into?"

"Only vaguely," she admitted.

"Could you stop talking about me as if I wasn't standing right here?" Joe demanded.

"See? He's bad-tempered. Attitude ridden. Mean as hell," Vince said ruthlessly.

"He's also fiercely loyal, generous to a fault, compassionate and the most wonderful man I've ever met, and you know it because he's your best friend."

Vince nodded slowly. "Yes, he is, and I care about him almost as much as I've come to care about you. My condolences, Caitlin."

Caitlin tilted her head, baffled. "For what?"

"You fell in love with him, didn't you?"

Her smile was both dazzling and wobbly. "Yes," she whispered.

And Joseph's heart stopped.

11

Vince's smile was bittersweet. "I'm glad for him, even if I am jealous as hell." He met Joseph's stunned gaze and shook his head. "Unbelievable, Joe. Your luck keeps holding."

Joe didn't know whether he'd call it luck or not, but either way, he still couldn't speak. Not with his body humming in disbelief, his eyes glued to the woman who'd just declared herself.

"You're the most courageous woman I know," Vince told Caitlin. "And I hope you're patient, too, because you certainly haven't taken the easy road."

She loves me, Joe thought, bowled over by the knowledge. This unbearably sweet, chaotic, intelligent woman loved him, and all he'd given her in return was a hard time and grief.

"I'll be okay," Caitlin said softly, looking at Joe.

He wanted to hold her, never let her go. He wanted to run like hell and never look back. She deserved better, far better. He'd never been able to handle intimacy. Never. To think he could now was foolish. Worse, he would hurt her. *He'd* get hurt.

The fear of it overwhelmed him, which was ironic. He

wasn't afraid of much. Just a lush, beautiful blonde whose smile and innate kindness knocked him for a loop.

Vince leaned close and gave Caitlin a hug. Joe told himself he wouldn't hurt his best friend unless he kissed her, but then Vince did exactly that, on the cheek.

Caitlin kissed him back, sniffed and opened the door for him. "See you Monday, Vince. Thanks. For everything."

Vince smiled once and was gone.

Joe didn't know whether he was relieved or terrified. Both, he decided a minute later when Caitlin turned around and walked into her empty living room. "Chastity's clearly finished," she said. "Everything's gone."

Maybe she could ignore what had just happened, but he couldn't. "Why did you pick me, Caitlin?"

"I wonder if she took the toaster?" She sighed deeply. "I wanted her to because it was an antique, but whoever buys it won't know you have to turn the bread halfway through or you get burned toast."

"Caitlin."

She was wringing her fingers, and her voice came low and fast. "Well, I'd hate to have someone pay good money for the thing and feel like they got ripped off—"

"Caitlin." He moved up close to her, knowing she was as nervous as he was.

"And the cord! Oh, God. I forgot to tell her it occasionally catches fire, and you've seen my luck with such things. Do you think I should call her? Because—"

"The damn toaster is gone." He grabbed her shoulders, whipped her around. "Now talk to me."

"I know the toaster's gone!" she shouted unexpectedly. "*Everything* is gone. Do you think I can't see that?" She threw off his touch. "I have eyes in my head, you know!" Her voice cracked. "I'm not a…complete idiot."

Then, to his utter horror, she burst into tears.

"Ah, hell," he said to the empty room, and pulled her into his arms. "I'm sorry," he said gruffly. "I'm so sorry."

"You're only sorry you're the one that's left to deal with me." Her tears soaked his shirt and destroyed his heart.

Selfish, he called himself silently, as quiet sobs shook her body. Holding her close, he ran his hands gently over her back and shoulders. Selfish to enjoy holding her so much, when she was hurting so badly.

"I'm tired of being alone," she said on a sniff.

Tell her, his conscience urged. *Tell her that her father didn't abandon her on purpose, that he had no choice. Tell her you're the jerk for not reading the letter sooner.* But he'd been asked to remain silent by the only man who ever showed him kindness and he couldn't break that promise.

Caitlin squeezed him, hiccuping, and she felt so small, so defenseless…so perfectly right in his arms.

"You smell like roses," she said finally, sliding her hands up around his neck.

It felt so good to have her touch him, he shuddered at the contact. "I should. I took a bath in them, remember?"

"I'm sorry."

"Those shoes were ridiculous."

"Hey, I needed my height. Extra boost of confidence, you know."

His smile faded as he stroked her hair and rubbed his cheek against the top of her head. He hated that she continually felt self-conscious about herself, knowing that a good portion of that just might be his fault. "Did I ever tell you I'm rather fond of petite women that I can tuck in close and wrap myself around?" He tightened his arms to prove his point.

"No." Her voice was breathless. "You've told me very little about yourself." Warily, she lifted her head. "Are you really?"

"Really." Of its own accord, one hand skimmed down her spine, cupped her bottom and very purposely rubbed her against the painfully hard part of him that could prove his point.

Her mouth opened, as if she couldn't get enough air.

"And here's the really ironic part," he told her in a stage whisper. "Curvaceous blondes are my wildest fantasy."

She lifted her head. Her curtain of gold hair tickled his chin. Those beautiful, drenched eyes of hers met his. And heaven help him, but he recognized some of the emotion there. Need. Hunger. Desire. His body reacted with matching emotions, fast and hot, leaving him shaken, for he'd never felt that way about anyone. "Caitlin...come with me?"

"Where to?"

"My place." He took her hand.

She resisted. "That's not a good idea."

"Probably not," he agreed. "But I'm not leaving you here alone." He hesitated, cupped her cheek and met her uncertain gaze. "Let's stop fighting this and follow through with it for once, okay?"

She bit her lip and studied him for a long moment, searching for he could only imagine what. Apparently, she found it.

"Okay," she whispered.

SHE FELL ASLEEP in his car on the way to his house. When she felt herself being lifted into a pair of strong arms, hoisted up against a hard, warm chest, she bit back her drowsy grin.

"Oh, Vince. I had no idea you felt so good."

Joseph's arms tightened around her and he growled, making her laugh. Her arms snaked around his neck, and she buried her face into his throat.

"Say my name," he demanded.

"Joe," she whispered obediently, winning herself a quick, hard hug. "Mmm. You smell good," she murmured, inhaling deeply.

"You're awake," he accused. "Why am I carrying you into my house?"

It was a lovely house. Small, inexplicably cozy.

And messy.

She had a quick view of high vaulted ceilings, airy rooms, magazines and books scattered haphazardly throughout... his home.

Uncertain yet tingling with anticipation, she closed her eyes again.

She had the weightless sensation of going up stairs. She held him tight and kept her eyes closed. "Did I ever tell you I fantasize about this modern-day pirate?" She felt him pause, could feel the weight of his curious stare. It almost made her giggle. "He's tall, dark and so gorgeous and he takes me into his cabin and bounces me onto the—" The sentence ended on a scream as he tossed her into the air.

She hit a soft, giving bed and bounced high. Her eyes flew open. They were in a large bedroom, with dark oak furniture. There were clothes and more books scattered around, not that the mess surprised her; she'd seen his office.

What *did* surprise her was that she was sprawled on the biggest bed she'd ever seen. With forest-green, soft, Joe-scented bedding that she wanted to bury her nose in.

He laughed roughly and followed her down on the bed. "Do I ravish you now, fair maiden? Or after I tie up your crew?"

"Now, please." The words popped out of her mouth before she could stop them. He lowered himself to her, bracketing her body with his arms.

And it was then that trickle of doubt spurted. Just a trickle, though, because he was tall and dark and oh so gorgeous. "Joe, wait a sec—"

"Pirates wait for no one," he growled in a voice that sent delicious shivers running over her skin.

His tough, lean body pressed against hers, holding her pinned where she'd dreamed about being. But that was her dream, not his. "Joe...this isn't just because you feel sorry for me, is it?"

He blinked, then knelt in the bed, pulling her up with him so that they were face-to-face. "What?"

"We both know I'm not exactly your type."

He stroked her cheek. "I told you I fantasize about you. I meant it."

"You had to say that."

She made a move to leave the bed, and he stopped her, putting his hands on her hips. "What is this? I want you. You have to know that."

"You don't just feel bad because I cried?"

"You're kidding me, right?" Taking her hand, he pressed it down between their bodies, holding it up against the fly of his jeans, and his erection. "If anyone should feel bad for anyone," he announced, his eyes crossing with lust when she caressed him through the fabric, "then feel sorry for me. For *this*." Unable to help himself, he thrust into her hand, groaning when she squeezed gently. "I've been in this pathetic state since the day you walked into my office weeks ago and smiled at me, and it has absolutely nothing to do with pity!"

"Oh," she breathed, her eyes bright and luminous, sensuous and innocent at the same time. Just looking at her had heat spearing his body, weakening his limbs with a needy languor.

She kept on touching him, forbidden delight and discovery lighting her face as her fingers explored him through his jeans. "I did this to you?" she asked in wonder.

"Yeah. *You,*" he said, grabbing her waist. "You. Only you, Caitlin."

Her eyes met his, full and warm. "I love you, Joe."

It should have turned him off to hear the words, but instead they had the opposite effect. "I can't give you more than this," he told her, his voice rough and torn as he pushed against her hand mindlessly. "No promises. I can't."

"I know," she whispered, sighing deeply when he flexed his buttocks again. "Don't worry, Joe. This is enough for me."

It wasn't, shouldn't be, and he wanted to tell her so, but then she planted her wet, open mouth on his throat and her fingers moved on him again, and he was lost to reason. Lost to anything but what she was doing to him.

Then she let him go, and he thought he would die right there on the spot. So much emotion swirled in her eyes; heat, need, desire...and then with one fluid motion, she pulled off her ribbed tank top with the happy face. She was wearing nothing beneath but glorious, proud, full curves.

"Caitlin." He said just that, just her name, because he could hardly breathe, but she covered herself with her arms. The most difficult thing he'd ever done was to bite back his own raging needs, to soothe and excite. He wanted to see her wild, out of control. For him. He ran a finger down her arm, watching as goose bumps rose. He touched her hair reverently, then eased it aside to kiss the sensitive spot beneath her ear.

His fingers, light as air, played on her throat, then moved to the back of her neck. Stroking, teasing, always barely touching, but still she covered herself, not wanting to stop, he knew, but not knowing how to make him continue.

With his large, warm, tender hands, he cupped her face and tilted it up. "You're so beautiful," he whispered. "So very beautiful, Caitlin." Then he kissed her, stealing any breath she had left. That warm, sexy mouth deepened the connection, his powerful body pressing into hers. When he finally raised his head, she moaned in protest.

"Be sure, Caitlin," he said softly. "I won't have you regretting this."

"I have nothing to regret," she promised. The words were no sooner out of her mouth than his head descended. Each kiss got hotter, wetter, deeper. He ran his hands down her arms to her elbows.

"Why would you try to hide such an incredible body?" he wondered hoarsely.

"Because I'm embarrassed." She closed her eyes. "I'm too..."

"Too perfect." He finished her sentence in a husky whisper. "Don't tell me you're hiding something. Tan lines? Freckles?"

"Both," she admitted with a choked laugh, which died on a harsh intake of breath when his fingers explored the soft flesh spilling out above and below her crossed arms. "Oh...*oh*. Joe, hurry."

"Don't rush me," he murmured. "I want to see and touch and taste each little bit as we go."

She had melted at his tender touch, but his words finished the job.

Gently, Joe took her hands and pulled them away from her body. His gaze held hers, and she'd never felt so exposed or so aroused in her entire life.

"No, don't do that. Don't be embarrassed," he told her. "Save it for when you sail down the stairs on your ass. Or when you blow up my coffeemaker. But not here. There's no room for it. Only for you, and me and what we make each other feel." Without another word, he lowered his head, splaying his hands on her bare back to draw her close, and opened his mouth on her breast.

Fire speared through her, and Caitlin bit her lip to keep any sounds she might make inside, but it was difficult, made more so by what he continued to do to her. With his tongue, he teased, using a maddening light touch, then suckled hard and strong.

She was burning up. Her toes were curling. Her insides were churning, shaking. So were her legs. She shook her head to clear it. Still, her body raced, each pulse a desperate, needy beat. "I feel...funny," she whispered, realizing she was holding tight to his shirt with a death grip.

"I feel overdressed." Straightening, he whipped his shirt off, and the light that had been too stark only a moment before became a blessing. Rugged, lean and rangy, he was quite simply the most magnificently made man she'd ever seen. His gaze held hers as his fingers went to the button on his jeans. It opened and...

Oh, how could she have forgotten? "Joe—" She let out a disparaging sound. "I don't know quite how to tell you this," she moaned.

His fingers stilled. "You could start by opening your eyes," he suggested quietly.

She did, then wished she hadn't. His body was incredible. His chest drew her fingers. She couldn't help herself, the tensed muscles, the light, springy hair that tapered down and disappeared into his open jeans...

Capturing her wandering hands in his, he looked at her. "Tell me now, before this goes any further. A change of heart?"

"Not exactly." Bravely, she met his hot, frustrated gaze. "I'm sort of a...virgin."

12

"Sort of?" Joe let out a choked laugh. "You're *sort of* a virgin? How is that?"

"Because I haven't done it before."

"Caitlin." His rough voice held a hint of a smile. "*How* is it you've never done this before?"

Self-conscious now, she turned from him and once again crossed her arms over herself. "I know you probably thought I had lots of experience. I let people think that because…"

"Because?"

This wasn't the time to shrink back and try to save her feelings, or her pride. "Because then they know I mean it when I say back off."

"Ah…the curse of being desirable."

"I don't understand it." She wished she had her shirt back, but in her haste to jump him, she'd tossed it dramatically across the room. "But nobody looks beneath the surface."

"Or past the checkbook," he said in her ear, making her jump.

"I guess you do understand."

"What I don't understand is why you were going to

let me have you." With terrifying tenderness, he pulled her back against his chest, crossing his arms over hers to hold her close.

It took every ounce of courage she had, but at this point, there was nothing to lose. Turning in those warm, capable arms, she met his questioning, and yes, still passionate, gaze. "Because I love you, Joe. I wanted you to be my first."

His eyes were bright, eloquent. "I thought we weren't going to make promises."

"I don't expect one back," she assured him, pulling his head down to hers. "Please, Joe. Love me. Just for now."

Her lips clung to his, warm and wet. Sensuous and innocent. *Just for now,* Joe promised himself. His eyes never left hers as he stepped out of the rest of his clothes. "Don't regret this. I won't be able to stand it if you do."

"I won't." Her gaze was glued on him, her eyes wide and huge as she unabashedly stared at his proud, heavy sex. "You're so beautiful, Joe. All virile and...hard."

On a laughing moan, he lay down, wrapped her in his arms and held her to him while his mouth ravaged hers again. "*Hard* being the key word here." He slipped his hands beneath her skirt, caressing her thighs, playing with the tiny panties he knew were covered with happy faces. "I've wanted to take these off since the moment I got a front-row view of them on the landing."

She closed her eyes, her face flushing. Laughing, Joe kissed her until she was flushed with passion, not embarrassment. He loved the texture of her—all soft and dewy, he discovered as he removed the last of her clothing. Loved, too, the way her body quivered at his every touch. Lowering his head, he nuzzled at her, kissing and nipping until she was squirming and burning and restless beneath him.

Lifting his head, he whispered, "Every time I was a jerk at work, it's because I wanted to do this." His thumbs made passing caresses over the tips of her tight, aching breasts, and he watched her body's response, the way she panted for air, how her nipples puckered and beaded. When he drew her into his mouth again, she arched off the bed and into his arms.

His hands ran down over her stomach, her thighs and back up between her legs. She caught her breath when he touched her there, then again when his touch deepened. Tossing her head back, she fisted her hands in the sheets and pushed up against his fingers, whimpering shamelessly.

"Good?" he asked.

"More."

She was the sweetest, most desirable woman he'd ever seen, and for the moment, she was his. "Yes," he promised. Her slippery heat coated his fingers and he moaned. "Yes, more."

Her body tightened as he stroked her slowly, every muscle clenched. His fingers continued their sensuous play, giving her what she'd wanted, and she whispered his name, her voice torn between need and panic.

"It's all right." He drowned in the pleasure of watching her discover desire. "I'm right here to catch you."

She was on a tightwire, grappling and struggling for balance. She hadn't expected this. Had thought it would be fast. Reckless. Even painful. What she got was hot, delicious sensation. "Joe!" She wriggled, but the heat just consumed her all the more. "Where's my *more?*"

"For someone new at this, you're awfully bossy." He kneeled between her legs. "I like that in a woman." He put on a condom before she could stop him. It wasn't that she didn't want to be protected, but she wanted to participate in everything. Before she could complain, he was kissing her again and she could participate in that, oh yes, she could.

Joe tasted her lips, her jaw, the precise spot on her throat where the pulse frantically leaped, then took her mouth again, shaken with the force of his own need. And those fierce little sounds that escaped the back of her throat were the most arousing he'd ever heard. He heard her sigh, then when he nudged at her hot, wet center, she gasped.

"Okay?"

"Yes," she murmured, opening for him. "More. You promised."

"Hold on to me, Caitlin. Hold on tight."

Her arms slipped around him. His mouth closed over hers as he slid into her inch by inch. When she cried out, he froze in terror that he'd hurt her, but she shifted her hips, lifting experimentally. "Oh," she breathed, drawing him in deeper, snugger, tighter. "Oh, I like it."

His hands shifted from her hips to brace on either side of her face where, from behind a haze of deep hunger, he watched her for any signs of pain or discomfort. She shot him a dazzling smile, and he saw only pleasure—dazed, dark pleasure.

"There's even more, isn't there?" she asked hopefully, making him both groan and laugh at the same time.

She met him stroke for mind-blowing stroke. And in her eyes, he saw everything he'd feared. Warmth, affection, acceptance, heat, need. Love. He saw her soul, and his mirrored back. He knew that alone should have brought the most fear of all, but miraculously, it didn't.

Beneath him, her eyes went wide, her mouth opened in a surprised O as she began to tremble and quiver. He tried to hold back, to prolong it for her, but his body finally betrayed him as she convulsed. Her shudder worked through him and became his, swirling and demanding, and he buried his face in her neck. She sobbed out his name as she climaxed, and clenching her fisted hands in his, he let himself go with her.

CAITLIN WOKE FIRST, to the sound of a light spring rain. Joe held her as he slept, her back to his front, his arms possessively tight. One of his large hands, fingers spread wide, was low on her belly. The other had tangled itself in her hair. One of his thighs was pressed between hers, and for a minute, she allowed herself to snuggle in deeper, surrounded by his warmth.

She'd made love, for the first time in her life. Giddiness welled, as did a blissful wonder. She'd never known… never expected it to be so spectacular.

He had made it that way, she thought, joy flooding her. He'd been fierce and wild, and gentle and tender. And afterward, he'd carefully cleaned her with a warm washcloth, expressing concern, but it hadn't been necessary.

She felt fantastic.

And ready for more.

His breathing was deep and even, and she decided to show mercy as she'd obviously exhausted him.

The scent of the rain on the air drew her, as did her curiosity about the house. She'd only caught a short glimpse of it. She slipped out of his arms, then stopped to admire his tough, rangy body, only half-covered by the sheet.

He was…heart stopping. And, for now, hers.

The air was hot, muggy, so she walked nude to his dresser and stopped short, baffled at the reflection. Her hair exploded around her face in loose curls. Her lips were red and swollen, her eyes bright with light.

She looked…like a wild woman in love, one who'd just been shown how much she was loved back.

Did Joseph love her?

She twisted to see the still sleeping form on the bed. He was magnificent, sprawled in all his glory. He certainly lusted after her, and she blushed remembering exactly how much.

But did he love her?

She sighed, suddenly discontent. She stepped out onto the dark patio. His house faced the ocean, giving her an incredible view of heavy waves lit only by whatever weak moonbeams managed to evade the clouds.

A jag of lightning flashed across the sky, and a second later thunder rolled. The roof of the deck was slatted and the cool rain fell through, wetting her. Shivering a little in spite of the hot air, she stood there, face upturned to the mist, loving the erotic feel of the cool drops landing on her hot body.

My God, JOE THOUGHT as he stepped onto the deck. *That's a sight.* Caitlin stood there with her head tipped back, the slim column of her neck exposed, her full breasts thrust out, her legs taut as she rose up on tiptoe, stretching. Her white skin glimmered and shone as the rain ran in small rivulets down her body.

Just standing there watching her take her own pleasure from the rain had him rock hard. He walked up behind her, slid his arms around her slick body. "I thought it was all a dream," he whispered in her ear, taking the soft flesh there between his teeth, drawing goose bumps to her skin.

Arching back, pressing her spine to his chest, she sucked in her breath when his hands spread on her thighs, streaked up her hips, over her belly and captured her wet breasts. "If it was," she moaned, "it's the best dream I ever had." His thumbs flicked over her rigid nipples, making her writhe, her hips rubbing urgently back against his.

"Caitlin." He slid his hand down, down past damp curls

and into hot, creamy heaven, thrilling to the soft, dark sounds she made. "Are you sore?"

"No, not yet," she murmured, gripping the railing in front of her for balance and grinding her hips in tune with his hand. "I had no idea…how it would be. I want more, Joe…more."

Whatever she wanted tonight would be hers. Whatever she needed, he'd find a way to give it. The rain fell unnoticed, and the night sang with the sounds of the ocean waves hitting the shore below them.

He kept her from falling as she came, quivering in the pale light, her skin aglow. He held her like that, just held her, with her bottom snugged up to his thighs, with their hearts racing together, and he had to fight against swiftly and greedily taking all that she offered. It wasn't easy, not with her hands urging him as she reached back and gripped his hips, and her body poised and waiting, silently confirming she yearned as much as he. The ache within him became primal and blinding as he absorbed the exquisite feel of her against him.

Nothing would ever be the same again.

Suddenly, there was no reason to rush; there was time. Time for everything. And oh, how he wanted everything, every whisper, every promise, every touch, every single second of this time with her.

Everywhere he touched, she turned something inside him to gold. Despite the misery of his past, she made him feel good, wanted, needed…loved. "You make me feel so alive," he said huskily, kissing his way along her jaw. "So alive."

She twisted her head, and her lips parted for his kiss. The urgency returned tenfold. She pressed back against him, restlessly running her hands up and down his thighs, trying to draw him inside her.

Too fast, he wanted to tell her. He wanted to savor, explore, but he couldn't be gentle or tender now. Nor patient, either, with her fingers digging into him, urging, demanding.

The darkness cocooned them; the rumbling thunder and flash of lightning provided their music. There was no other sound except the frantic roar of their own hearts and harsh, needy breathing. One last time, Joe brought his mouth down to hers, taking her stunned cry into his throat as he gripped her hips and sheathed himself into her from behind, filling her. Not just with his body; even in his confusion, he understood that.

Caitlin threw her head back against his shoulder, her body bowing in slim arch with strain and wonder and abandon. Even as part of his brain struggled to register that he didn't want to love her, didn't want to need her, she was taking him away to a place where there was no reality. Where love didn't hurt. Where he could let himself go.

He closed his eyes and did just that. He'd known, hadn't he, that it would be like this with her. No restraints, no boundaries. No hurt. Nothing and no one but the two of them, soaring as high as the clouds.

"I HAVE NO IDEA why I waited so long to do that," Caitlin said conversationally a short time later. "It was the most fun I've ever had."

"Fun?" He pulled on a pair of sweatpants and laughed shortly. "You nearly sent me to another world, and you thought it was fun?"

He watched her blond head poke out the neck of his shirt as she put it on, and his blood surged again at the way she looked wearing his clothes. "You know what I mean," she said, lifting her gaze and smiling at him.

His throat closed. "Yeah."

"I…uh…you know. Had an orgasm." She blushed gorgeously and he laughed.

"*An* orgasm?" He laughed again. "Princess, you most definitely had more than one."

"Is it always like that?"

His amusement faded. It had *never* been like that. "No, not always."

She was looking at him with such emotion, he nearly lost it right there. His lungs seemed to collapse. He needed her, so damn much. Fear welled, but he beat it back. She wouldn't know, *couldn't* know, unless he told her. And if he didn't tell her, he had nothing to fear. Nothing at all.

But she deserved more than a quick toss in the sheets. She needed a man who would give her a future, a man who could give in to his emotions and love her as she deserved to be loved. She didn't need him further screwing up her life. Hell, she already thought she was in love with him. Delusions, of course. No one could love him, not really. He was trouble. Had an attitude. A temper. He could be a real selfish bastard. He'd once walked away from his family without looking back. He'd taken everything Edmund had given him without questioning Edmund about Caitlin, and what she might need. Caitlin didn't know this, didn't understand, or she could never believe herself in love with him.

He had to walk away now. Had to forget that she could make him laugh, could make life seem more important than work. He had to get over how her chaotic world was as fresh as springwater when compared to his, which was stagnant, dead. He had to forget that her way of living revived his, gave him back the joy of being. She'd wormed her way into his heart, spreading happiness like wildfire, and he hadn't even noticed it happening. He *had* to forget, or the realization of exactly what it would cost him to walk away would kill him.

She took his hand, and that simply loving, trusting gesture had him swallowing hard.

He'd betrayed Edmund by failing to protect Caitlin. He'd betrayed Caitlin by taking her love and innocence without means to repay it. Any minute, fate was going to come knocking and swipe away any semblance of happiness.

She led him down the stairs. "I'm starving," she said. "I hope you have more food in your house than I do in mine." In the entryway, halfway between his kitchen and the living room, she came to a grinding halt. "I've never seen your place."

He let out a laugh. "Should've opened your eyes when I was playing pirate and hauling you upstairs."

But Caitlin didn't crack a smile. She stared at the beautiful glass-and-stone foyer, looked through the kitchen and then sank to a large window seat in the front room, which overlooked the sea. "You never told me you lived at the beach, too," she said with mock calm while her heart drummed painfully.

"I didn't know where you lived until yesterday."

It was a day for truths, and she had to have this one. "My father loved the beach. He gave this place to you, didn't he?"

A shadow crossed Joseph's expressive, rugged face. "Yes. Years ago. When I graduated from the college he bullied me into attending."

"I see." Pain slashed through her, and she didn't quite manage to keep it out of her voice. "I'm sorry. I…have to go."

In three strides, he caught up with her at the door. Gently, his heart already dying, he turned her to face him.

"I didn't know he didn't pay yours off, Caitlin. I swear to you, until that day we had lunch, I didn't know. Come here. You'll see." He dragged her back through the living room into the kitchen. On the table was a file, which he opened. "The deed for this place," he told her, lifting it up for her inspection.

Attached to it was a quit-claim notice, which even she knew meant Joseph was signing this house over, and out of his name. *To her.*

"I don't understand why Edmund had paid mine off all those years ago, and hadn't done the same for you."

"I do," she said sadly. "It was my own fault. I moved around a lot, was a fickle little thing. He never believed I'd stay in one place for long."

He tossed the document to the table and took her shoulders so he could see into her face. "Whatever his reasons, I can't keep this place while you lose yours. It's wrong, and so was I."

"Wrong? How were you wrong?"

He'd gone a little pale. "I should have done this a long time ago. I'm ashamed of myself that I didn't. I'm giving you this place."

"No." She backed away from him, holding her hands out to ward him off, because one more touch would have her crumpling, and she had to be strong. "You're not giving it up for me." She walked out of the foyer, and he followed her into the living room. "My father gave it to you," she said, turning around in the large room. "He wanted you to have it."

"I can't keep it." He watched her pace. "You're hurting and I want to make it better."

Caitlin knew there was only one way for Joe to make it better, and that was for him to love her back as hopelessly as she loved him. While she suspected he might feel that way, she was afraid that he was so used to being able to rely on only himself, he'd never be able to tell her. "You can't do this. He loved you, Joe."

"Yes. And I...loved him," he said softly, the words grainy and rusty, as if he'd never said them out loud before. He looked open, and more vulnerable than she thought possible.

He *could* love, she thought with a rush of joy and hope. And knowing that, she knew anything, anything at all, was possible.

"I loved him," he repeated. "God, I did."

Through a haze of tears, Caitlin reached out and hugged him. "I know you did," she said brokenly. "I know."

He clung close and so did she, their bodies warm and snug and comforting. It started out that way at least, but as the seconds ticked on, and as Caitlin thrilled to be needed by him, the embrace turned decidedly sexual. The smooth, sleek skin of his back drew her fingers, and her hips instinctively melded with his.

"Caitlin."

His low voice turned her on, too. Everything about him turned her on. He was unpolished. Physical. Sharply intelligent. Fascinating.

And fiercely aroused.

He looked at her, and it was far more than the heat and hunger that drew her. Whether he knew it or not, he did *need* her, needed her strength and affections. Her love.

She wanted to give it.

She slipped her arms around his neck at the same time that he caught her up against him. His body was strong and hard and grieving. The combination was irresistible.

"Again," she whispered, kissing his jaw, his ear, whatever she could reach. "I want you again."

"No, it'll hurt you," he protested softly. "You'll get sore."

"Don't make me seduce you," she said, and he laughed, turning his face so that their mouths met, only it wasn't the gentle kiss she'd been expecting. Instead, it was deep and wet and long and had them both straining for more.

"Please, Joe," she whispered. "You'll never hurt me."

He moaned, his forehead against hers. "I can't resist you, not for anything." He dragged her down to the thick carpet, then took her face in his hands and kissed her again, a carnal mating of their tongues, a mimic of what he really wanted to do to her. He touched her first with his hot gaze, then opened the shirt covering her, spreading it wide.

Slowly, he lowered his body to hers, grace and power blending into one. He took her to new heights by just touching her with his magic fingers. He tore off his sweats so they were skin to skin. He was sensual and uninhibited, and he encouraged the same from her, caressing and kissing every inch of her until she was panting his name.

When he slid down between her thighs, replacing his fingers with his lips, she arched up and begged. It wasn't necessary; his open mouth unerringly found her. One stroke from his nimble tongue and she exploded. Instantly. Without control.

Chest heaving, body slick with perspiration, hair sticking to her face, she looked up at the ceiling and blinked in stunned surprise. Her body rippled with aftershocks. "Wow."

"Again," he demanded, cupping her, stroking her back into a frenzy, back to the point of no return, until bright lights blinded her, until her body went taut as a bow, then shuddered again and again.

"Wow," she repeated when she could finally manage as she lay limp and replete on the floor.

Joseph's skin was also slick when he levered himself

above her and bridged her body with his arms. "Such a profound statement."

She ran her hands through his hair. "Then how about *more?*"

"Caitlin—"

"Don't make me beg again."

He entered her, then, watching her flushed face carefully. She sighed with pleasure. He pushed deeper. Her breath quickened and so did his, and eyes locked with hers, he pushed deeper still. When he was fully seated within her, they both moaned.

He pressed his forehead against hers. "Tell me you're okay."

"I'm...so much more than okay."

He began to move and she raised her hips to meet his hungry thrusts. Though each one threatened to toss him over the edge, he held back, waiting for her.

When she climaxed, she dug her fingers into his skin and cried out his name, shuddering long and hard. It was more than he could take. Burying his face in her neck, he allowed himself to follow her into oblivion.

"OKAY, YOU CAN seduce me," he gasped, and she laughed.

They stared at each other, and their smiles faded slowly.

"Please, let me do this for you," he whispered. They were lying entwined on the soft carpeting, looking at the high ceiling, listening to the rain pound the roof. "Please let me give you this place."

"You know, I think I've figured something out." She sat up and slipped his shirt back on with a smile. She loved wearing his clothes. "I don't think my father meant to forget me. He just wanted to show me something."

Guilt stabbed at him, and he wished with all his might Edmund hadn't asked for his silence. She looked so beautiful sitting there covered only by his shirt, still flowing from their lovemaking.

Beautiful and brave.

But all he could think about was the secret he was keeping from her. The secret his mentor—her father—had asked him to keep.

She was right. Edmund hadn't forgotten her; he'd tried to protect her, the only way he knew. Through Joe.

And Joe had let them both down.

His heart hurt just looking at her. That unwanted panic surged again when he realized what was happening to him. That despite his promises to himself, he just kept falling for her deeper and deeper.

He loved her.

"I think my father just wanted me to learn to support myself, you know?" I always resented him saying that, and because of that resentment, I never bothered to learn when he was alive. But he was right. I can see how selfishly I'd been living. This has helped me grow up, and at twenty-four, it's about time."

He stared at her. "How can you be so generous? So understanding?"

"It's just facts." She reached out and hugged him. His heart broke.

Sorry, Edmund, he pleaded silently. *Forgive me, but I have to do this*

He had to tell the truth. "Caitlin." His voice was hoarse, and for the life of him he couldn't force himself to return her sweet smile. "I have to show you something."

He drew her to her feet, using the excuse to hold her close one more time, for he held no illusions.

This would be the last time.

"It's upstairs," he said. "Will you come with me?"

"Anywhere," she said simply, and his chest tightened all the more.

In his room, he went to his jeans, which were still lying on the floor. Slipping them on, he pulled out Edmund's letter from the pocket.

Caitlin recognized her father's writing. "What's this?" she asked, looking at him.

"Read it."

"Oh, my God," she breathed, sinking onto the bed as she did just that. "He ran out of money.... He asked you to take care of me." She closed her eyes on the mortification. "And I thought I was doing it on my own." She let out a choked laugh. "Not only did he make you give me a job—he had such a low opinion of me that he thought you would have to help teach me to support myself!"

"No, no Caitlin, it's not like that—"

She leaped off the bed, and though he thought he'd been prepared for her to walk out of his life, he'd been wrong.

He couldn't let her go.

He caught her at the door, barely. "Wait. Caitlin—"

"No." She ripped free, his shirt flying up above her luscious thighs. Her wild hair swung in a curtain when she whipped around to face him. "You knew all along his money was gone. You called me princess, you made fun of me, and you knew!"

"No, no, I didn't. I saw the note for the first time yesterday. I know how this all sounds to you, but you've got to listen." He grabbed her shoulders and jerked her close, as if he could shake the belief right back into her. "Before you came into my life, all I thought about was work. I ate, slept and drank work."

"You still do," she said bitterly, shrugging him off and backing to the door. "What a fool I've been. I thought you were starting to come around, starting to care for me."

"I was. *Am!*"

"Right."

"Caitlin," he said in a grating voice, coming after her, letting pride go because he had no choice. No choice at all. "You have no idea how difficult this is for me to say, but it's the truth. I care for you. More than I ever have for anyone."

"I don't think so. I think this is guilt. It's just you fulfilling a stupid promise you made to my father." Her lovely eyes filled. "And because he meant so much to you, you'll do anything to see the vow through."

"He *did* mean a lot to me. But you've got the promise thing all wrong—"

He was talking to air.

When he caught her on the stairs, she spun on him. "Did you guys get a good laugh at my expense?" Her eyes were stark with pain. "Tim and Andy. And Vince. Was it all a joke? Their help? Their friendship?"

"No. No, Caitlin. God. They worship you. You've got to know that."

"I know nothing anymore," she said sadly, backing from him. "Except that apparently I've been such a burden to you that you couldn't even explain the truth to me."

"You read the letter. He asked me not to tell you. Whether it was pride or love—"

She let out a hard laugh. "Don't fool yourself. He loved *you*, Joe."

She made it to the bottom of the stairs before he caught up with her and hauled her back against him. "It was far more than just a promise," he grated into her ear as she struggled valiantly against him. "And you're not going anywhere. Not even if you did manage to put some pants on."

"Yes, I am."

"You don't have a car."

"I'm a pro at public transportation, believe me."

"Forget it." He entertained some half-baked idea about holding her down on his bed and proving to her in the only way he knew how to show her how much he cared.

"In your mind, you owed him," she panted as she wiggled and shimmied to free herself, grunting when he simply slung her over his shoulder.

"It started out that way, yes. Damn, you're heavy. Ouch—" He snarled through his teeth when she bit him on the shoulder, hard. "But I *did* start to care about you. Hell! I couldn't stop thinking about you." He carried her up the steps, back into his room.

Tossing her to the bed, he watched her eyes darken with anger when she bounced.

"You only thought about me so much because of all the trouble I caused," she accused, furious. Hurt.

When he knelt next to her, she crawled away.

"Don't touch me." She ran around the side of the bed, jerked her skirt off the floor and slid it over her legs. "Don't ever touch me again."

"Dammit, Caitlin."

"No, I mean it," she said when he came after her. "Don't touch me now—I won't be able to resist you if you do." Biting her lip, she looked wildly around, then shoved her bare, petite feet into his large tennis shoes. Her anger faded at the look on his face. "This isn't all your fault," she allowed. "It's mostly mine, actually. I'm an idiot to have fallen for you."

"I fell for you, too," he said quietly.

She straightened and tugged down the hem of his shirt with touching dignity despite the fact that only a fraction of an inch of her skirt stuck out the bottom, and she looked like a little girl playing dress-up. "It came far too late, Joe."

Now he knew real, gut-wrenching fear. The kind he

hadn't felt since he'd been a kid with nowhere to go and nothing to eat. "What do you mean?"

"I mean that I have to go."

He reached for her again, but she backed away. Nothing had ever hurt as much as that. "Don't do that," he beseeched her, fighting nasty by going in low and snagging her to him. "Don't back away from me—I can't take it."

"I feel like you betrayed me, Joe. I can't forget that."

"And I can't let you go," he said softly, gentling his hold. With minute care, he cupped her neck and drew her forward so that his mouth could find hers, quietly, slowly, then deeper, until he felt his insides start to crack apart at the emotional pressure built up there. His hands framed her face, then slid down her neck, over her shoulders to mold her body, drawing a soft, needy sound from her.

Then she shoved back, her eyes wide and luminous. "Don't kiss me like that."

"Like what?"

"Like—" Her voice cracked. "Like you love me." Covering her mouth with a shaking hand, she walked away, only to stop, hand hovering over the doorknob when he spoke.

"Don't go, Caitlin."

"I can't stay here with you—it would hurt too much. I want more from you than just...this. I want trust. And love. If I stay, I'll make both of us miserable, and I refuse to do that. I deserve more, Joe, and so do you."

"Wait. Please—" With horror, he realized how close he was to actually begging her. Begging. *God.* He'd been through some unbelievably tough spots before, but he'd never resorted to begging.

She looked at him then, *really* looked at him, and he knew she was seeing past the exterior to the real him. To his deepest of souls. In her eyes, he could see the flicker of life. Of hope. Of love. Hard to accept, when he still hadn't quite let himself believe that she could really love him.

"What should I wait for, Joe?"

The words stuck in his throat.

When he didn't speak, the hope in her eyes went out. Simply extinguished. Liquid brown eyes cold for the first time since he'd met her, she left the room, shutting the door quietly behind her.

All Joe could do was try to swallow past the lump in his throat and watch her go.

He'd ruined everything, and with his eyes wide open.

All because he'd waited too long to trust her with the heart he'd protected from harm for years. All because he'd waited too long to tell her he'd finally, truly, irrevocably fallen in love.

Hell, maybe he should have begged.

13

ALONE IN HIS OFFICE around 4:00 a.m., Joe finally cracked his computer program. It simply clicked into place. Once upon a time, he would have jumped up and down, shouting and whooping for joy.

Now the victory was hollow and meaningless.

Yes, he'd been working for the better part of three years on the office system he knew would redefine software as most knew it. And yes, he'd once measured his success by it.

Success meant nothing now. Nothing at all without Caitlin to share it with.

Swiping his hands down over his haggard face, he looked around at the darkened office. The only light came from the glow of his computer. The only sound was from the coffeemaker down the hall—which was running perfectly smoothly now that the wiring had been fixed.

Still, what he wouldn't give for Caitlin to be here blowing it up at this very moment.

Because only then would everything be perfect.

He'd once harbored great dreams on this program. It would make him famous. Make him a somebody. Give him wealth and security for the rest of his life.

Now he didn't care about any of that. All he wanted
was to be a somebody to a beautiful, caring woman named
Caitlin Taylor, who wanted nothing to do with a cold jerk
like himself.

He couldn't blame her.

Shoving back from his desk, he stalked toward the door,
suddenly needed fresh air.

Once outside, he stepped around the sleeping homeless
man on the stoop and watched the early morning. Tipping
his head back, he studied the stars.

A cool breeze rumpled his hair. In the distance, he could
hear the drone of the cars on the freeway, and knew he'd
get better scenery at home on the beach, where he could
feel the cool ocean spray and smell the salt on the wind.

But at home, he'd be reminded of his failures. He'd
probably stand in his bedroom and fantasize about having Caitlin back in his bed, golden hair spread on his pillow, her dark eyes wide with sensual wonder. Just thinking
about it brought back the scent of her, the satiny feel of
her skin against his.

If he closed his eyes, it was so clear in his mind. The
huge bed. Sighs and murmurs, the whisper of clothing
floating to the floor. The gentle, full spring wind teasing
the curtains and blowing the air over their heated skin…

He'd driven her away, and the way he saw it now, he had
two choices. He could be a complete fool and live, suffer
with his decision to keep his love to himself.

Or he could do what he'd sworn never to do—beg.

HE'D SEARCHED THE entire world for her. At least it felt
that way. With humbling defeat, Joe tossed his keys aside,
plopped down in his chair and set his head on the desk.

It was late afternoon, and he had to face the devastating facts.

Caitlin had disappeared.

"Still no luck, Joe?" Andy asked from the doorway.

Joe didn't lift his head, but knew Tim would be hovering there, as well, waiting for news. "Nope."

"You looked in her condo?"

Only six times. "Yep."

"And you checked your place again, right?" This from Tim, sounding worried.

Worried was a good thing, Joe decided, because if either Andy or Tim was hiding her, he would have to kill them. "Yes, I checked my place again." He'd left it unlocked, actually, hoping against hope. But she hadn't shown.

"Did her father have a place?"

"It's been sold, but yes, I checked there, too. And the hotels and motels in the area." And the hospitals, the police station, and out of sheer desperation, three of the closest shopping malls. He'd even driven to Amy's apartment, after he'd begged the landlord for her address. No one had answered.

Caitlin had vanished, and he'd never in his life been so sick or guilt-ridden.

"So you screwed up already, huh?"

Vince. He'd been suspiciously absent earlier this morning. Joe surged to his feet, rage ready. "Tell me where she is."

Vince shot him a half smile. "Flattering that you think she'd come to me." His smile faded to disgust. "All you had to do was love her, Joe. She's like the most perfect woman ever made. What was so hard about giving her your all?"

"Tell me, damn you."

Both Tim and Andy wisely slunk back, out of sight.

Vince just shrugged. "I don't know any more than you do where she is, but I'll tell you this. If I find her first, you won't stand a chance in hell."

Joe searched his face for any sign of deception and found none. He sank back to his chair in defeat. "You really don't know where she is, do you?"

Stuffing his hands into his trouser pockets, Vince leaned back against the wall and shook his head. "Do you think she's all right?"

Joe's anger abruptly drained. "God, I hope so." Shoving his fingers through his hair, he leaped up again, unable to sit still. He started pacing. "I'm the biggest idiot on earth."

"Nah." Vince managed a grin. "Well, maybe. But at least you're the richest one. I can't believe how much they're going to pay for that system, Joe. Not to mention the royalties. I just can't believe it."

"All we have is a very small, preliminary commitment from one phone call. They still have to test it, prove to themselves it does what I say it does," Joe warned soberly. "I hope you're not disappointed I decided to sell it rather than market it ourselves."

"Are you kidding? If it works out, you just set me and the twins up for life." Vince's joy faded. "But how about you? Are you set up for life, as well?"

Joe looked out the window. Below, the city was flowing smoothly into evening traffic. The streets were crawling with commuters, seething with activity. He sighed. "Not until I find Caitlin."

Two days later, Joe was out of his mind with torment. How could Caitlin have just disappeared into thin air?

It amazed him, the turn everything had taken. In just two short days, he'd gotten a request for a complete new system, one that would keep him busy for a long time to come. This, on top of a bid for the system he'd just completed. They'd offered about five times what he'd expected, which should have been the thrill of a lifetime. If Edmund were alive, he'd be cackling over the fact that suddenly Joe had more money than he.

But Edmund wasn't alive, Caitlin was gone and the victory meant nothing.

His phone rang and he leaped at it, heart pounding. "Yes?" he barked, hope cruelly flaring.

"Joe, could you come up here?"

Darla. Hope deflated, leaving despair. "I'm busy."

"You always say that."

"I can't face the tax stuff right now, Darla," he said quietly. Outside his window, two flights down, a young woman walked, holding a toddler's hand. The little girl, awed by the size of the buildings around her, craned her head upward and seemed to stare right into Joseph's eyes.

God, I want one of those, he thought as his heart constricted. *I want a family, and I want it with Caitlin.*

"Please come, Joe," Darla said into his ear, her voice no longer friendly, but urgent. "You won't be sorry."

He stared at the receiver after she hung up. Darla never asked him for anything unless it was absolutely necessary. So it was with a sigh that he left his office and headed toward the elevator.

When he entered Darla's suite minutes later, she rushed out of one of her offices and yanked him into another before he could draw a breath.

"What the —"

"Shush." Darla locked the door and shoved him into a chair.

"Darla," he said slowly, carefully, straightening. "This is flattering, but—"

"Shut up, Brownley." Darla slapped her hands on her slim hips and glared at him. "I can't believe how slow you are." She paced the room. "I promised not to get involved and normally I'm pretty good at promises, but I'm reneging on this one. It's going to cause problems, but I think maybe it's worth it."

He was getting dizzy watching her pace. "What the hell are you talking about?"

"I haven't got the details figured out yet. She's much, much smarter than I gave her credit for, but I think if you—"

Joe went still. "Darla."

"It should work. I think if you really play it up right, she'll feel so sorry for you, she'll *have* to give in. For some reason, she's a sucker for you, which does work in your favor."

It was difficult, very difficult, to remain calm with his heart blocking his windpipe. "You know where Caitlin is."

Darla stopped pacing and looked at him as if he were an idiot. "Of course I do."

Slowly, in order to not kill her before she gave him the information he needed, he advanced on her. "Tell me where she is. Afterward, you can tell me why you kept it from me for nearly three days when you knew how much this meant to me."

Darla's eyes went soft with regret, but she kept the presence of mind to back up. "I'm sorry, Joe. But she was so hurt, and you really messed things up. She begged me to keep quiet, but now, after watching her work while trying not to mourn over you, I think I did the wrong thing by promising not to tell you. I think she really loves you. And I know you love her too, way deep down in that black heart of yours."

He came closer, and her words came faster. "So could you do me a favor, a really big one?" She rushed her words. "Could you go out there and make my new full-charge bookkeeper-in-training smile? Could you turn her grief into joy so that I can get some real work done?"

That stopped him short. "You hired Caitlin?"

"Well, you've seen what she can do with numbers. Besides, I like her." Her face softened. "A lot."

"But—"

"You should see the mind that lurks behind that ridiculous come-hither haircut…my God, Joe. She loves numbers almost as much as I do. She can't answer the phones too well, and she tends to distract my male clients all to hell, but you should see her reconcile a checkbook. A girl after my own heart."

He was jerking the door open, nerves and hope singing through his veins. "You can't keep her—she's mine."

"Wanna make a bet?"

When he growled, she laughed, "Let the best boss win," she said diplomatically.

She smiled when he slammed out. "I'm such a hopeless romantic," she whispered, and sank into her chair to get some work done.

IT WAS LATE AFTERNOON by the time Caitlin finished sorting out the bank account of one of Darla's clients. It had been a mess of mismatched checks, wrong deposits and untotaled columns. At first, she'd panicked, but after looking closer, she'd gotten excited.

It *was* a mess, but it was just a matter of shopping around for the right numbers—and no one understood shopping better than Caitlin Taylor. Besides, somehow, the mess appealed. Maybe because she so understood the misguided logic that had created the disaster in the first place. Maybe because she loved to sort and add and organize. Maybe just because she felt thrilled about feeling so useful. So purposeful.

It should have made her very happy. It shouldn't have had her gaze covered in a sheen of unshed tears.

"No," she muttered, blinking them ruthlessly back as she stuck her pencil into the electric sharpener. "I won't cry another tear for him. Not one."

"I don't blame you."

She nearly started right out of her chair at the sound of that familiar, unbearably sexy voice behind her.

"Hi," he said softly when she looked up at him. Slowly, he shut her office door. He walked over to her desk while her heart raced. He looked the same. Stone-washed faded jeans fitted to that long, lean, mouthwatering body. Simple white T-shirt stretched across his chest. Brown wavy hair falling over his forehead, as wayward as the owner. But it was his eyes, those light blue, all-seeing eyes, that stopped her heart.

They held her, caressed her, refused to let her go.

"Are you going to sharpen that pencil until it's gone?"

With a soft oath, she jerked it out of the sharpener. "What are you doing here?"

He smiled at her, then took a little bow. "Your new secretary at your service, ma'am."

14

CAITLIN COULD ONLY stare at him. "I'm sorry. I don't understand."

Joe leaned a hip against her desk, propping his weight against it. "It's simple. You're so busy working the accounts, Darla hired me to...answer phones for you. And..." His gaze searched the room, and she wasn't so far gone in her own misery that she missed the nerves and tension in his eyes.

"And?" she prompted, uncertain.

He lifted a shoulder. "And whatever else you need."

"What if I don't need anything?"

Now he looked desperate, as well as stressed. "I can make coffee," he added, brightening. "Real good coffee."

She let out a little disbelieving laugh, but had no idea what to say. Her fingers fiddled on her desk for something to do. Grabbing another pencil, she shoved it into the sharpener.

"Are you going to sharpen all your pencils now?" he asked conversationally. "Because I could do that for you."

"I don't need any help from you."

"I understand." His gruff voice clearly said the opposite.

So did his hungry gaze as it swept over her. "I certainly brushed *you* off enough times, didn't I?"

"Is that what this is about?"

"Partly." He gave her a little smile. "You have no idea how good it is to see you, Caitlin."

"I've...been busy."

Undeterred, he slid closer, and his gaze was the most soul-shaking, heart-wrenching one she'd ever seen. "You scared me to death, you know," he said quietly. "I'm not sure whether to throttle you or kiss you silly."

Unable to sit and calmly talk after all that had transpired between them, she surged to her feet. With lithe grace, he rose, as well, and they ended up toe-to-toe...face-to-face.

"Neither appeals," she said quickly.

He touched her cheek gently, tenderly. "Why don't we kiss and make sure."

It took every ounce of self-control she had not to throw herself at him. "There's nothing left, Joe."

"I'm sorry you feel that way."

"No," she said, her eyes stinging. He'd not stopped touching her in that way he had, the way that told her how much he cared. "That's how *you* feel."

"You're wrong. There's our future, for one thing."

She might have scoffed, except he was looking at her as though willing her to understand. She didn't. "We have no future, Joe. The things I said—about loving you. I was mistaken." She met his gaze and wasn't at all satisfied to see the pain her words had caused. She faltered, and knew if he didn't leave now, she'd crumple. "Please go."

The phone rang, and before she could reach for it, Joe smoothly scooped it up. "Ms. Taylor's desk... No, I'm sorry. She's unavailable at this time. A problem with your account?" He listened seriously. "I see. Okay. Hold on,

I'll get her." Without taking his eyes off her, he hung up the phone.

She gaped at him. "Are you crazy? That's not how to put someone on hold."

"Oops," he said mildly. "Sorry. Would you like to talk now?"

She let out a baffled laugh. "Do I have a choice?" She wished he didn't look so good. Wished she didn't miss him so much that she was shaking with it.

He looked at her bleakly, all cockiness and self-assurance gone. "Where have you been, Caitlin? Have you had a place to stay? Enough money to get by? Dammit, are you even eating?"

"God, don't." She made herself busy at the shelving unit against the wall. "Don't talk to me in that voice. It makes me hurt."

He followed her, his big body sheltering her with warmth. "I hate it that you hurt. I hate that I caused it."

"Please," she begged him, unwilling to break down in front of him. "Please, just go. I can't handle this—"

"If you'd just listen for a minute—"

"I *have* listened to you! All my life, I've been listening to someone, blindly following. Well, I'm through with all that!" She was shouting now and she didn't care. "I'm listening to myself for a change!"

He held her close when she started to shake with anger, but then her anger was gone and it was grief making her tremble. "I'm listening to myself."

"The way I should have all along."

It was the steely quiet in his tone that made her look at him. "What do you mean?"

His hands gentled on her, but he didn't let go. "I'm sorrier than I can say, Caitlin. You tried to tell me so many things—how you needed more to do on the job, that your father had pretty much deserted you...the way you felt about me. I didn't listen," he said with disgust aimed at himself, "because I couldn't handle how you made me feel."

"And how did I make you feel?"

"Terrified," he said without hesitation. "Caitlin, I know next to nothing about letting people close to me. Even less about families and love. I was never close to anyone until your father. I taught myself to hold back, to protect myself, because it was easier. I couldn't get hurt that way."

"That's no way to live," she told him huskily. "*I* can't live that way."

His smile was warm and completely unexpected. "I know. You throw yourself wholeheartedly into absolutely everything you do. You give it your all, one hundred percent of the time, not worrying first about whether you're going to get hurt or not. It's one of the things I love most about you."

Afraid to read too much into his words, she crossed her arms over her chest and backed up a step, out of his reach so he couldn't touch her. So she couldn't touch him.

"I cared when I didn't want to," he said. "I worried when I swore I wouldn't. And, dammit," he said roughly, his voice breaking, "I really need you to break in any time here and tell me you meant it when you told me you loved me."

Tears filled her eyes as she stared at him mute. Panic filled him. "Wait!" he said quickly, slapping his forehead as he remembered. "Wait a minute. I have to tell you first. God, I really stink at this." He drew a deep, ragged breath and met her drenched eyes. "I fell in love with you, Caitlin. No matter how many times I told myself I couldn't, that I wouldn't, I did." Lifting her hand to his lips, he kissed her knuckles. "I love you hopelessly. Will you stay with me forever? Be my wife?"

She looked at him for an eternal moment, for once her eyes shuttering her thoughts from him. "I don't want to go back to work for you," she said finally.

What did that mean? he wondered wildly. But then, beyond the tears, he saw the teasing light in her expression. Relief, joy and a thousand other surging emotions rushed through him.

"No offense," she told him teasingly as a tear slipped down her cheek, "but Darla pays better. Much better."

"I'll triple your salary," he said without skipping a beat, cupping her face and swiping another tear away with the pad of his thumb. "Quadruple."

She tilted her head as she considered. "I get to do your accounting. All of it."

"Okay, but I'll make the coffee," he said quickly, flashing a sudden grin as his heart threatened to burst. "Caitlin. Tell me. Tell me you love me quick, that you forgive me for being such a fool. I'm dying here."

She smiled, a brilliant radiance spreading across her features. "I forgive you for being a fool. And I love you with all my heart."

"Thank God," he murmured, yanking her against him. He kissed her, his mouth open and warm, receiving and giving, full of enough promises to last a lifetime.

Lifting her head, she looked up at him, taking a moment to bask in the joy of their love. "Let's talk benefits."

Eyes dancing with love and laughter, he pulled her close. "Anything you want, Mrs. Brownley-to-be. Anything you want."

"Well, there's just a couple of little things...." She pulled him close and whispered her heart's wishes.

He made them all come true.

Epilogue

THE LETTER CAME one week after their wedding. Caitlin stared at her father's familiar handwriting and her pounding heart landed in her throat.

"What's the matter?" Joe came up behind her, slipped his arms around her waist. Leaning over her shoulder, he frowned. "That's Edmund's writing. How—?" His arms tightened on her in reaction. "Where did that come from?"

"The mail." She patted his hand, knowing the gruffness in his voice was grief. "My father's attorney sent it to me." Quickly, with fingers that shook, Caitlin ripped open the envelope.

As she read, her heart warmed, tightening in her chest until she thought she might burst with love and happiness. She whirled to face Joe, her eyes burning, her throat thick. In his gaze, she saw equal emotion, and knew he'd already read the note. "He loved me," she whispered.

"Very much," Joe whispered back, bending to kiss her softly. "So much that he hid away a trust fund for you. He just wanted to be sure you'd be okay without him. Without his money."

"It says here that he always knew I was smart, tough—" Her voice cracked a little. "But he wanted *me* to know it, too." She smiled through a haze of tears. "He'd have loved that we found each other. He was so proud of you."

Joe cupped her face and looked down at her with love swimming in his eyes. "He'd be so proud of you, too."

Caitlin sighed. "I can't imagine what we're going to do with all that money."

"No?" Joe smiled. "A year ago, you wouldn't have given it a second thought."

"I'd have shopped until I dropped." She smiled. "Joe, how do you feel about setting up a charity for women who've been dumped on?"

"You mean divorced?"

"Yeah. Or deserted in any way at all." She grinned. This was the delicious part. "We could train them to make it on their own. Teach them important skills." She tucked her tongue firmly in her cheek and gazed up at Joe with adoring affection. "You know, such as respect for their employer, making coffee, or...how to pick the proper business attire."

He gave a shout of laughter and hugged her close.

Suddenly serious, she leaned back. "I want to do this, Joe. We can train them in bookkeeping. *Anything.* Just so that they don't feel worthless or helpless. What do you think?"

His breath caught because she could still dazzle him with just a look. "I think I've never been more proud, or loved you so much, Caitlin Taylor Brownley." He bent to give her another kiss, his love, his life.

* * * * *

HER PERFECT STRANGER

To Bruce and Leslie,
for all your expertise, patience and,
most of all, friendship. Without you,
this book wouldn't have happened. Thank you.

1

HE'D NEVER FORGET his first glimpse of her. Or his second. She walked in as if she owned the place, and in spite of the chaos around him, Mike Wright's gaze went straight to her.

It was all indelibly imprinted on his mind: the harsh storm outside pounding against the fogged windows of the hotel's pub; the lights flickering overhead as the electricity spiked with the repeated thunder and lightning; the loud strains of Bruce Springsteen blaring from the speakers mounted on the walls; and the even louder voices of the crowd around him talking, laughing, flirting.

He'd been preoccupied, thinking about the reason he was in Huntsville, Alabama, in the first place — his life's work, flying space-shuttle missions. The primary pilot of STS-124 had broken his leg parachuting and the first team backup had contacted hepatitis. All of which left Mike, once the secondary backup, as primary. He'd been called home from Russia, where he'd been on loan from NASA to the Russian space agency for the past decade.

Mike loved being an astronaut, loved his testosterone-run life. But he loved women, too. All of them, all shapes and sizes and colors and temperaments, and everything else faded away the moment she stepped foot into the place—the storm, the crowd, the noise, everything.

She was wet. Drenched, actually, her dark, dark hair plastered to her head, her clothes molded to her body.

Another poor, unsuspecting victim of Huntsville's weather.

He could empathize, having just come from Russia's much more predictable climate. But this woman didn't look like anyone's poor, unsuspecting victim, not with all that attitude, fire and rage spitting from her eyes.

Drenched *and* inconvenienced, Mike guessed. And furious because of it. Amused, he watched as she pressed on through the thick crowd, and in spite of her petite stature, people moved out of her way.

It might have been the fact she was a woman, when most of the patrons were men. On-the-prowl men at that. But Mike thought it was most likely her queen-to-peasant look, which was icily effective.

She worked her way closer, heading directly toward the bar, and by coincidence, him.

"Something hot," she demanded of the bartender, setting one hand down on the bar as she dropped her bag, establishing a spot for herself where there was none to be had. She looked to both sides, left then right, clearly expecting someone to get off a stool so she could sit.

Grinning now, Mike rose. "Please," he said, gesturing for her to take over his seat.

"Thank you." As if she wasn't dripping a river of sleet and rain onto the floor, she sat and tossed back her hair. When the bartender slid what looked like an Irish coffee in her direction, she nodded her head regally and sipped. And then sighed. Sinfully. Her shoulders relaxed slightly, as if she'd just dropped the weight of the world.

After a good long moment she appeared to realize Mike

was still standing next to her. Her dark-blue eyes were cool and assessing, in direct contrast to her wet, incredibly lush, incredibly sexy body.

"No coat?" he asked, referring to the fact that she wore only a black, long-sleeved silky blouse and skirt, both of which were so wet they couldn't have been tighter if she'd painted them on. What should have been a very conservative, businesslike outfit became outrageously erotic, especially given that she had a body that could make a grown man drop to his knees and beg.

"Someone stole it at the airport." She grimaced. "I hate airports. Let's just say this is a day better forgotten all around."

She didn't have the Southern drawl of the people around him. Another misplaced traveler, he thought, just like him. "Got caught by surprise in the storm, did you?"

"Yes, and I hate surprises."

Her voice was as cool as her eyes. Low and slightly husky. But combined with all those feminine curves, she became one irresistible contradiction. Fire and ice. Tough, yet sexy as hell.

Though Mike had planned to have only one beer, which he'd already had, before going up to his room and crashing for the night in preparation of the crazy week ahead, he didn't budge. And when the guy behind him vacated his bar stool, Mike took it for himself.

"Don't bother," the woman said without even looking at him as she continued to sip her drink, staring directly ahead.

Mike made himself comfortable, which included smiling at the pretty female bartender. "Don't bother what?"

"Trying to charm me out of my panties."

Mike laughed. This woman was truly sexy as hell, gorgeous as sin, cool and regal, *and* funny. A rarity. "Now why would I try do to that?" he asked innocently, though now that she'd planted the thought, he could think of nothing else.

"Why? Hmm. Maybe because I have breasts? I don't know." She shrugged. "It's a male genetic disorder, I guess."

Mike laughed. "You mean I can't help myself? That's a handy excuse, indeed."

She looked at him then, a hint of a smile on her lips. "That's right. As a man, you can't help yourself, you're just a helpless slave to your body's cravings. Will that help you sleep at night?"

"Oh, yes. Thank you." Mike cocked his head and studied her. She was warming up, no doubt thanks to her drink. There was a blush to her cheeks now, and when she crossed her legs—remarkably well-toned legs, he couldn't help but notice—they appeared to be drying nicely.

"To be quite honest," he said. "I hadn't entertained the notion of charming you out of your panties at all."

She slanted him a doubtful glance.

"Really." He lifted his hands in an innocent gesture. "Before you came, I was just going up to bed."

"Don't let me stop you."

But she did. Everything about her stopped him cold, and it wasn't just that her nipples were pressing against the material of her blouse, or that her skirt clung to her perfectly rounded hips. It wasn't just that she smelled like heaven and sin all in one, or that he knew instinctively that her skin would be soft and creamy and in need of being warmed up by his hands and mouth. He couldn't name exactly what kept him there watching her, why she fascinated him so.

Everything in his home country fascinated him, and he enjoyed being back after so long away, even given the work ahead of him. He needed lengthy training for the upcoming mission, training that would keep him busy day and night until launch, only four months off now. He'd be far from his own place, which happened to be a suitcase more often than not these days. In fact, he was no longer certain where home really was. He and his four brothers were close, but they were also scattered across the globe, in various military branches. So was his father.

His mother, a native Russian, had died when Mike— named Mikhail by her—was very young, which was probably why, when he'd had the chance to go to Russia after his stint in the Air Force, he'd jumped at it, wanting to understand the heritage he'd missed. He'd welcomed the opportunity to stay there, in the cosmonaut space program, working on the International Space Station. It was a life style he loved, but he suddenly realized how isolated from female companionship he'd been lately.

A sharp bolt of lightning startled the large, noisy bar into an instant of collective silence. Thunder rolled immediately on its tail, and after another instant of stunned quiet, the room went back to its dull roar.

The woman next to him pushed her drink away and sighed. She shivered once, then crossed her arms. "Well. Back to work."

Yeah, he should be working, too. He had plenty of reading to do. From now until launch, he'd be living and sleeping this mission, running like crazy to catch up with his crew—whom he'd not yet met—and who'd been training together for a year and a half already. He looked forward to meeting everyone involved, but at the moment, as the woman next to him shivered again, work and everything that went with it were far from his mind. "You have business at this hour?" he asked, slipping out of his jacket and putting it around her shoulders. "What do you do?"

Those midnight-blue eyes shot his hands a sharp glance, causing him to lift them from her shoulders. "I have some reading to catch up on," she said, snuggling deeper into his jacket. "Thanks for the coat."

"Reading?"

"I don't really care to discuss it."

"Touchy about work," he said with an agreeable nod. "Duly noted."

"Good."

"How about your name? Are you touchy about that, too?"

Reaching once more for her drink, she tossed her head back as she downed the last of it, then licked her lips in an uncalculated, outrageously sexy move that made Mike want to groan. "Tonight," she eventually said, her full, bottom lip wet now from her own tongue, "I'm touchy about everything." But she made no move to get up. "I don't want to talk about my job, my name, my life. I don't want to talk about politics or headlines." She lifted those amazing eyes to his. "Still want to have a conversation with me or have I scared you off yet?"

There was more than a little dare in her expression, and Mike, the youngest of four boys in a military family, had never, not once in his life, walked away from a dare.

Lightning struck just then, and when the thunder came right on its heels, everyone in the room oohed and aahed.

Not the woman sitting next to him, though. Her gaze remained intense and direct and right on his, so that he hardly noticed the ruckus going on outside. He did, however, notice the growing crowd, as more people made their way in from the storm. Which was fine by him, as it forced him slightly closer to the woman still waiting for his answer.

"I don't scare easily," he eventually said.

"I'm losing my touch then."

"Tell me your name."

"Why?"

"I feel the need to call you something."

"Fine. Call me Lola." She lifted a brow in what might have been either self-deprecation or wry humor. "Yes, tonight Lola will do."

Oh, definitely, she was warming up. Her skin was glowing and rosy. And her hair was starting to curl as it dried, with little wisps falling in her face even though she kept shoving them back.

"Usually men quake in their boots when I walk by," she noted casually. "I have quite the reputation for being terrifying at work."

"Ah, but we're not talking about work, remember? And not your real name, or life, or politics, or headlines."

At her own words repeated back, her lips curved. "You're not a local. You don't have the slow Southern ways. And you don't have the accent, either, that lazy, drawn-out way of speaking that makes so many women want to swoon."

He sent her a lazy, drawn-out smile and drawled in a perfect imitation of an Alabama local, "I can make up the accent, if it'd make you swoon."

"Is it real?"

"The smile? Or the accent?"

"Either."

"Are you trying to charm me out of my panties?"

"You have quite a memory," she said, but smiled at her own expense. "I'll have to quit giving you things to make fun of me with."

"I wasn't making fun," Mike assured her. "Much."

"Hmm." She studied him with a sidelong glance. "You've very neatly avoided telling me if you're a local or not."

"Maybe your need for anonymity tonight goes both

ways." Without thinking, he lifted a hand and stroked her cheek.

At the contact, she went utterly still, as if his touch had stunned her every bit as much as it had stunned him. And it *had* stunned him. He'd touched plenty of women in his life, some he'd known no longer than he'd known her, but never had his entire body quivered at that touch as it did now.

She searched his gaze long and hard, as if assessing him for something very important. Maybe…honesty?

He *was* being honest. Here, amid the crowd, sitting with the most arresting woman in the place, he didn't want to think about work, either. He didn't want to think about anything other than what he was doing, which was enjoying the company of a beautiful stranger.

She seemed to come to a conclusion about him. She nodded thoughtfully, then uncrossed her legs. Her stockings made the most arresting silk-on-silk sound, and for the longest moment he couldn't get his mind wrapped around anything but the thought of what her legs would feel like without the stockings. "Another drink?" he asked.

"That's how a good number of the people in here are going to get in trouble tonight." She glanced around. "Look at those women. Lonely. Drinking. Easy prey for all those men watching them."

"Maybe they want to be prey."

A sigh escaped her, a sound of…longing? "Yes," she said, so softly he had to lean closer. "Maybe so. Maybe they don't know how to just go after what they need, even if it's not practical."

"Are we talking about sex?" He grinned as she raised an eyebrow. "Because really, sex can be quite practical. It's a great stress reliever, for one. And spectacular exercise. Not to mention it's just a feel-good sort of thing."

Her lips quirked. "You're speaking from experience, of course."

"Oh, no. A man should never kiss and tell."

That made her laugh, and she looked surprised at the rusty sound, as if she didn't do it often. "I need to get a room," she decided, slapping her palm on the bar as she reached for the bag she'd dropped at her feet. "There was a crowd at the front desk before."

He glanced at the very large—and getting larger by the moment—throng of people. "You don't have a room yet?"

"No, I wanted to get warm before standing in line."

Which was the last thing she said before the lights went out.

"Don't panic," came the low, unbearably sexy voice of her perfect stranger. "I've got you."

And he did. He'd slid off his bar stool to stand right beside her, his hand reaching for hers. Corrine could feel the heat of him, the strength in the tall, leanly muscled body that she'd been trying not to notice since he'd first spoken to her.

He wasn't her type.

Which was damn laughable, because it had been so long, she didn't actually remember what her type was. At work, a man with a cocky, knowing smile and such a laid-back manner would drive her crazy.

But here it was the opposite.

At work she was serious, intense, and…okay, a perfectionist. She freely admitted that. She wasn't a sexual creature, not at all. In fact, working as a woman in a man's world, she tended to ignore her sexuality and the needs that went along with it, for long periods of time.

Hell of a time for her libido to lift its head.

"The power will come back on in a moment," he reassured her as everyone around them seemed to panic. "Nothing to be worried about."

Corrine wasn't worried, and it wasn't just his bone-melting voice making it so, but the fact that she didn't worry about things out of her control. It was a supreme waste of time, and she hated wasting anything, especially time.

Someone trying to get out of the bar jostled her. She wouldn't even be in this madhouse if she hadn't had to fly here from Houston for an emergency meeting of the utmost importance—meeting the new pilot. After this she could only hope there weren't any delays in her next project—commanding upcoming space shuttle mission STS-124. As it was her team would have to work hard to bring the replacement pilot on board.

Given the angry, disturbed, upset voices around her, general panic seemed imminent, so Corrine both forgave and ignored the person who'd pushed her. But she didn't intend to be pushed again.

"I'm going to make my way to the front desk," she said, turning her head toward where she imagined her stranger's ear would be. Making herself heard in the uproar was difficult. "I'm going to get a room and just sleep the power outage away—" *Oh God.* Her mouth brushed skin. *His ear,* she thought, but it was hard to think at all because her body tingled with the most mind-numbing awareness.

Lust.

She recognized it, cataloguing the fact in her technical mind. But it didn't stop the phenomenon.

"I'll come with you." That was all he said, but in the dark, his voice seemed even lower, even more husky and sexy, if possible. Before she could figure out how to lose him, he'd taken her bag and was tugging her toward the door.

There wasn't much light. None from the windows,

which looked out into the pitch-black, stormy night. But since the generator hadn't kicked on, the bartender had lit candles along the length of the bar, and was doing her best to calm people down.

With her hand in the stranger's large, warm one, Corrine followed. An odd thing, following, something she as a leader didn't often do. But this man seemed to be a leader, as well, and she let him muscle his way through the mass of people. She had to admit, in a very sexist sort of way, that walking behind had its advantages. First of all, he smelled delicious, all woodsy and male. And second, even in the dark she could make out his broad shoulders and strong back. If only the light was slightly better, she could check out his—

"Uh-oh," he said, turning around so abruptly she plowed into him. He slipped one of his hands to her waist, holding her upright with ease as she caught her balance. "Looks like quite a few people beat us to the punch."

He was right.

Here in the lobby of the hotel, candles and battery lanterns cast an almost surreal light. The receptionist had a long line of people in front of her, and she looked harried, harassed and near hysteria.

In less than three minutes, the line started to dissipate. Far too quickly. Around them the grumbling increased, mimicking the force of the storm outside, as the wind and rain slashed against the walls, making it nearly impossible to hear.

Nearly.

"They're out of rooms," groaned the woman in front of them. "Now what?"

Corrine listened to the storm ravaging the hotel, and shivered. The thought of going back out there and finding another place to stay really irritated her, because damn it, she'd just started to dry off. That she'd told her assistant not to bother with reservations for the one night until her barracks room was ready was coming back to haunt her now. She marched up to the desk. "I want a room," she said coolly to the now teary receptionist.

The woman merely hiccuped.

Corrine briefly entertained the idea of ordering the woman to get a grip, that she should be helping people find other rooms in other hotels, or at the very least, looking sure and confident so people would stop yelling at her, but there was no point. "Check one more time," she said instead, in that voice of authority that always had people cracking. "I'll take anything."

Next to her, her stranger stirred, setting a hand very lightly on the base of her spine. At the touch, Corrine's every nerve leaped to attention and turned her knees wobbly.

"I don't think she has anything," he said quietly in her ear, causing all sorts of tremors inside her belly and other, far more erogenous, zones. "Or if she does, she's too worked up to find it."

Corrine sighed and nearly melted into the hand that was lightly, so lightly, rubbing the aching spot at the base of her spine. She caught herself just short of purring, and straightened, locking her traitorous knees while she was at it. "I know." She looked toward the double doors that led out into the night.

They opened and more people pushed their way in, seeking shelter. Rain and wind pelted everyone within ten feet of the doors. "It's back out there, then," she said with a shiver. "To find another place." She'd have to get a cab first, which wouldn't be easy in this weather. She'd be wet to the bone within two seconds. The thought wasn't appealing, but she had no choice and wasn't one to cry over spilled milk.

Intending to bid her stranger goodbye, she turned to him, but he spoke first.

"I have a room," he said very softly. "And I'm happy to share it with you."

2

CORRINE STARED AT her perfect stranger, shocked. Although it was dark all around them, she could feel his searching gaze on her, like a caress. In the depths of his warm, blessedly dry jacket, she shivered.

Not from the cold now, but from something far more complicated.

Another woman joined the nervous young receptionist behind the desk. "I'm the manager," she said to Corrine. "We're terribly sorry for the inconvenience, but as you can see, with no power and the generator not operating properly, we're in no position to get you a room or help you find another place. You can wait the storm out here in the lobby or make your own arrangements."

Wait the storm out? In this cold, dark, noisy room with all these other unhappy people?

Or she could hike back out there and try to catch a cab.

Some choice.

The man behind her stirred, just enough to have his thigh brush the back of hers, and everything inside her went still, then hot.

He'd offered his room.

And his bed.

Probably his body, too.

Please, her own body begged her brain. *Oh, pretty, pretty please.*

"Ma'am?" The manager looked at Corrine, impatience shimmering. She had other people to cater to at the moment, to smile at and try to appease.

What to do?

Corrine had been born to rule. Just ask her parents, who'd called her Queen Bee since day one. Her mom, a biochemist, and her father, a cardiologist, joked that it was in her genetic makeup to be the boss.

Corrine had to admit she'd lived up to their predictions.

Maybe if she'd been raised by people who hadn't understood her, who hadn't encouraged her to do whatever she wanted to do, be whatever she wanted to be, she might have turned out to be a holy terror, but truthfully, she wasn't spoiled at all. Shortly after her family had moved to Houston when she was a child, she'd dreamed of becoming an astronaut. She worked damn hard for what she wanted, and never gave up until she got it. No matter if it was being high school valedictorian, or graduating from college a year early, or entering the Manned Space Flight Program at NASA because she was determined to fly space shuttles. She'd not only entered, but had succeeded beyond everyone's expectations.

Except her own, that is.

Thanks to unwavering tenacity, sheer stubbornness and damned hard work, she'd risen through the ranks, flown on a record four missions to date as pilot, and was now going to be only the third woman in history to command a mission.

So maybe she was confident. And okay, a little tough. But to make it in space and aeronautics, traditionally run by men, she had to be. Corrine knew she used that toughness to purposely scare and intimidate the people around her, but she'd never have made it so far if she hadn't.

In that spirit, she considered demanding a staff room, but something happened. The man's fingers, still on her waist, spread wide now, his thumb skimming over her side, then her belly, making the muscles there quiver like crazy.

"I have a room," he said again quietly, her perfect stranger. Her perfect, mouthwateringly gorgeous stranger, who had an unbelievably sexy voice, with sexy eyes, sexy hands and an even sexier body to go with it.

What his fingers were doing to her system should have been illegal. She could no longer even see straight, she was so consumed with lust for this man, who was more handsome than the devil, thrillingly rough around the edges and full of promised sin. He had a slow, sensual smile that lit up the night. He was intelligent, humorous, and he wanted to share his room with her.

"What do you think?" he asked.

That she was crazy. That she had an intensely structured, controlled schedule for the next months. She was too mature for this.

Too…busy.

Oh damn, but that sounded pretentious. Why couldn't it be simple? Why couldn't she be as entitled to one night of frivolity as anyone else? She'd been too long without this sort of connection, and she deserved it, deserved one night of pure selfishness and pleasure, where no one would bow to her, kowtow to her commands or try to brownnose. She was entitled to be a woman once in a while.

Wasn't she?

As calmly as possible, she turned back to the manager, on the off chance this had all been some mistake.

But the woman was shaking her head. "I'm sorry."

The relief Corrine felt surprised her, but she was always honest, maybe to a fault. In light of that, she had to admit, at least to herself, that she didn't really want a way out of this. She'd flown into Huntsville to deal with an emergency. Whatever it was, it was big, and it would affect both her and the space-shuttle mission she'd lived and breathed for a year and a half now.

For these remaining months she wouldn't have any time to herself. None. This was it. This one last night.

It scared her how much she wanted it.

Turning in the dark, she bumped into his chest, and could tell by his quick, indrawn breath that she affected him every bit as much as he affected her. *Silly,* she wanted to tell him. *Juvenile. We're acting like hormonal teenagers.*

His fingers played again at the base of her spine. And all those hormones unleashed by her own hunger leaped and jerked within her. Breathing became optional. She wanted to melt to the floor in a boneless heap of jelly.

It should have been embarrassing. Awkward, at the very least. There should have been fear and doubt, for a million different reasons; that she didn't even know his name should have led the pack.

Instead, the strangest feeling of *rightness* flooded her.

In the dark she craned her neck, trying to see his face clearly. She couldn't, and she felt more than actually saw his slow, easy smile.

Everything inside her reacted, helplessly.

Oh yeah. She was absolutely in the right place with the right man. "Yes," she said.

"Yes?"

She inhaled deeply. "Yes, I'd like to share your room."

The receptionist and manager had both leaned close to hear her answer, and then looked like maybe they wanted to cry in relief. "His key will work," the manager said. "The electronic keying system is on emergency power and is one of the few things actually operating right now. You'll have no problem getting into the room."

Behind them, the crowd was growing impatient.

Her perfect stranger, who smelled like heaven and had a touch nearly as divine, didn't say a word, just took her hand, lifted it to his lips and then, still holding on to her, took the lead.

And for the second time that night, and for only the second time in her entire life, she followed.

MORE THAN ONCE in his life Mike had been accused of being cocky and confident, yet laid-back and easygoing. Sometimes downright lazy.

But as anyone who'd ever worked with him could attest, he was actually a very controlled man. It wasn't often he lost that control, but he nearly did now. He had an incredibly beautiful woman by the hand and was taking her to his room, and he had no idea what she expected.

The guys would laugh hysterically at that, he knew, for Mike had quite the reputation, especially when it came to women.

But the truth was, much of that bad-boy rep was hype, at least in the past few years, when he'd been far too busy to live up to it.

Through the dark, he glanced at her over his shoulder and found her watching him. He squeezed her hand and smiled.

She returned both the squeeze and the smile, and his body actually twitched with excitement. With any luck at all, his fantasy and reality were going to commingle tonight.

They crossed the large, noisy lobby carefully, winding their way through the unsettled crowd.

"Are *all* these people stranded?" she wondered aloud.

Mike didn't stop, but squeezed her hand again. "Looks like it."

"This is terrible."

It was, and he felt badly, too, but not enough to invite more up to share his room. In the midst of work, work, work, he'd somehow found a little something for himself. Frivolous. Dangerous even, considering the day and age and all the problems associated with recreational sex, but there was something about this woman that told him she was different.

A soft glow from various lanterns and candles lit the way to the elevators, which of course weren't working. There were people there, too, staring with dismay at the closed doors.

Mike's room was on the sixth floor.

It could have been worse, far worse. "We have to take the stairs," he said regretfully, pulling her up beside him. He felt bad, though not for himself. Given the physical demands of his job, not to mention the rigorous training he was constantly put through, he could take the stairs in two minutes without breaking a sweat.

But she wouldn't find it so easy. Her wet skirt, while not skimpy by any means, had to be confining, and those heels…well, they showed off her mouthwatering legs, but they couldn't be comfortable. In the dim light, her damp hair shone. Her skin did, too, along with her eyes, which were filled with deep, dark mysteries. "Six flights of stairs," he added apologetically.

She murmured noncommittally.

"We'll take it slow," he assured her, and could have sworn she laughed. But when he peered through the dark at her face, she was smiling slightly.

"Ready when you are," she said.

When he opened the door to the stairwell, an inky

blackness greeted them. To reassure the woman next to him, he once again took her hand. "Don't worry," he said, pulling from his pocket a pen that was also a flashlight. When he flicked it on, she looked at him in surprise.

"You actually carry a flashlight? In your pocket?"

Yes, he carried a flashlight. And a hand-held electronic organizer. And a state-of-the-art cell phone that could download from the net and retrieve his email. He was a techno-geek and couldn't help himself, but in his defense, he'd spent years and years in Russia, far from his home country. His toys somehow made him feel closer.

"You must be an engineer," she decided.

"I am not."

Her lips were curved, her eyes lit with humor, and she was so beautiful she took his breath away.

"Are you sure?" She was still teasing. "Now that I think about it, you look like one."

"Do you really want to know?" he asked softly, suddenly wanting to tell her about himself, wanting to hear all about her in return. It was silly, dangerous even, because with that additional emotional connection, he knew whatever they shared this night was bound to be the most powerful affair he'd ever had.

She stared at him, searched deep in his eyes for God knew what. And then, finally, she shook her head. "It's tempting," she whispered regretfully, lifting her hand to gently touch his mouth. "But no. I don't want to know."

For a long moment he didn't move, hoping, wishing she'd change her mind, but then the moment passed and he forced a smile. "I like to be prepared," he said, directing the flashlight ahead of them. *And please, God, let me be "prepared" with a condom in my shaving kit.*

"Prepared." She let out a little laugh, again a slightly rusty sound, as if she didn't do it often, and he smiled back.

Make that a box of condoms, he thought.

They started up the stairs. At the top of the first flight, Mike paused. "Need a rest?"

"After one flight of stairs?" She shook her head. "Tell me I don't look that fragile to you."

She was petite but not frail, not with all those wonderful curves and a face so full of life. "You don't look fragile to me," he said after a good long look that stirred his body.

"Smart answer."

They climbed another flight, and when Mike again paused at the top, she lifted a brow. "Do *you* need to rest?"

He smiled and they started on the next flight, but at a burst of wild laughter ahead of them, he once again slowed to a stop. Sprawled across the stairs, two men were sharing a flask of what had to be pretty potent stuff, given their wide, slack, idiotic grins.

"Looksy there," one said, slurring his words as he nudged the man next to him. "Now that's the way to pass the time, matey." The drunk leered at Mike and gave an exaggerated wink. "Don't need to tell you to keep warm, huh? You've got your heating blankie right there with you."

Both men laughed uproariously, and as they did, slipped down a few stairs, to fall together in a heap. It made them laugh even harder.

"Feeling no pain, I see." Mike stepped over them and helped her do the same.

The next flight of stairs began the same way, but then they heard a strange, heated moaning, then rapid panting. Mike didn't know what he expected to find. A fight, maybe. Someone stabbed or shot, someone in labor...he couldn't tell from the frightening sounds. He was prepared for anything, though, and tried to keep the woman behind him to protect her.

But she refused to be kept there, even for her own good. She evaded his hands and stayed stubbornly by his side.

The sounds came from a couple, and it wasn't a fight or severe wounds, as he'd feared, but a wild mating. Clothes were half torn off both of them. They were writhing together against the wall, and given the scream of pleasure that tore from the woman's lips, they were also deep in the throes of orgasm.

Mike looked at "Lola," but she didn't close her eyes or seem embarrassed. She just stared at the couple in front of them, as if mesmerized.

They had a perfect view. The woman was wedged up against the wall; the man could touch and grab at will, which he was doing. Her breasts were bare, and bouncing wildly in the man's face, which elicited plenty of encouraging groans from both of them. His hands snaked up her skirt, where he held her hips so that he could thrust into her, time and time again.

"Now! Now!" she shrieked. "Oh, Billy, *now!*"

"Yeah," said Billy as he pounded into her. "Yeah, baby."

"Ohh." Breasts jiggled. Her bottom bounced. Skin slapped against skin. "Oh, Billy, I'm going to come again!"

"Yeah, baby. Me, too."

Together they let out more shrieks and cries, and then moaning gutturally, they slumped together.

The woman standing next to Mike let out a strangled sound of her own. "Can we get past them, do you think?"

She sounded…breathless, and her palm in his had gotten warm. Almost sweaty.

Mike knew the feeling. He had never considered himself voyeuristic, but witnessing this couple, with Lola beside him, his desire kicked up a degree. He was so hot, so hard and so unbelievably ready he could hardly nod. "Come on," he muttered, and together the two of them started running.

Up the fifth flight, then the sixth.

At the top, Mike stopped, certain he'd gone too fast this time.

"If you ask me if I need to rest," she said seriously, "I will smack you."

She wasn't even winded. Neither was he, but hell, they'd come a long way up.

"And if you marvel about what good shape I'm in," she continued, "when you're obviously in just as good a shape, I'll—"

"I know," he said. "Smack me. Don't worry, I'll restrain myself and admire your strength later. Come on."

They made it to his door. No one was around, and the hallway was pitch-black except for the light from his trusty flashlight.

Taking out his key card, he looked down into her face. She was watching him with an unreadable expression. Slowly he reached out and stroked a finger over her cheek, her jaw. "Are you sure?"

"Already sorry you asked me?"

"Are you kidding?"

"Well then, I'm not sorry I'm here." She lifted a hand, too, and touched his face, ran her finger over his lower lip, over his jaw so that his day-old growth of beard rasped loudly in the silent hall. When she rimmed his ear, he sucked in a harsh breath, every muscle tight and tense.

"Are we going to stand out here all night?" she asked. "Or go in and…"

"And?" he pressed, stepping closer and running his fingers down her neck now, delighting in the shiver that wracked her. He stroked his thumb over the pulse dancing wildly at the base of her throat.

"And finish this," she whispered, her eyes closing, her head falling back slightly to give him more room. "Let's finish what we started the moment we looked into each other's eyes. Okay?"

"Oh yeah. It's more than okay." And with his body—and heart—buzzing, he put his key card in the slot.

3

THE ROOM SEEMED darker than the hallway. Dark but warm, and somehow inviting.

Definitely their safe haven from the storm.

Corrine stepped into the room and moved silently to the window. Pulling back the shades didn't let more light into the room. The blurry window was streaming with rain and sleet, but this high up, with the windows sealed, the night and the storm were eerily silent. She could barely make out the city below, and it was easy to believe they were anywhere, anywhere in the world, all alone.

He came up behind her, not touching, just...there. "I'm not married," he said. "Or attached." When she craned her neck and looked at him, he gave a little smile. "I know, you don't want to talk about yourself, and you don't want to talk about me, either, but I just wanted you to know that."

She had a hard time imagining this man without companionship. "You're unattached?"

He shrugged. "I see women. Nothing serious has come my way. Not yet, anyway."

She was selfishly relieved. She'd never been married, and hadn't been attached in so long she'd almost forgotten what it was like. Oddly enough, given such a lack of romance, Corrine's life was made up of men. But even being with men on a daily basis, she'd never been more aware of one in her life than she was right now. She felt surrounded by him, her perfect stranger, and she shivered again, though it had nothing to do with fear or intimidation or cold, everything to do with stark, demanding need.

If that need hadn't been so strong, so undeniable, so utterly reciprocated, she would have died of embarrassment, because Corrine Atkinson didn't need anyone, never had. But it *was* strong, it *was* undeniable and it was most definitely reciprocated. "I'm not married or attached, either," she said, turning toward him. "If nothing else, you deserve to know that."

His smile was slow and nearly stopped her heart. "Good," he said.

More lightning flashed, but the thunder was muted, almost as if it was happening in another time and place.

"I love to watch a storm," she said, suddenly nervous enough to let him in, just a little. "Especially at night."

"It's different at night," he agreed. "More intense. When you can't see, the other senses kick in, so you feel it more."

Exactly. He understood.

Which caused even more nervousness. "My mother hates this weather. It messes with her hair." *Where had that come from?* Corrine never shared herself, any part, including her family. To share meant opening up, and that wasn't her way.

Before she could cover up that slip with a light joke, he stroked her hair. "It only makes yours all the more beautiful."

Uncomfortable with compliments, she lifted a hand to the long, tangled mess, which had gone wild the moment she'd stepped out of the cab.

"I love the curls," he said, and stroked it again.

She felt the touch to the tips of her toes. "I usually keep it confined." Another personal fact, damn it. Her hair was one of those things about herself that she'd change if she could, like webbed feet or short, fat fingers. "I leave it long because I can pin it back. If I cut it short I look like a mop."

He laughed.

Good Lord, who'd given her tongue permission to run off with her mouth?

"It's so soft." He tucked a particularly wayward curl behind her ear, his fingers tracing down along her jaw.

She could no longer breathe.

His hand danced down her throat to the lapels of his jacket, which he drew more tightly together.

He thought she was cold.

The gentleness of this man floored her, along with his size and shape and his utterly confident masculine air.

"I can sleep on the floor," he said quietly, and the tenderness in his voice, combined with the careful way he was touching her, nearly did her in.

"No, I—"

He put a hand to his chest. "I wanted you here more than I wanted my next breath, but now that you are here, I don't want to rush you."

She stared at his hand, but that wasn't what drew her eyes, not really. It was his chest, which was broad, muscled and calling for her hands.

She tried to remember the last time she'd been drawn to a man, but couldn't. She saw attractive men all the time, and not one of them had ever sparked an interest in her.

This man wasn't causing just a spark, he'd started a full-blown wildfire, and it wasn't simply his physical beauty, though that was nothing to sneeze at. It wasn't his smile, though that alone had been enough to set her hormones raging.

There was just something about him, so big and tough, yet so…gentle.

He'd probably laugh at that, or maybe get embarrassed. And yet again, maybe not; he seemed to be a man embarrassed by very little.

"You're not rushing me," she finally said.

He flashed his smile, then set his hands on her shoulders and turned her away from him again. In what started out as a light, sexy touch, he kneaded, then found the knot of tension at the base of her neck that she was rarely without these days. With a rough sound of empathy, he dug in.

She nearly melted to the floor, unable to contain her soft moan of pleasure as his fingers unerringly zeroed in on the place she needed them most.

"Mmm, you're so tight. Try to relax a bit." He smoothed the muscles all the way down her arms and out toward her fingertips, then started again at her neck. He did that, over and over, with infinite patience, until she had to grip the windowsill to keep from sliding to the floor in a boneless heap of massive gratification.

"Better?"

"If it gets any better," she said, "I just might explode."

"Promise?" As if rendering a woman completely out of control was an everyday occurrence for him, he laughed huskily when she let out another helpless little moan.

And it well might be for him, but not for her. Certainly not for her. When was the last time she'd had sex? She tried to remember, but his fingers were working their magic and now she could feel his chest, his thighs, brushing her back and legs, making her even weaker.

"It's very late," she said.

His fingers stilled, then he carefully stepped back. "Yes, it is. You'll want to go to sleep."

She turned to him, her heart in her throat. "I think maybe this is worth being tired for."

He'd been wearing a solemn expression, but now she saw what he'd been hiding behind that in case she turned him down. Stark desire and need, even fear—everything she was feeling was in his gaze, and there was no way she could resist it, no way she wanted to.

She'd given herself this night, and she wasn't going to take it back now. But even in their anonymity, there was something they had to discuss. "I don't have any protection." She actually blushed; she hadn't done that since grade school. "I wasn't...expecting this."

His smile was sweet and self-deprecatory. "Neither was I. I'm just hoping that in my shaving kit I still have... Hold on." He vanished into the bathroom, and she saw the quick small flash of his penlight. Then he was back, relief shining in his strong features as he held up two condoms.

"Two." She went a little weak in the knees. "Well..." She was actually breathless. "It's rumored two of anything is better than one, right?"

He let out a low laugh, then his mouth brushed her cheek. She turned toward him. Their lips connected once, then again, making her sigh. "You taste just the way you smell," she murmured, not really meaning to say it out loud. "Like heaven."

A sound escaped him, one that might have been humor mixed in with hunger, and slowly, slowly, he eased his jacket off her shoulders before drawing her close and moving her against him.

She nearly died of delight right then and there, because his body was large and hard and so thrilling she tipped her head back and wordlessly asked him to kiss her again.

He did, but she needed more. She had since she'd first

set eyes on him, and it wasn't entirely loneliness now, but a hunger she'd never experienced before.

Cupping her face, he continued to kiss her, more deeply now, touching her as if she were special, precious. Feminine.

She wanted to be all those things to a man, *this* man, if only for a night. He fascinated her. He was beautiful and physical. He was dangerous, if only to her mental health. And he was hard and aroused, for her.

Perfect.

She wrapped her arms around his neck at the same time he caught her up against him. His mouth was firm, demanding in a quiet way that reminded her of his voice. But he didn't press her for more than that simple connection of their mouths, and she realized that he wouldn't.

If she wanted more, which she most definitely did, she would have to take it. It wasn't that he didn't want her in turn; she could feel that he did, could feel the satisfying bulge between his powerful thighs. And his restraint made her want him all the more.

Later she would wonder what had come over her during that dark, stormy night, but for now, safe in his warm, strong, giving arms, there seemed no better way to satisfy the emptiness deep inside her. "More," she said, sinking her fingers into his hair, lifting his head to look deeply into his melting brown eyes.

"More," he promised. Still holding her, he turned toward the bed.

She felt a moment's hesitation when he laid her on the sheets, but then he pulled off his clothes. Oh, how she wished there was light. But when he set a knee on the bed, then crawled toward her, she was able to catch sight of his incredible body and forgot everything else. His chest was broad, tapered down to a flat belly that she itched to touch. His thighs were long, taut with strength, and between them, he was hard and heavy.

Fully aroused.

He was a stranger, so that nothing about any part of him was familiar, yet she lifted her arms and welcomed him closer as if they'd known each other forever. His mouth took hers, more hungrily this time, and his hunger fueled hers. As if it needed fueling!

The heat spread, and when he undid her blouse, and then her bra, gliding both off her shoulders, she found herself panting, her hips already pressing insistently toward his. He excited her beyond belief, and if she could think, which she definitely couldn't, she might have been horrified at her lack of control.

And yet it never occurred to her to stop him, not then, and not when he slid the rest of her clothes off and his condom on. Not when he cupped her face in his big hands and kissed her, deep and wet and long. And certainly not when he touched her first with his eyes, then his fingers, then his mouth, and then finally, oh finally, sank into her.

Outside, the storm continued to rage, while inside one of not such a different nature took its course, as well. Reality had little chance, between the flashes of lightning and the flashes of bare, naked hunger. The friction of his thrusts and the greed of her own body shattered her. It might have been terrifying, how far he lifted her out of herself, if he hadn't been right there with her. She was still in the throes of a shockingly powerful orgasm—her third!—when he buried his face in her hair and found his own release.

MORNING WAS BOUND to come, Corrine knew, but damn it, did it have to arrive so soon?

Bright orange-and-yellow rays of sunlight filtered

through the crack in the curtains, casting an almost surreal light in the room, assuring her that the storm had passed.

Definitely, morning. And with it, responsibilities.

Damn.

She lay in the embrace of her perfect stranger. They were both deliciously, gloriously naked, pressed skin to skin, heat to heat. For an indulgent moment she just looked at him as he slept on, at all his masculine beauty, wondering at the hard, leanly muscled body that had brought her to paradise and back so many times in the night.

His eyes were closed, his face relaxed, his chest rising and falling evenly. His firm mouth brought back memories of what he could do with it, and made her body tingle all over. His lashes were dark, long and thick, resting against his strong cheekbone. His jaw had darkened with stubble, the same stubble that had rasped so satisfyingly over her skin all night long.

He was curled around her, one arm gallantly being used as her pillow, the other tightly anchoring her to him. His fingers cradled her breast possessively. From this angle, she couldn't see much below his waist, but she could feel him pressed to her, every delicious, rock-hard inch of him. She sighed with pleasure. He was amazingly tough, strong, hard in all the right places, and so beautiful it almost hurt.

Just looking at him made her heart contract. He was someone she could have allowed herself to care for, if she ever allowed such things. But she couldn't, at least not now, not with her all-consuming mission coming up. Some other time, perhaps…

Though she knew that was a lie. She'd always told herself that someday she'd allow Prince Charming into her life, but the timing was never right.

But damn it, when? *When* would it be right?

Her heart constricted again, but she ignored it. In her

not-so-humble opinion, she had it all, the way her life was right at this moment. She had great parents who supported her incredibly busy lifestyle, and she had the best job in the world.

True, she didn't have her *own* family, not a husband or children, but she didn't have time for that. She did have needs, like any other normal, red-blooded woman, but those needs were easily met. When she felt the occasional itch, she went out and got it scratched. Carefully, of course, but she wasn't shy.

Just like last night.

And now she would go on with her life. Content. Happy. Fulfilled.

Just as she wanted to.

So why, then, didn't she extract herself? Why did she lie there panting after a man who should have been out of her system by dawn's first light? She couldn't say for certain, but reflecting on the matter would have to come another time.

She had to go.

Slipping out from beneath his arm wasn't easy, but she was a master at stealth. Still, she couldn't help thinking *If he wakes up now, it's fate.* No way could she look into those warm, inviting eyes and walk away. Especially if he flashed that equally warm, inviting smile and reached for her, which she imagined him doing, then imagined her own open-armed response…

He didn't budge.

Tempting fate, she leaned in close, softly kissed his cheek.

I'll never forget you.

For a moment she stood by the bed, yearning and longing for something she couldn't put a name to. But even if she could, it was no use.

She was simply no good at matters of the heart. Dressing quickly and quietly, she hesitated one last time at the door.

Then, picking up her bag, she finally left, knowing she had no choice. No choice at all.

4

As always, Mike slept like the dead and awoke by degrees. It was a great fault of his, being so slow to shake sleep. Over the years he'd gotten both ribbed about it and in real trouble, not the least of which was the time he'd slept through his first "SIM"—space shuttle simulation pilot test. He'd been in Russia, and had just battled a week-long flu, which he'd kept silent about so as not to have to give up the chance. The test had been agonizingly long, and his "landing" required a predawn wakeup. Thanks to his cold medications, he hadn't made it, and as a result, the autopilot had kicked in for the simulated event, "demolishing" the entire landing strip and center, "killing" over one hundred people.

That particular mishap had caused him years of jokes at his expense, not to mention requiring some serious kissing up. He'd practically had to beg to be kept in the program.

And now, when he finally managed to crack his eyes open, and saw the bright sunlight pouring in through the hotel window, he knew before reaching out that he was alone.

Still he stretched, touching her side of the pillow they'd

shared when they hadn't been rolling, tangled and heated and breathless, across the sheets.

It was cold.

She'd been gone for a while then, and he had no one to blame but himself for the odd mixture of real regret and not so real relief.

As he rose and showered, Mike reminded himself that he had no time in his life for any serious entanglements. Having to fill in for this mission as pilot, when the mission had been in the planning stages for so long, meant he had months of catching up to do. He knew better than to think it would be a piece of cake. It was going to take every single second of every single day until launch to pull this off.

First, he had to get through the initial process of inserting himself into an already established team. They were in Huntsville to immerse themselves in this critical project. In a week, they'd move on to Houston, where they would stay until launch time, with occasional trips back and forth to Kennedy Space Center in Florida.

He was looking at a whirlwind of activity.

Which meant this was not the time to be considering a personal attachment. That was actually a good thing, as he'd never wanted a personal attachment.

But last night, what he'd shared with that woman…now *that* could have been the first time he might have actually paused and considered anything close to a relationship.

But she was gone, and he had to work, so it was over.

Which didn't explain why after his shower he stood staring down at the rumpled bed, yearning and burning for something just out of his reach.

He dressed and ate as if it was just any other morning, and everything was normal. Same old, same old.

But it wasn't. He wasn't.

He knew he had last night to thank for that. He'd known

from the moment she'd set foot in that bar, soaking wet, head high and eyes bright, that she was going to shake things up.

She'd done that and more; she'd shaken him to the core. He tried not to think about that, and also about what he could have felt for her, under different circumstances.

How could that happen, he wondered, after only a little conversation and some good sex?

Okay, *great* sex.

Regardless, it wasn't like him to be mooning on the morning after. He'd always been the one running. But *she'd* left *him,* without a word or note, and he would have sworn that's exactly what he wanted.

So why was he entertaining other thoughts, about things like relationships and family and white picket fences? He had missions to fly and hopefully someday command. A wife and kids sounded nice, but for far, far, *far* down the road. Not now.

At 0900 hours on the dot, he entered the Marshall Flight Center. He expected to leap right into work, expected to be whisked into the whole rush of it immediately.

He didn't expect a conference room filled with smiling people and good food— usually an oxymoron when it came to government-provided meals.

Though he'd spent very little time in the United States since his Air Force days, many of the people milling around were familiar to him. The space industry was like that—very incestuous. Even during the Cold War, when politicians from one country wouldn't speak to, or even recognize, politicians from another, science had managed to remain universal. As countries, Russia and the United States might have ignored each other for years, but their scientists hadn't. They'd been sharing the designing and planning of expeditions and experiments since the very beginning, and nothing had changed since.

Few people on the outside realized how closely Russia, Japan, the United States and many other countries were working together to build the International Space Station, and even now, just thinking about it made Mike's chest swell with pride at being a part of it.

"Welcome, Mike!"

He found his hand being energetically pumped by Tom Banks, an old astronaut training buddy who now worked in ground control. Mike was surprised to see Tom had lost some hair and gained some weight since those training days.

"I heard the good news!" Tom was grinning. "You're back in the States, filling in for Patrick." His smile faded. "Poor guy. Can't believe he biffed it so badly parachuting. Sporting three pins in his leg, did you hear?"

"Ouch." Mike wondered exactly how selfish it was of him to be grateful for the miracle of that mishap, and also the fact that the backup pilot had contracted hepatitis.

Probably pretty damn selfish.

But he'd been training for exactly this opportunity for years. He'd been in space twice before and couldn't wait to get back up there. So far, all he knew was that the mission would carry and install the third of eight sets of solar arrays that, at the completion of construction in 2006, would comprise the space station's electrical power system, converting sunlight to usable energy. It was a project he was intimately familiar with, as he'd been working on it in Russia for years. "How is it all going?"

"It's going," Tom said, nodding. "They're thrilled to have you, as your reputation precedes you."

That, Mike knew, could be good or bad.

"Hey, heard about last year," Tom said. "How you limped back after the payload fire midflight."

Limped. Kind word for nearly losing it, as in crashing back to earth, becoming fish food, biting the big one. Thanks to some quick thinking on Mike's part—and he was convinced anyone on that team could have done the same, he'd just gotten there first—he'd managed to contain the fire and put it out before it destroyed them beyond repair. "I don't care to repeat that experience," he said in grand understatement.

"You were a lucky bastard, that's for certain. All of you."

"Have you met your team?" Tom turned to the two men who'd just come up to them. "Mike Wright, meet Jimmy Westmoreland, Mission Specialist-One. And Frank Smothers, Mission Specialist-Two."

As it turned out, Mike had met both men before. They'd come to Russia several years back to study some of the communications equipment for the space station in its planning stages, so it was more of a reunion than anything else. A few moments later he was introduced to Stephen Philips, the fifth member of the team and their payload specialist.

"You've met everyone now," Tom said. "Not bad for your first ten minutes here."

"I haven't met the commander." Oddly enough, Mike felt his first flash of...not apprehension; that was far too strong a word for a man who felt so utterly comfortable in his world. But just as the space industry was notorious for its small population of overeducated overachievers, it was also notorious for its big egos, and no one, absolutely no one, made it to commander status without a significant sense of self-importance.

Added to that was yet another problem.

This commander was a woman.

Everyone knew Mike loved women. He cherished them, dreamed about them, wanted them, enjoyed them.

Take last night, for example.

But working for a woman? As in, directly beneath one?

He didn't want to think of himself as biased or sexist, but honest to God, he couldn't imagine why a woman would want to be commander of the space shuttle, he just couldn't. It took strength, a tough-as-nails demeanor and, well, *balls.*

"Corrine Atkinson?" Stephen craned his neck, as did Tom and the others. Unlike Tom, Frank, Jimmy and Stephen were of average height or taller, and leanly muscular. They wore the short, short buzz cut that screamed military, and all of them had the look of tough, rigidly controlled, well-trained athletes.

Unfortunately, astronauts on the whole were not nearly as serious-minded as their reputation might lead the general public to believe. In fact, for the most part they were great pranksters and troublemakers, not one of these guys being an exception.

"The commander is here somewhere," Stephen assured Mike. "She just came in from Houston."

"She flew in to meet you, in fact," Frank said, far too innocently. He ruined it by grinning. "Don't worry. We told her all about you."

Jimmy joined in with his own evil grin. "Yeah. We started with that time we came to Russia and you brought us to that party, remember?"

God help him, he did.

"And those women jumped out of a cake," Jimmy added, though Mike already knew the rest.

"They were some great lookers," Frank said. "But then we found out they were prostitutes. You tried to send them home, Mike, remember? They didn't have a ride, so we offered to give them one—"

Mike groaned at the recounting of the bachelor party for one of his comrades. "Tell me you didn't tell her this."

"Oh, yes. We did. She especially liked the next part." Frank grinned. "You remember...the naked part."

"Okay, that was *not* my fault." Mike rubbed his temples. "And when they pulled their guns to rob us, we didn't get hurt. Did you tell her that, I hope?"

"We were safe only because they had a crush on you," Jimmy pointed out. "They *still* took our wallets and cash."

"And our clothes," Frank added. "Don't forget they took our clothes and then our keys, and left us by the side of the road."

"It started to rain," Jimmy recalled with a shiver. "Hard."

"Yeah." Frank smiled in fond remembrance. "Good thing it wasn't winter."

"The commander," Mike said weakly. "She found that story particularly fascinating, I suppose."

"Oh, yeah."

Everyone but Mike doubled over with laughter.

Great. Just great. Mike hadn't even met the woman and he was probably on her shit list.

"There she is now," Stephen said, pointing across the room.

She had her back to them. All Mike could tell from the view was that she was rather petite. No other details, except she'd pulled her hair back in a severe bun that reminded him of Mrs. Stestlebaum, his strict, terrifying first-grade teacher.

Commander Corrine Atkinson appeared to favor boxy business suits that didn't show nearly enough of the female body to suit him, and hid any curves she might or might not have.

"Come on, I'll introduce you," Tom said.

Mike drew in a deep breath, feeling resigned, but not sure why. So she dressed a little stiffly. So she liked to torture her scalp with unforgiving hairdos. It didn't mean she would be difficult to work for.

He hoped.

"Mike?"

"Yeah," he said to Tom. "Coming." But he didn't move.

Frank laughed and slapped him on the back. "It's just the boss, big guy, not the guillotine."

But Mike knew that sometimes they could be one and the same. Together, moving as a team already, they strode forward to introduce him, the other men smiling, relaxed in a way that suddenly Mike couldn't have imitated to save his life.

Strange, given how much he enjoyed smiling and being relaxed.

He didn't understand it, at least not until he got within two feet of her and she turned to face him.

CORRINE GOT THAT funny tingle at the base of her skull, the one that warned her that something exciting—good or bad, she couldn't yet tell—was about to happen.

The inkling was right on, she discovered, as she slowly turned and faced the group of men standing there smiling, all of whom she knew, some better than others.

With the exception of the one in front.

Her perfect stranger.

The man with the wicked eyes and even more wicked hands, the one she imagined would headline her fantasies for years to come, was standing right there in front of her.

Only now he wasn't in worn jeans and a clean T-shirt, sitting at the bar tapping his foot in tune with the music as a storm raged outside. Now he wasn't looking alone and sexy, and just a tad bit dangerous to her mental health.

Now he was…oh, definitely still sexy and just a tad bit dangerous to her mental health—but no longer alone late at night.

He was surrounded by her team, looking for all the world as if he belonged there, looking as if he'd been *born* there.

"Commander Atkinson? This is Mike Wright," Tom said proudly. "In the flesh."

Flesh. Oh, she knew his flesh. *Intimately.* And at just the thought, she blushed.

Blushed.

Unimaginable. She opened her mouth, maybe to deny this could really be happening, maybe just to let out an indignant squeak, but thankfully, he spoke first.

"*You're* the commander?" He looked as sick as she did. "Commander Atkinson?"

At least he was every bit as stunned as she. Which didn't help things, not one little bit, not when her perfect stranger was… Oh my God.

On her team.

He was a subordinate. He was going to have to take direct orders from her, and as she knew damned well, he wouldn't like it. He was strong and tough and his own man…and this couldn't be happening, this couldn't really be happening.

She couldn't have accidentally slept with someone she was going to work closely with. God, *more* than closely, they were going to be practically glued at the hip for the next four months. This was some sort of cosmic joke. It had to be.

A nightmare.

For the first time in her life, she was truly speechless, with no idea of how to react.

But she could see he did. In fact, he was already reaching out his hand, not to shake hers as a stranger would, but to hold it and squeeze gently, in that very familiar way he had, a way that would scream to anyone watching what they'd been to each other, only hours before. "You're—"

"Mike. Mike Wright."

He had a name. Fancy that. She jerked her hand away and carefully schooled her features into a cool passivity. "Nice to meet you."

He wasn't only surprised at her civil tone and refusal to acknowledge that they knew each other, he looked shocked as well. But she couldn't register that at the moment; all she could think was...*he* was Mike Wright!

Not her first choice for pilot, or even her second, but those men had been taken from her by circumstance. When American-born and Russian-trained astronaut Mikhail Wright had been suggested for emergency secondary backup, she'd agreed, because his amazing talent and precise control were well known. Though she'd never met him, she'd thought he'd be perfect.

Perfect.

God, he was. He had been. And now she'd pay the price.

"It was very good of you to leave Russia and your projects there to come join our team," she said evenly. "Thank you."

He just stared at her.

"Well..." Her voice trailed off, because for just a moment she wasn't the commander, but Corrine the woman, the one who'd let a man in, and because of that had seen possibilities she couldn't imagine.

The situation couldn't be worse. Well, okay, actually it could; everyone in the room could know she'd slept with him.

That would be worse.

If her team found out, she'd lose her tough, intense edge, at least in their eyes. All her control would be taken away, and much of their respect, and that would be a fate worse than death because of how hard she'd worked to get where she was.

Straightening both her spine and her resolve, Corrine forced a little smile, hoping he got her silent message and urgent plea. "You'll want to get started immediately. First we'll acquaint you with what we've been doing. You've got an all-day meeting with the mission specialists, whom I see you already know."

Frank and Jimmy beamed.

Mike never took his eyes off her, his big, leanly muscled body taut as wire. He said nothing.

"Then tomorrow, at 0800 hours, we'll get started on our SIM," she said, referring to their simulation in a huge tank of water that projected the approximate weightlessness of the environment in space. She was already wondering how she could get out of that exercise herself. "After training together for a week, becoming a team, we'll leave for Johnson Space Center, where we'll stay for the remaining months before launch, training on a daily basis."

He still just stared at her, his mouth grim, and in the depths of his fathomless eyes she saw things she didn't know how to respond to—surprise and shock, not to mention bitter disappointment at the way she'd handled this impossible situation.

Finally, after a long, hard moment in which she sweated buckets inside her far too stuffy suit, he slowly nodded, every inch of him serious and businesslike in a way that made her want to cry.

"See you then," he said, in a voice made of steel. Turning on his heel, he left the room, and Corrine could only watch him go.

And wonder at the odd sense of loss she experienced.

THE REST OF the day was pure torture, and it was only day one. She had months left to go before she could be alone to lick her wounds and get over it.

Get over *what* exactly, Corrine wasn't sure, but she wasn't going to allow herself to think about it, not yet.

Not surprisingly, she ran into Mike twice more before the end of the day. Each time was more difficult than the last. The first was after his initial mission meeting. She happened to have the bad luck—which seemed to be following her around!—to be walking down the hallway as he came out of the conference room.

His shirtsleeves were shoved up; his hair was ruffled as if he'd run his fingers through it often. But his gaze went right to hers, and it was hot.

There were people everywhere, leaving her with no opportunity to do anything other than ask him about the meeting. He responded in kind, revealing nothing, for which she was grateful.

But as she walked away, quaking inside with so many unnamed emotions, she felt his gaze on her, and continued to feel it long after he was out of sight.

The second time she ran into him was in the middle of the night. The entire team was being housed on-site; each team member had a private bedroom, but they shared three community bathrooms.

Unfortunately for Corrine, she always seemed to need a pit stop around midnight, and this night was no exception. She left the bathroom and walked down the darkened hallway, plowing into a solid chest.

"Corrine."

There was no other voice in the world that could make her knees wobble. No other voice that could evoke so many thoughts and emotions that she quivered in response.

"We have to talk," he said.

"Not here." Panic such as she'd never known welled up in her, because with *this* man she felt weak. Vulnerable. *Not allowed.*

She couldn't talk to him about their "problem," not yet, not until she had a better grip on her emotions and could fully control herself. He would *never* again see her without that control.

Memories flashed through her mind. She'd totally lost it with him, let him do anything and everything. She'd been spread-eagled and open on the hotel bed, with him kneeling over her, using his fingers, his tongue, his entire body to make her cry out and beg. That he'd cried out and begged, too, didn't matter. His control wasn't at question here, hers was.

"Talking won't help," she said. "It's done."

"It doesn't have to be."

What was he implying? That he wanted her again? How was that possible, now that he knew who she was?

Didn't matter. She didn't want it to happen again. She wanted to move on, as if she'd never allowed her weakness, her loneliness, her momentary lapse of sanity to occur. "It's over, Mike." Saying his name helped. Her perfect stranger had a name and an identity to go along with that long, hard, warm body she'd worshipped all night long.

"Just like that?" he asked. "Fast as it started?"

"Yes."

"Harsh, don't you think?"

"That's life." She forced herself to remain cool when she had the most insane urge to ask for a hug. "Goodbye, Mike."

"You can't say goodbye to me. I'm on your team."

"I'm not saying goodbye to you as my teammate."

He shook his head and looked at her in a way that made her want to weep. "And I'm not saying goodbye to you as my lover—"

She set her finger on his lips, barely able to speak. "Don't say it," she begged. "Don't say anything."

He took her hand from his mouth and gently, so gently it brought up the tears she'd been fighting down, kissed her knuckles. "I won't," he said. "Only because I don't have to. We're not finished yet. And I think you know it."

Then he was gone.

5

AFTER THEIR MIDDLE of the night run-in, Mike slept poorly, haunted by visions of his new commander and her cool, cool eyes and even cooler voice.

Damn it, where had all that iciness come from? And why had she refused to acknowledge him and their night together, if only between them? Try as he might to make sense of it, he couldn't.

He understood the obvious. She was ashamed of what they'd shared. But why did that hurt?

As for how *he* felt, he was having a hard time reconciling the woman he'd held all night in his arms—the woman who'd showed him such passion and hunger—with the cool cucumber he'd been introduced to today.

Giving up on sleep, he got out of bed before dawn, still feeling insulted and angry, whether that was rational or not. With hours to spare before he had to be on site, he paced his room. Damn it, he'd wanted this opportunity, had worked for it for years. He wouldn't let her ruin it.

He knew how he was going to spend the day—hell, probably the next week. He'd be in the water tank. It would be tedious, time consuming and restricting; they'd be in full scuba gear.

He couldn't wait, but first he had to get rid of some of this restless energy. He could hit the weight room or take a swim, but as he'd be spending every waking moment in the water for the foreseeable future, he decided to run.

Mike had left his room and was walking down the hall when Jimmy's head appeared outside his own door. Looking rumpled and tired, Jimmy took one look at Mike's running gear before he groaned. "Perfect. You're going to make us all look bad for the—" he glanced right, then left, then lowered his voice to a conspirator's whisper "—Ice Queen."

"Who?"

Frank stuck his head out another door, a fierce frown on his face. When he saw Mike and Jimmy, he grinned sleepily. "Hey, just like old times. You're going running? Wait for me—"

"No," Jimmy said quickly, but Frank had already disappeared back into his room. Jimmy sighed. "Damn it, now I'll have to come, too, just to keep the two of you in line."

"Wait," Mike said. "About this Ice Queen thing—" But Jimmy had already shut the door in Mike's face.

He'd wanted to be alone, to burn off this undeniable, restless energy and to think, but he was destined for company now. Maybe that was for the better. Maybe he could stop thinking and just try to enjoy.

Frank and Jimmy were both dressed and ready to run within two minutes, and just as all three men started down the hallway together, yet another door opened.

Dressed in loose running shorts, a baggy tank top and aviator sunglasses that completely blocked her eyes from view, the commander herself emerged. She saw Jimmy and Frank first, both of whom happened to be standing in front of Mike, and she smiled. "Hey, guys. Up for some company?"

Then Mike stepped out from behind them. For lack of a better greeting, he lifted his hand and wagged his fingers at her.

Her expression froze. "Hello," she said flatly.

Hello. That was all she could manage. Not *I'm sorry I'm ignoring you.* Not *I didn't mean to deal you the biggest shock of your life.* Not *Wow, just the other night you made me come half a dozen times. Can you do it again?*

Instead she looked through him, as if only thirty hours ago he hadn't had her every which way but Sunday.

Frank hitched his head toward Mike. "We dragged his lazy butt out of bed, Commander. We're forcing him to run this morning so he can be in as good a shape as you."

Jimmy jumped right in. "He didn't want to come, ma'am. You should have heard all the new words he taught us, even though we asked him nicely."

Mike watched as good humor warred with wariness on Corrine's face. He still couldn't get used to knowing her real name, but it suited her. Just as the team suited her. Evidently, they'd gelled as a group during their time together. Their camaraderie bode well for the mission.

It didn't bode well for him. For one, he hated being the outsider. He didn't mind the work entailed to catch up; in fact he would thrive on the challenge of it. But damn it, he wanted her to like him, not look at him as if he were some sort of deviant.

He didn't understand how she could go from soft, laughing and full of heat to hard as nails, unsmiling and totally controlled.

Oh, and then there was the kicker—she was his commander. He'd seen her naked, sprawled out beneath him and whimpering for more, and she was his damn boss.

"Let's go," he said as lightly as he could. "Let's see

who keeps up with who. And just so you know," he added to Frank and Jimmy, "I plan on outrunning both of you."

His friends simply exchanged knowing smiles.

Which only doubled Mike's determination.

They started off at a quick pace. Not that Mike couldn't easily maintain it, but he remembered Jimmy and Frank as not being the most disciplined of men. Curiously enough, they were disciplined now.

Corrine stayed with them, silent and determined, and he wondered how long she could hold her own. Wondered, too, how she would give in. Would she gracefully drop back, or kill herself trying to keep up? He told himself he didn't care. Either way, it would give him great pleasure to see her sweat.

At the twenty-minute mark no one had even slowed, but Mike was starting to sweat. Jimmy and Frank, too, especially since they'd kept up a steady stream of banter all along about the exploits they'd shared with Mike in Russia.

"You should have seen the crowd after we landed in '97," Frank said to Corrine, who might or might not have been listening, as she never slowed her pace or glanced over. "The Russian women couldn't get enough of Mike. He's a huge celebrity. They yell and cry for him as if he were Mel Gibson."

Jimmy snorted. "Yeah, tough job we had, fighting them off for him. And then there was that one who sneaked into his shower in the hotel room. Remember, Frank? Remember how he screamed like a pansy?"

"She scared the hell out of me," Mike said in his own defense, sending a sheepish glance at Corrine.

She didn't so much as crack a smile.

"Oh, you poor baby," Jimmy said, now gasping for air. "Hey, can you still get a different woman every night if you want?"

"Uh…" Another glance at Corrine assured him she was listening, after all; her face had definitely gone a shade redder. What he didn't know was whether she was exhibiting embarrassment or anger. "I never had a different woman every night."

"Right. You took Sundays off."

Definitely anger, Mike decided, as Corrine's face darkened even more.

Frank and Jimmy took great delight in his growing discomfort, but they had no way of knowing they were innocently revealing parts of him he absolutely, positively didn't want exposed in front of this woman.

Apparently he hadn't yet made the switch from Corrine's lover to her teammate. He was going to have to do that sooner or later.

At the forty-minute mark, he started huffing, but refused to show it, distracting himself by watching the commander's tush swing gently to and fro with each stride.

The clothes she wore were a crime, he decided. She had an incredible body, lush and curvy in all the good spots, tough as nails in others. He knew this, as he'd personally kissed and sucked and stroked every single inch of her.

But both yesterday in her stern suit, and now in the loose jogging clothes, she hid it all.

That alone was going to kill him, if not the pace. And then suddenly, mercifully, both Frank and Jimmy slowed to a walk, waving them on.

Mike glanced at Corrine, more than ready to let her concede defeat, because there was no mistake to be made here, this was some sort of pissing contest, and he intended to win.

She never even glanced at him, just stared straight ahead, her legs and arms pumping for all she was worth. And she'd hardly broken a sweat.

"Tired?" he asked as casually as he could while sucking serious wind. "Because we could slow down."

"Feel free," she said, and actually picked up speed, starting to leave him in her dust.

Holy shit, was all he could think, kicking into as high a gear as she had.

She was going to kill him.

"Please don't continue for my sake." She actually had the nerve to toss that over her shoulder in an even, controlled voice that only fueled his frustration.

He could hardly breathe, much less answer. "I'm fine," he said through his teeth.

"Suit yourself."

They went another mile in silence while he stewed over the fact that at the hotel he'd suggested she rest while climbing a damn flight of stairs.

After a while, she shot him a glance. "Oh for God's sake, Mike. Stop, would you?"

"No."

"You're just being stubborn."

True, but damned if he was going to admit it.

"What if I ordered you to stop?"

"You can't do that."

"Why not?" She shoved up her glasses to rest on top of her head, and her clear, midnight blue eyes stared right at him.

That he could remember when they were cloudy and opaque with lust really ticked him off.

"You can't order me to do anything," he said. Or rather, gasped. "We're not working at the moment."

Her jaw tightened, but she didn't break stride. "I should have known. You're going to be a male chauvinist pig about this."

"What?"

"You can't work for a woman, right?"

"Ha!" he gasped, but then had to go quiet to concentrate on getting oxygen to his poor body. "I can work for a woman. And—" And he was fresh out of air. "I'm... not...a...pig."

"Male *chauvinist* pig."

Okay, now she was *trying* to rile him, but before he could accuse her of that, she slowed, then finally stopped. Ignoring him, she went about a series of stretches to cool down, while Mike just concentrated on staying conscious.

He found himself watching her as she spread her legs, then bent over, her palms flat on the ground.

For just a moment, her shorts tightened across her tight, curvy butt and his hands actually itched to touch.

How was it that he hadn't noticed what incredible shape she was in? He couldn't believe it, but she was actually in better shape than he was, and he was pretty damn fit.

"Look," she said, suddenly straightening and looking him right in the eye, somehow managing to stare down her nose at him at the same time, even though she was nearly a foot shorter than he. "I can see you're going to have problems working under me, but get over it. You're our third and last choice. There is no one else. I won't compromise the mission."

He didn't know whether to be flattered or insulted, so he brilliantly stood there like an idiot.

"Your reputation precedes you," she continued, blowing a strand of hair out of her face that dared defy its confines. "Both in and out of the space shuttle. I'm well aware of your profile, but I didn't expect to have problems so soon."

He blinked and straightened, breathing trouble and screaming muscles forgotten. "Excuse me? *Problems?*"

She just looked at him.

"Are you referring to the fact that we've been naked together?" he asked bluntly.

That chin of hers thrust even higher into the air, and she pointed at him. "And I want you to stop that."

"Stop what, exactly?"

"Referring to…you know."

"Being naked?" he asked, feeling wicked and angry, which didn't make a very good combination. "Or having sex?"

She whirled and walked away.

Because she was moving along at a good clip, and because he couldn't walk without whimpering, he let her go.

But they still weren't finished, not by a long shot.

THE TEAM SPENT the day in the water simulator, working some of the experiments they'd be taking up with them. Although heavy equipment was weightless in space, it still wasn't easy to move around.

Corrine knew the general public had no idea how strong an astronaut had to be. To relocate a large mass, which described all of their equipment, you had to apply a large force, taking care to exert it precisely or the object would twist and turn uncontrollably. An equally large, well-directed, controlled force was required to stop any motion.

In other words, brute strength.

Even something as simple as trying to screw a bolt into a piece of equipment required finesse. That sort of maneuver couldn't be done while floating in the cabin. Anchors were needed, or footholds, in order to apply force, which required special techniques, special tools, special processes, and often the coordinated efforts of a teammate. Everything, even the easiest of tasks, had to be practiced over and over and over again.

One of the biggest challenges they faced was that a true

space environment couldn't be simulated exactly on earth. Hence the "SIMs" in large bodies of water, with astronauts in scuba gear. It was the closest they could come to the real experience, even with today's vast technological advances.

Corrine climbed into bed that night, thinking things had gone well. That is, if she discounted the dark, questioning looks she'd gotten at every turn from her pilot, Mike Wright.

She still couldn't believe her rotten luck. How was it that she couldn't even manage to have an anonymous affair?

If Mike had his way, it wouldn't be anonymous at all! She couldn't have that, absolutely could not let the others on the team know what she'd done with him in a moment of selfish weakness.

And what she'd done was still interrupting her sleep. She couldn't close her eyes without feeling his body brush hers, without remembering how he tasted, or the incredibly sexy sounds he made when he—

She flopped over in bed yet again and stared at the ceiling, but an almost unbearable sense of loneliness came over her. Why now? This was the life she'd willingly chosen. She'd known it would be a dog-eat-dog world, that she'd be forgoing any indulgence of her femininity to make it. She'd known that, had even craved it—she who'd never quite mastered being…well, a woman. So what was this sudden longing to be just that, to let someone in, to be vulnerable, soft? Giving. Even loving.

With Mike.

Wow, that thought came from nowhere and extinguished any amount of sleepiness she might have mustered. She flipped over again, but the damage had been done, Mike was back in her mind. And all she could think of was how he'd looked coming out of the water simulator earlier, when he'd stripped out of his cumbersome gear down to nothing but a pair of wet, clingy swimming trunks.

Sleek, wet and muscular, that had been Mike, standing there on deck.

She'd taken one look at him and had lost every thought in her head. He'd known it, too, damn him; she could still see the slow, baby-here-I-am smile he'd sent her.

This had to stop. She'd had him once and that should be enough. It should be over.

But it wasn't.

She couldn't even look at him without having that stupid, adolescent, weak-kneed reaction, and it was really making her furious.

She'd read his personnel files, shamelessly soaking up his private information. He had four brothers, all in the military. His father, too, was a military man. His mother, a Russian, had died when Mike had been only four, so it was no wonder he was so incredibly masculine. He'd grown up in a house full of Y chromosomes, and then had gone into an industry overloaded with testosterone.

That was a problem, she decided, rolling over to punch her pillow. Because while Mike definitely knew how to treat a woman—he had, after all, made her purr more than once—he had no idea how to do anything other than pamper a female, much less work for one. To work beneath her command was going to be utterly foreign to him, and with both of them needing their control…well, it wasn't going to go smoothly, this mission, she could see that.

What she couldn't see, exactly, was what to do about it.

She wasn't herself around him. She had a hard time sticking to that cool, icy facade she favored, mostly because he saw right through her.

She hated that.

With a sigh, she heaved herself out of bed for her usual

middle of the night run to the bathroom. It was annoying, but then again, if she'd just sleep the night through like normal people, instead of obsessing, she wouldn't have to go at all, would she?

The hall was silent, both when she crept into the bathroom and when she came out two minutes later. Which was why she nearly screamed when she ran into a solid rock wall of a chest.

Even as those big, warm hands came up to steady her, she knew. "Mike," she said in a breathless whisper, blinking through the dark.

"Fancy meeting you here."

"You have a weak bladder, too?"

"I don't have a weak anything."

"Everyone has a weak something."

"What I have," he said softly, reaching up to tug on her ponytail, "is a weakness for long dark hair flowing wild and free, and dark-blue eyes melting with desire when they look at me, instead of two icicles."

"I'm going back to bed."

"Not until we talk."

"It's late."

He flicked the light on his watch. "Actually, it's early. I've been listening for you, Corrine. We need to get this over with."

"Maybe you'd rather try to beat me at my morning run again."

He scowled. "So I underestimated you."

"You thought me nothing more than a fragile doll."

"This isn't what I wanted to talk about."

"I bet. Look, Mike, this is never going to work. Surely you can see that. You have a problem with me being the commander of this mission."

"What I have a problem with is you pretending you

don't know me. You pretending we didn't sleep together, that we didn't make love—"

She slapped his hand over his mouth and whipped her head to the right, then to the left, making sure no one could hear them. "Damn it," she breathed. "Could you stop talking about it? Why do we have to keep talking about it?"

Grabbing her hands away from his mouth, he held them at her sides, slowly backing her up against the wall until she had the cool plaster at her back and his hot, hot body at her front.

She hadn't given much thought to her pajamas—men's flannel shorts and a loose tank top. As they were her favorites, they'd been washed to a thin softness. Thin enough to feel every inch of him, and her body seemed to recognize how much she'd enjoyed those inches, because she closed her eyes in order to better concentrate on the sensations.

"Corrine," he whispered, his voice low and rough now, as if he, too, couldn't help himself. "I don't understand you. Help me understand. Why can't we just…be? Why do we have to ignore this?"

Why? He had to ask why? There were a million reasons, starting with the fact that they had to work together professionally, with no personal hangups between them. The mission depended on it. NASA counted on it. Billions of tax dollars were at stake. There could be nothing dragging them down emotionally. "There is no 'this,'" she said with a finality she didn't feel.

He ran a finger over her jaw, down her throat to the base of her neck, where her pulse had taken off. "Liar," he chided softly as her nipples beaded and thrust against the material of her shirt.

"Mike."

"Yeah."

She let out a disparaging sound. *Oh, Mike.* Why couldn't she forget? What was it about what they'd shared in the dark, dark of the night with no music and no candles, no romantic devices, nothing but the two of them turning to each other? They'd needed nothing but each other, and that scared her.

Hell, it terrified her. "There *can't* be a this," she whispered.

"Oh, there's a this." His finger continued its path over her collarbone to her shoulder, nudging the edge of the tank off it. Stepping even closer, he dipped his head and nipped at the skin he'd exposed, while his fingers continued their seductive assault on her senses.

Thunk. The back of her head hit the wall as she lost the ability to hold it up. "Mike—"

"How can you ignore me?" He dipped his head so that she could feel his breath on her skin. "After what we shared?"

"It was…just…sex," she panted as he dragged that clever mouth back up her throat now, feasting as he went, his fingers toying with the edging of her top, and the curve of her breast.

"Yeah. Sex. Great sex." He waited until she cleared her glassy gaze and looked at him. "I made you come, remember?" His hips slid to hers. "Over and over, until you were screaming."

She was going to scream now. "Stop." Since she wanted to mean it, she put a hand to his chest. "I want you to forget all that. If we're going to make this work, you have to forget."

"Corrine—"

"*Forget,* Mike." And while she still had the strength, she wrenched away. But instead of going back to bed, she went into the bathroom and cranked on the shower.

Cold.

As she stripped and stepped beneath the icy spray, she could swear she heard Mike's soft, mocking laughter.

6

THE MEETING WAS not going well. Corrine knew this, and she tried to get a handle on things—things being mostly her own emotions. But with Mike sitting there so calm and put together at the conference table, it was all but impossible.

She could feel his eyes on her, searching and intense. And though it had to be only an illusion, she thought she could smell him, all clean, sexy male. She certainly could feel him, and he wasn't even touching her.

She'd dreamed about that, his touching her. He did it far too often. Always in such a way as to seem innocent, of course. A brush of an arm here. A thigh there. Here a touch, there a touch, everywhere a touch.

She was losing it

"Facts are facts," she said into the tense silence. "We've been asked to conduct these experiments, and we will."

"But we can complain about it, at least. They're not NASA based, or even university experiments," Frank said. They'd been having this bickering session for an hour. "It's a bunch of elementary students from Missouri, and they want to test *seeds*. I think we can all agree that, with the unknown time factor involved in repairing the already installed solar panels, combined with constructing the new ones, we have better things to be worrying about than kids with seeds."

Both Jimmy and Stephen nodded. Corrine looked at Mike.

He returned the look, his expression closed, and said nothing.

"I hear what you're saying," she said, a bit unsettled by how that simple exchange could rattle her wits. "But these kids—middle school, not elementary—won a national contest in D.C. It was a publicity stunt, designed to bring the public's attention back to the space shuttle and the International Space Station in a positive way." That she personally agreed with her team—that they had far better uses for their very limited time in space—didn't matter. Her hands were tied. She had no choice. "We have to do this. The president promised we would."

"Commander, surely he could—"

She shook her head at Jimmy, hating that she couldn't find her cool, purposeful calm with Mike sitting there watching her. This should be easy, persuading her team to do whatever she wanted them to do. She shouldn't feel their bitter disappointment in her inability to change the unchangeable. "The president personally asked NASA for this favor, and we agreed."

"Yes, but when we agreed," Stephen pointed out, clearly annoyed, "it was *before* we knew about the additional time problems we were going to face, both in transport and on the station."

As the payload specialist, he had viable concerns regarding the time constraints. Corrine knew this, which didn't make her tough stance any easier. The International Space Station, or ISS, had had its share of problems, the current and biggest being the defective solar panels already in place. Since astronauts were housed on the ISS on a permanent basis, repairing the problem was crucial.

No one wanted to spend critical hours every day of their ten-day flight babysitting the students' projects, which included exposing seeds, hair, bread, hamburger and even bubble gum to the weightless environment of space to see if they were affected by the change in pressure, altitude or anything else.

"We still hadn't figured out how to add the required replacement parts to our payload without crushing the original load," Jimmy said. "Much less allow time for the repairs Stephen has to perform." He lifted a troubled gaze to both Corrine and Mike, who as commander and pilot, together would run the ship. "We're running out of time."

"Not to mention, maneuvering into the tight area of the ISS is going to take a miracle," Frank added. "Are you prepared for that? Prepared to tell the other countries in this mess with us that we couldn't figure it all out because we were too busy handling amateur science experiments?"

"You don't understand the pressure NASA is under to have the public on side in this huge tax expense," Corrine said evenly. "The microgravity of space has become an important tool for developing new and sophisticated materials." She purposely didn't look at Mike, so she could let her famed iciness fill her voice. She was in charge here and had the final say, whether they liked it or not. "And the public is losing interest."

"Good," Stephen said, and both Jimmy and Frank laughed.

"Not good," Corrine corrected. "We need a total of forty-three flights to build the ISS. That's quite a bit of taxpayer money."

"We're already committed as a nation," Stephen said. "It's too late for them to decide they don't want in. I'm with Frank and Jimmy. Dump the experiments."

"Stephen," Mike said softly. "This isn't a democracy."

Corrine took a deep breath but didn't look at Mike. He was siding with her, apparently. Because he agreed, or because she'd slept with him? She hated that she questioned it. "We're not ditching the experiments."

Stephen's jaw tightened.

Jimmy looked irritated, too, but asked calmly, "Can we agree to shelve them if we have a problem up there?"

"We'll make that decision when and if the time comes," Corrine said.

"Well, let's work on the timetable then," Stephen said, still grumbling. In a low mutter he added, "And make sure nothing conflicts, especially a PMS schedule. Geez."

The rest of the men appeared to fight for control of their facial expressions, and lost. Jimmy and Frank grinned.

Mike wisely looked down at his clamped hands.

But Corrine was infuriated, anyway. Why was it if a woman had a strong opinion, or needed to get her group under control, she came off as a moody bitch? But when a man did so, he was merely acting within his rights as a male in charge?

The unfairness wasn't new to Corrine, but for some reason, today it hit hard. She chalked it up to a lack of sleep, *not* the unquenched heat Mike had kindled within her body last night, and used her don't-mess-with-me expression to stare down the men.

Jimmy and Frank were unhappy, to say the least. Stephen looked equally so. "I think this stinks," he said. "For the record."

"It doesn't matter what you think," Mike said evenly.

Fair or not, at his defense of her, Corrine felt smoke come out of her ears. She didn't want any heroics here, she wanted...she wanted— Oh hell. She wanted *him,* damn it!

"Obviously we need a break," she said, standing. "Now's a good a time as any."

Mike was the last to the door, and she stopped him. "I want to talk to you."

"Do you?"

"I don't need defending." She knew she sounded stiff and ungrateful, but as she was both at the moment, she couldn't help it. "Especially in front of my team. Not now, not ever."

"It's my team, too," he said softly. Too softly. "And I won't let anyone talk to you like that. Not now, not ever," he said, mocking her words, while somehow utterly meaning what he'd said.

If she'd had more sleep, she would have seen it coming and deflected it. But as it was, she'd been sidetracked by all that heat in his gaze, so that when he cupped her cheek and stroked her jaw with his big, warm and oddly tender hand, all she could do was stand there and tremble like a damn virgin.

"Corrine."

"No," she whispered.

"You don't even know what I was going to say."

"I don't want to know."

"I'm going to tell you anyway."

"Please, don't."

"Please." His lips curved. "The only time I've ever heard you say that word was when I was buried inside you and—"

"Mike!"

His eyes darkened. "And that, too. The way you say my name. Makes me hard, Corrine."

"I'll be sure never to say it again," she said through her teeth.

"I want you." He shook his head, clearly baffled. "God, I still want you."

She crossed her arms, desperately striving for normalcy, which was impossible with this man. He set her body humming without even trying. "We were talking about what happened in this room a few minutes ago. About the fact that you came to my defense when I didn't need it."

"No, *you* were talking about that. *I* wanted to talk about something entirely different. Or not talk." His eyes flared with an unmistakable desire. "Not talk is okay, too."

This was far worse than she could have believed, because how could all this…this *heat* still be between them? They'd had each other, more than once! It should be over. *Done.*

And where had her anger gone? How was it that whenever she so much as looked at him, she lost every thought in her head? And how in the hell was she going to keep it to herself?

"So many worries," he said quietly, holding her face while he forced her to look into his eyes. "Share them with me."

"Yeah, right," she managed to answer weakly, pushing away his hands. "I can't."

"*Won't* you mean." He watched her pace the room. "Why are you doing this? Why are you this warm, soft, passionate woman with me, and yet with your team you're so…"

She whirled on him. "So what?"

"Hard," he said bluntly. "You're hard, Corrine."

That hurt, and she had to swallow before she could talk. "If I have to explain it to you, you'll never understand."

"Try."

She looked into his earnest face and for some odd reason felt her throat tighten. "Mike. Not here."

By some mercy, footsteps came down the hall.

"Later then," he agreed. "But, Corrine? There *will* be a later."

AT LEAST THE afternoon session went more smoothly, though the damage had been done. Corrine was as uptight as she could possibly be.

Everyone else seemed willing to move on from the morning's scene, however, so she put all her remaining tension behind a cool smile and a hard determination.

After all, she had work to do and a mission to whip into shape. The solar array wings they'd be carting into space had to be treated with kid gloves, both while packing and transporting, and then while constructing and assembling on the space station.

Each of the mission members, Corrine, Mike, Stephen, Frank and Jimmy, had a specific job, and each job was critical, requiring months and months of planning, and then months and months more of actual, hands-on practice. For instance, while attaching the very large solar array wings, each of which, when fully deployed, would stretch two hundred forty feet from wingtip to wingtip, Corrine first had to maneuver the shuttle into position so that they could open the payload bay and work in there. That alone— shifting a space shuttle in the available window at the ISS— would be an amazing feat.

Stephen and Mike would operate the robotic arm. Frank and Jimmy, both of whom had extensive technical training, would do the actual repair. Three space walks were required, and each time, the robotic arm would be used as a movable platform for an astronaut to lie on. That astronaut, Jimmy in this case, would be strapped in, with Corrine directing Mike and Stephen into maneuvering Jimmy where he needed to go. The integrated equipment assembly measured sixteen by sixteen by sixteen feet, and weighed twelve thousand pounds. It required very precise teamwork, all done in a weightless atmosphere, hovering between the tight corridor of the space shuttle and the ISS, while wearing a bulky, hundred-pound spacesuit.

Mind-boggling, when she allowed herself to think about it. She and the others would literally have their lives in each other's hands.

Practice. Definitely practice.

As pilot, Mike spent much of the day right by her side. They weren't alone, not even for a second. Though every inch of skin was literally hidden from view—everything but their eyes, through the viewing lens on their mask—she was so aware of him that every time he so much as drew in a deep breath, she knew it. If he looked at her, she felt it.

And when he accidentally—or maybe not so accidentally—brushed up against her, her senses went into overdrive.

She didn't like it.

She ignored it.

She did so by remaining cool and in control, refusing to be baited or sidetracked. Once, when the rest of the team was on the other side of the large mechanism they were using to hoist the huge pieces of equipment, Mike planted himself in front of her, purposely looking directly into her mask as his gloved hands slipped to her hips and gently but deliberately squeezed.

They were separated by layers and layers, and yet she felt his fingers as if they were skin to skin. Her eyes fluttered closed, her heart picked up speed. And she actually ached. *Ached.*

When she forced her eyes open, she expected triumph to flare in his own deep, dark-brown gaze, but all she saw was his own response, which mirrored hers.

After that, it got harder and harder to ignore him. As a result, maybe she worked them all a little harder than she might have, but she told herself she was a perfectionist and simply expected the best out of them.

That they were delivering that best went a long way toward easing the knowledge that the rest of the team didn't especially like her. But they respected her, and had the same work ethic she did, so that would have to be good enough.

Besides, she was used to not being liked. Not many understood her drive, her need to succeed. At times, she didn't understand it herself. Her parents supported her; her friends supported her. All her life she'd been loved and cherished. It wasn't a lack in any of those things that drove her but a simple, overriding hunger for success.

And she would have it.

MIKE WAITED IN the dark, in the hallway, silent and tense and listening for Corrine's standard midnight run to the bathroom.

It was stupid, even pathetic, especially when he had no idea what he wanted to say or do.

Actually, that was one big, fat lie.

He knew *exactly* what he wanted to do to her, and it involved no clothes, a bed and lots of moaning.

What was this crazy need he had for her? It made no sense. Especially when she'd made it clear she wanted to forget she'd ever known him. He should want to forget her, too, given what a tough, no-nonsense commander she was.

But he couldn't forget. And so he waited.

She didn't disappoint. Just past midnight, she came out of her room, wearing her men's boxers and tank top.

Shrinking back into the shadows, he watched her as she

walked with her frank, here-I-come gait until she disappeared into the bathroom.

When she came back out, yawning broadly, he grabbed her.

She nearly screamed, but quickly controlled herself. And while he admired her control on the job, he didn't want her in control now, he wanted her hot and bothered and unsettled, which happened to be the only time he got to see the woman he suspected was the real Corrine Atkinson.

She fought him, but he used his superior strength to haul her closer until they were chest to chest, thigh to thigh, and all the delicious spots in the middle were meshed together.

Ah, just what the doctor ordered.

"What are you doing?" she whispered fiercely.

Hell if he knew. "How about this?" And he captured her mouth with his.

Immediately she went utterly, completely still, and he knew he had her. If she'd fought him, he'd have let her go instantly. If she'd given him any sign that this wasn't where she wanted to be, he'd have stepped back and gone to bed. He might have been hard as steel and frustrated beyond belief, but he would have gone.

She didn't give him that sign, but she didn't kiss him back, either. He wanted so much more, wanted to see her eyes slumberous and sexy with the same hunger he felt, wanted her body humming and needy for his, wanted her to look at him the way she had in his hotel room, the look that told him he was the only one who could possibly do it for her in that moment.

He thought maybe he wanted even more, but that idea unsettled him, so he concentrated on the physical craving instead. Her mouth was warm and tasted exactly as he remembered. Gentling his hold, he smoothed his hands up and down her back while nibbling at her lips, teasing as he sought the entrance she would have to willingly give him.

It wasn't until he said her name softly, cupping her face so that he could look deep into her eyes, that she let out a quiet hum and slid her arms around his neck. "Mike."

He let out a rough groan when she tilted her head, searching for a deeper connection. And he gave it to her. Within two seconds that connection was not only deeper but scorchingly hot. Corrine had one hand fisted in his hair, holding him tight as if she thought he might back away.

Fat chance.

Her other hand slid around his waist, her fingers slipping beneath his T-shirt to the base of his spine before stroking up his bare back. A simple touch, even an innocent one, but it set him on fire. His hands were busy, too, dancing down her arms to her hips, sliding beneath her shirt to glide along bare, warm skin he couldn't get enough of. Their kiss was long, wet, deep and noisy, but just as he brought his hands around to cup her breasts, one of the bedroom doors behind them opened.

Corrine froze and he felt her horror. Silently swearing at the loss of her hot body and their privacy, he put a finger to her lips and quickly backed her into the bathroom.

Like two teenagers they stood stock-still in the dark room, listening.

Nothing.

"My God," she whispered. "I can't believe I— That you— That we—"

"Nearly ate each other up?"

"Don't say it."

She sounded disgusted, and it made him mad at her all over again. Why, he wondered, did he care about this woman? Why did he care that his teammates were grumbling about her cool and controlled demeanor, that they didn't see the real Corrine as he did? Why did he care that beyond the facade she showed the world, she had the deepest, most soul-wrenching eyes he'd ever seen?

"We nearly...*again.*" She closed her eyes and rubbed her temples, and her abject misery fueled his growing temper.

"You can only have sex with me as a stranger? Is that it?"

"We were not having sex!"

"So when you were writhing and panting in my arms only a minute ago, tearing at my shirt, whimpering for more, pawing at me, demanding more...what was that?"

She tried to stare him down, but he didn't stare down easily. He could see the wheels turning in her head as she strove for a way to make this okay in her little dream world, where they didn't have this shocking need for each other.

"All we did just now was kiss," she said finally, nodding her head as if she could live with that particular fantasy.

Time to pop her little bubble.

"Honey," he said with a disbelieving laugh, "if that was just a kiss, I'll eat my shorts."

"It was!"

"How is it then that you were two seconds from coming, and I'd barely even touched your breasts?"

He didn't need light to see the hot flush of anger on her face. "You're impossible!" she spat. "I really hate that!"

"And you're ashamed of what we did. I hate that."

They stared at each other, but there was nothing left to say.

7

THE NEXT DAY was spent in one meeting after another again, and by the end of it, Corrine was mentally drained.

It wasn't the work; she loved that. It was Mike.

She couldn't forget how he'd looked when he told her he thought she was ashamed of what they'd done.

She'd let him believe it, and in doing so, had hurt him.

See? *This* was what happened when one acted irresponsibly. And having sex with a stranger in his hotel room definitely constituted an irresponsible act.

But it was the oddest thing...she couldn't truly bring herself to regret what they'd done. Not one moment of it. She sure as hell wasn't ashamed, either. Which meant, for honesty's sake, she had to set the record straight. Then and only then could she get on with life and put her full concentration into this mission.

It took a while until she was free of the bureaucracy and red tape she had to dance through all day in her meetings with NASA officials, scientists from no less than five other countries, and a representative for the students' experiments, but finally she went in search of Mike. Her intention was to straighten this out, which in no way explained why her body was humming at just the thought of seeing him again. Nope, she attributed that to hunger.

She couldn't find him. She couldn't find any of her team. As a last resort, she hunted down Ed, one of the administrative assistants.

"They're out to dinner," he said.

"They?"

"Your team."

Was that pity in his eyes? It was hard to tell, as he vanished as soon as he'd answered, reminding her that most of the assistants lived in terror of her.

For no real reason, she told herself. Yes, she was usually in a hurry. And maybe sometimes she could be...well, abrupt. It wasn't anything personal, though.

But her team going off without her, now *that,* she was pretty certain, was personal.

No biggie. She didn't want to eat with them, anyway.

Much. Besides, she had work to do.

She stayed late to prove it, but she knew damn well a small part of her was wondering if any of them would come back after dinner to see how she was doing.

Ah, geez. Pathetic. She hated that she'd been reduced to thinking such nonsense.

Get over it and move on.

THAT NIGHT SHE lay awake, staring at the ceiling. The mission was far from her mind, which was otherwise occupied by a tall, leanly muscled, beautiful man who, when he smiled could talk her into jumping off a cliff.

Maybe he'd be waiting to pounce on her in the hallway, she thought at midnight, leaping to her feet, her heart racing in anticipation. But as she made her way to the bathroom, as slowly and loudly as she dared, no one grabbed her. Not then, and not when she came out.

She was alone, truly alone, just as she'd always wanted to be.

BEFORE HE KNEW it, their week at Marshall Space Flight Center was over. Mike and the rest of the team were leaving for Houston and the Johnson Space Center, where they would remain in training until mission launch at Kennedy Space Center, Florida.

There was much left to be done. At Johnson Space Center, each of them would be run through their paces. Over and over again. Loading. Unloading. Constructing. Repairing. Reconstructing. Takeoff. Landing. Going through each possible scenario, and just when they thought they were close to done, they'd be ordered to do it again.

NASA took it all very seriously. Having had painful, painful failures in the past, mistakes that had cost billions, not to mention the taxpayers faith, they didn't care to repeat any of those mistakes.

Mike understood this all too well, and still he loved his job. He loved everything except the fact he was working for a woman he wanted to kiss stupid, and he couldn't quite get that out of his head.

He planned to travel to Houston the way he'd traveled to Huntsville, piloting himself in his honey of a plane, which he'd rebuilt himself.

Frank had also flown himself into Marshall, so he flew himself out. But Stephen and Jimmy jumped at Mike's offer to come along with him.

And to his shock, so did Corrine.

She appeared on the tarmac, her bag on her shoulder. "You have room for one more?"

"Absolutely." At the sudden, awkward silence, Mike glanced at Stephen and Jimmy, both of whom shrugged noncommittally. Their faces had been wiped clear of the laughter they'd just been sharing over some obscene joke, but even *they* were professional enough not to quibble if their commander wanted to horn in on their ride.

With Stephen and Jimmy preoccupied admiring Mike's work on the Lear, Corrine moved close. "I wanted to talk to you."

"You've said that before." Mike lifted a brow. "And haven't really meant it."

Shifting from one foot to the other, she let out a half laugh, and he realized with some shock that she was nervous. Corrine never looked nervous, and his curiosity twitched. She seemed so put together in her business suit, revealing none of her lush curves and warm softness. He remembered both so well that her armor didn't matter, and his curiosity wasn't the only thing that twitched.

Damn her anyway, for standing there killing him, for being so heart-wrenchingly beautiful. "Talk away then," he said with far more lightness than he felt.

"Okay, good. Thanks." She set down her bag. "You've been avoiding me."

Yes, he had. Self-preservation. But damned if he was going to tell her that. Mike Wright avoided no one. "How is that possible? We've been working side by side for over a week now."

A breeze blew over them, but Corrine had her hair tightly back and beaten into submission. Not a strand moved, not as it had that night they'd been together, when her mane of hair had flowed over his hot flesh, teasing him with its silky scent.

"Yes, we worked together," she agreed. "But we haven't…"

It was wrong to pretend he had no idea what she was trying to say—wrong, but ever so satisfying. "Yes?" he coaxed. "We haven't…?"

She let out a huff of breath. "You know. Talked. Or…"

Even more satisfying was her blush. "Are you referring to our hot, wet, long kisses? Or the hot, wet fun we had in my hotel room?"

Her eyes darkened. Her mouth turned grim. "It was a mistake to bring this up. I'm sorry." She went to step past him and into the plane, but he stopped her.

"It was wrong," he said in a harsh whisper. "Because you don't really want to talk about it. You want to forget it ever happened. You're ashamed—"

"No." She put a hand to his chest, deflating his sudden anger with just one touch. "I'm not ashamed. That's what I wanted to tell you. I'm sorry I let you think it."

For a moment, she actually let him see inside her, past the aloofness and into the woman he'd held so closely that night. It gave him a funny ache in his chest. "Why do you do that?" he whispered, unable to help himself from stroking her arm. "Why do you let them think of you as the Ice Queen? I know you're not."

Her eyes widened; her mouth opened, then carefully shut. "What?"

His stomach fell. "Nothing." God, she didn't know what they called her. "Nothing at all."

"What?" she finally said again, very, very softly. "What did you say they call me?"

His fault, that devastating, stricken look in her eyes, and though she managed to hide it with amazing speed and grace, he couldn't have felt worse. "Corrine—"

"Never mind." She straightened her shoulders, lifted her chin high. "No need for me to be insulted when it's the truth."

"Wait…"

"No, let's not. We have a meeting this afternoon and need to hustle."

"Yes, but—"

"You going to fly this baby or what?" she snapped, stepping aboard. She nodded curtly to the others, without an outward sign that she'd just been brought to her knees.

"Final inspection complete?" she asked Mike when he slid into the pilot's seat.

"Done. Corrine—"

"Don't." Sitting there next to him in the cockpit, as if she belonged there, she proceeded to grab his clipboard and start the preflight check.

He grabbed it back. "I've got it."

She picked up his headphones and would have put them on, but in *his* plane, *he* was in charge. He took those from her as well.

"Route?" She ran her hands over the controls.

"I know how to get us there." He brushed her fingers away from the instrument panel.

She shot him a look of annoyance. "Then do it."

He ignored the tone of that remark, because he understood she was hurt. But with her obnoxious, controlling attitude, he was damn close to forgetting how lush and warm and giving she could be.

He didn't like it.

In fact, he downright hated that aloofness, and decided to destroy it. He waited until they were in the air and Corrine was fully relaxed, lost in her own little world. Perfect. She was reading an aviation magazine, deeply engrossed, when he reached over and put his hand on her thigh.

She nearly leaped out of her skin.

Oh yeah, he thought, wisely keeping his grin to himself, his good humor restored. He'd gone at this thing all wrong. Letting her build up her defenses wasn't the answer; driving her crazy was, and apparently he could do that with just a touch.

"Could you hand me a tissue?" he asked, gesturing toward the small box next to her right hip. Before he removed his hand from her thigh, he stroked her, just once.

She fumbled and dropped the tissue, then jerked when she finally handed it to him and their fingers touched.

He smiled, and her gaze went to his mouth.

Bingo, he thought, pleased with himself. Very pleased. For the rest of the flight he touched her whenever possible, when no one else would see. He even managed to suck on her earlobe for one delicious second.

She nearly leaped out of her skin then, too, but she didn't say a word. Just glared at him while the flush on her cheeks and her shallow breathing gave her away.

He expected great satisfaction to course through him, as he'd indeed shattered her aloofness, but since she was clearly furious at him for doing so, it was somehow a hollow victory.

In Houston, things were different. Everyone on the team but Mike lived there, so they had their own home to go to every night. NASA had booked a hotel suite for Mike, so there were no more clandestine, late-night bathroom "meetings" in the barracks.

Corrine missed them.

A week into their training at Johnson Space Center, she knew she had a problem. It wasn't the team; they were working well together. More than well, mostly because now that she knew they thought of her as the Ice Queen, she used it to her advantage. She wasn't there to make friends, she told herself, but to lead a team.

Once again, the problem was Mike.

He was driving her crazy. Yes, he'd kept their secret; he hadn't told a soul about their wild night of passion. But he was no longer ignoring her. Well, that wasn't true. To anyone else, anyone who didn't know of their past, Mike and Corrine were working together. Period. They'd see nothing but a professional link as the two of them continued trying to make their mission a success.

Their chemical attraction remained secret because somehow Mike managed to keep his expression perfectly even, his every thought hidden behind his cool, assessing eyes. And still he strove to drive her insane with hidden touches. Often. All the time, as a matter of fact. Just a finger over her skin. A whisper of a wicked smile. A brush of his thigh to the back of hers. A million different things, each designed to drive her right out of her living mind with lust.

She couldn't take it anymore. You didn't have to be a genius to know he was trying to make a point, but she was already hot and aroused every single second of every single day, so she couldn't figure out what that point was supposed to be.

After one particularly long, hot, frustrating day, after spending hours and hours attempting to coax one of the robotic arms to do as it was told, Corrine snapped. She and Mike had been side by side for hours at a time. All that time she'd been breathing his scent, feeling his own frustration mount.

He was currently on his stomach, stretched out on the platform, toying with the apparatus they were trying to operate, *trying* being the operative word. Jimmy and Frank were below him; Stephen was in the control room watching the computer images. All of them were deep in concentration. Only Mike drew her gaze.

His dark hair was ruffled, from fingers plowing through it, no doubt. His sleeves had been shoved up long ago, revealing tough, sinewy forearms, tense with strain. Every muscle in his sleek back was delineated and outlined by his damp shirt. That back alone stole her breath, then she allowed her eyes to drop lower.

It shocked her how easily he pulled her out of work mode. This had to stop or she was simply going to go up in smoke.

At the end of the day, she calmly—or so she told herself—followed him out into the hall. "I can't do this," she said to his retreating back, making him stop. "I'm so on edge I can't stand myself, Mike. We have to…"

She steeled herself to look cool and composed, but he whipped around and grabbed her hand, opened another door, to a storage closet, then pulled her into the dark space.

"Mike—"

His name was pretty much all she got out before he hauled her up against him and kissed her, hard. It took her exactly one instant to wrap herself around him like a second skin and kiss him back, just as hard.

Something happened in that desperate moment. It became so much more than a kiss, and far more necessary than breathing. Closing her eyes to the dark around them, to the fact that this was really, really stupid, Corrine concentrated only on Mike, on his rough groan as he felt her with his hands, at the taste of him, at the contact of his big, hard body against hers. After a long heated moment, during which their hands fought with clothing to get as close as possible, she came up for air. "Mike."

He pressed his forehead to hers, his breathing ragged. "I know." He thrust his hips to hers, his frustration evident in the size of his erection.

"Mike…"

"Please, Corrine, don't turn back into the commander. Not yet. You just sounded so…turned on. I had to touch you."

Touch her he had. Her body was still thrumming with

a burning desire, on the very edge, but she pulled back. He sighed and dropped his hands.

"You go first," he said, sounding strapped for air. "I'll stagger out when I can walk. It should only take about an hour."

She smoothed her clothing, imagining how she must look, all rosy and swollen-lipped. "We have to stop. You have to stop."

"Stop what, exactly?"

"Stop...touching me. You know, brushing up against me by accident."

"We happen to work within very close confines."

"Yeah, well, it doesn't have to be *that* close. And stop looking at me," she added, ignoring his startled laugh. "I mean it. You look at me and I can't think, Mike."

"Stop touching you, stop looking at you. Is it okay if I still breathe?"

Now she'd hurt his feelings again. "I'm sorry."

"Just go, Corrine."

With as much dignity as she could, she went, horrified by her yearning to dive back into the closet and attack him like a hormonal teenager. And horrified that anyone, anyone at all, could have innocently opened the storage closet and found them, locked in their ridiculous, uncontrollable passion.

8

PASSION WAS ONE great big mystery to Corrine.

She'd felt it to some degree over the years of her adult life, but only in a limited way. Such an irrational emotion required letting go of the reins of control. While she could loosen her grip on those reins, she'd never entirely let go.

As a result, when it came to matters of the heart, she'd always been able to take it or leave it.

This time, however, there was no taking it or leaving it. *It* had taken *her,* and it had the clamp of a bulldog's jaws.

But she hadn't been born stubborn for nothing. She was tenacious, too, and if she wanted to walk away from what she felt for Mike, well then, she'd walk away. She was in control.

This was her life.

She had to repeat that to herself during the next week, often. They were deeply embroiled in the mission, working with prototypes of their real cargo. At the moment, they were trying to nail down the unloading process—a tricky, dangerous, huge undertaking complicated by the fact that no one had ever done it before.

Daily run-throughs were critical. If they messed up in space, not only would they toss away billions of dollars, they would further delay the completion of the International Space Station, perhaps indefinitely.

Couldn't happen. As a result, total and complete dedication was essential. Corrine was certain she had her team's total concentration; her own was debatable. Horrifying, the way her mind wandered. Horrifying and humiliating, because more often than not, where it wandered was straight into the gutter.

She wanted Mike, and she wanted him naked.

"Commander's mumbling to herself again," Frank said from far above, on the platform that put him at eye level with the robotic arm they were still attempting to master.

Jimmy, on his belly next to Mike, who was also spread out on the platform, brow furrowed as he worked, laughed. "She always mutters."

"I do not." Corrine climbed the ladder to reach them. Everything in this hanger was to scale, which meant huge. If she let herself think like a civilian, look around with an untrained eye, she felt like an ant.

"Actually, you do," Stephen called up from ground level, where he was watching the computer monitor carefully. "You mutter a lot. It's how we gauge your mood."

Mike, all stretched out, muscles bunching and unbunching as he worked, laughed, but bit back his smile when she looked at him with a raised brow. "I don't know anything," he said, going back to his work.

Yeah, right.

At least they didn't know *what* she'd been muttering about. There was some relief in that she'd managed to keep everything a secret.

They'd managed.

She had to give Mike credit for that, because for whatever reason, he'd abided by her wishes. She watched him now, watched as for the first time they managed to slide the robotic arm—with Mike on it—into the absolutely precise spot, the one that would allow the solar panels to be correctly unloaded.

Perfect.

It was a huge accomplishment, worthy of a celebration, and as a huge smile split her face, Corrine turned to her team. They turned to each other.

Jimmy slapped Frank on the back. Stephen whooped and hollered, then high-fived the other men when they came down.

Corrine watched, a pang in her heart, until Mike came down, too, and craned his neck.

Across the twenty feet or so that separated them, he looked right at her. The ever-present heat was still there, simmering and igniting a slow burn in the pit of her belly, but there was more, too. There was the thrill of what they'd done, and the need to share it with each other.

He took a step toward her, a slow smile curving his lips.

Everything within her tightened in anticipation.

Then Stephen reached out for Mike, halting his progress, and the connection was broken.

Corrine stepped closer, wanting to join the testosterone-fest, be part of the backslapping and whooping.

But while they all turned to her, still smiling, still proud and filled with excitement, each one of them refrained from physical contact. It didn't help to know it was her own damn fault, that she'd kept them on the wrong side of her personal brick wall.

It also didn't help to watch Mike, so excited, and so damn sexy with it. How was it that he could be so comfortable in his own skin, all the time? He fit into this world like a piece of the puzzle, and why shouldn't he?

He had a penis.

Great. She was in her thirties and had penis envy. Pathetic.

She turned away, and had nearly made it to the door before she felt the touch on her elbow. She didn't need to look to know it was Mike, that he'd somehow broken free of the pack. Not when her entire body shivered at that light touch.

What would he say, she wondered wildly, if she told him what she'd just discovered about herself, that she was jealous, pathetically jealous of what he so effortlessly had with the team? That she no longer enjoyed her solitude?

"Corrine," he said in a low, husky voice that scraped at every raw nerve and made her shudder again. "We did it."

"I know." She didn't look at him, couldn't.

He touched her again. Standing behind her as he was, with his back to the team, no one could see how he stroked the small of her back. Just a few fingers, nothing more, and it shook her to the core.

"I'm going to go upstairs." To the control room. Where there would be more ecstatic people, but them she could handle. "I want to see if—"

"*We did it,* Corrine. I think that deserves a hug, don't you? Or maybe even more. What do you think?"

Nervous now, she let out a little laugh. "You're crazy. I can't touch you here."

"Why not? The rest of us did."

Had he read her mind, or was she just that transparent when it came to him?

"Why would anyone think anything of it?" he asked reasonably.

Yes, why would they? All sorts of excuses danced in her head, but at the root of all of them came the truth. "It's not them, it's me. I don't know what happens to me around you."

"I do. I threaten your sense of control." His broad chest brushed her shoulder. "You threaten mine right back. Did you ever think of that?"

She studied the door. "No."

"This isn't going to go away," he said quietly. "We might as well just go with it."

"You mean sleep together again."

"Hell, yes," he said fervently.

She laughed then, but since it sounded half-hysterical, she brought her hands up to her mouth. "Oh, God, Mike. I don't know what to do with you."

He turned her to face him, looking deep into her eyes. "Yes you do. You know exactly what to do." When she only stared at him, probably wild-eyed and wide-eyed, he let out a long, slow breath. "You're torturing me. You know that?"

"*I'm* torturing *you?*"

"All these stolen touches and wild kisses—"

"Then stop—"

"I look at you with your hair up, in these severe clothes, and I want to see the *other* Corrine. Without the mask of the job, without the icy control. It makes me ache."

"Mike—"

"*Ache,*" he whispered. "I'm staying at the Hyatt hotel. Suite—"

"No," she quickly gasped, putting a finger to his mouth. "Don't tell me—"

"Six forty-four," he said around her fingers. He grinned. "Sixth floor again. Can you believe the irony? I'm hoping it's a lucky sign."

She groaned and closed her eyes. "I didn't want to know that."

"Yes, you did."

Yeah, damn it, she did.

As if fate was mocking her, the day ended early, leaving Corrine with two choices. She could go home and see what she could cook up for dinner.

Or she could catch a movie, as she'd been wanting to do for months.

She pulled up to her complex and stared at the building. She hadn't gone food shopping; she'd have to make due with cold cereal and the television for company.

Mmm, so appealing.

Well, it was her own fault, being so wrapped up in work that she no longer had a private life. She could go see her parents, who'd welcome her with open arms. But much as she loved them, that didn't appeal at the moment, either.

Going to the Hyatt to see what Mike wanted, now that appealed.

Only she knew what he wanted; yes, she knew exactly. It was the same thing she wanted.

But what then? Would this almost desperate need for him go away?

Telling herself it would, it had to, because she couldn't stand it otherwise, she ran into her condo to change, then ran right back out again and drove toward the hotel.

The knock at the door startled Mike. His heart began to race, and though he told himself it could be anyone, anyone at all, he hurried toward the door, holding his breath, wondering, hoping…

And then he was looking into Corrine's eyes and seeing everything he felt mirrored right back at him: need and wariness, and even fear.

"I don't know what's happening to my perfectly planned out life," she said, clearly baffled. "I can't concentrate, can't think, can't do anything except daydream about you, and—" she straightened and pointed at him "—it's all your fault."

"That's funny."

"There's nothing funny about this."

"It's funny because I'm having the same problem," he said. "And I was pretty certain it was all *your* fault."

She let out a little disbelieving laugh. "Yeah, right. You're having the same problem."

"Can't eat, can't sleep, yadda, yadda," he said, narrowing his eyes when she laughed again. "Now *you're* amused."

"Yes, because you're having no trouble at all concentrating and thinking! I know because I've been watching you. You look cool, calm and collected, and I've got to tell you, Mike, it's really ticking me off."

Now *he* laughed. And hauled her close, taking her mouth, her body and his own life into his hands, because he was going to have her again, he had to have her, and now. Given the hungry sound that ripped from her throat, she felt the same way.

He deepened the kiss and she met him more than halfway. It was a bigger thrill than what they'd accomplished today at work. Sinking his fingers into her hair, he freed it from the clip that held it captive. She dug her fingers into his scalp, too, holding his head prisoner to the kiss he didn't want to escape from, anyway. They were gravitating toward something hot and out of control, their bodies sliding and grinding against each another, their hands fighting for purchase, when Corrine pulled back to draw a breath. He pulled back, too, and she bit his lower lip. Heat spiraled through him and he reached for the zipper on her sweater.

But she put her hands over his.

Barely able to see through the sexual haze she'd created, he shook his head. "We're stopping?"

Her breathing was as uneven as his strained voice, her eyes glazed, her mouth full and wet. She looked very un-commanderlike, and he thoroughly enjoyed that. "We're right in the open doorway, Mike."

Oh. Oh yeah. He'd forgotten. They could have been on the moon for all he remembered. "See? Proof positive you make me lose my mind." He pulled her in, stopping only to slam the door before leading her to the king-size bed.

She came to a grinding halt, staring at it. "Are we making another mistake?"

Hell yes, but he wasn't about to admit that now, so he pulled her around and kissed her again, kissed her long and thoroughly, until he could barely recall his name and knew she couldn't either. Then and only then did he go for the prize once again—the zipper on the form-fitting sweater she wore. His knuckles brushed her skin as he worked it down, down, down, discovering halfway that his sexy commander wore nothing beneath. Bending, he put his mouth to her throat. Her eyes slid shut as he nipped and sucked his way down to the base of her neck.

"Mike…wait."

He tasted her soft, creamy flesh.

She moaned.

"Now?" he asked hopefully, still tugging on the zipper.

"I don't know." She pulled his T-shirt free of his waist-band and over his head. Then stood blinking at his chest. "How come you're so perfectly made?" she asked seriously, lifting her hand to run her fingers over the muscles that twitched with her every touch.

"God designed man this way so despite our stupidity, women couldn't resist us. Is it working?"

She nodded slowly. "Undoubtedly."

"I'm sorry I'm hurting you at work, Corrine. I don't mean to be."

"I know." She stared at his body with what looked like befuddled arousal.

"Now?" he asked in a voice very close to begging as he fingered the zipper between her breasts.

"Okay," she whispered. "Now."

Ziiip. He spread the sweater open, pushing the material from her shoulders to hang from her elbows. Looking down at her, he found even his ragged breathing went still. Everything went still, except his heart, which chose this moment to ache like hell. "You take my breath away, Corrine."

She put a hand over the one he'd pressed to his heart. "Mike—"

"No, I mean it. Look at you." Reverently, he reached out and touched the tip of one beaded nipple. She let out a sexy, helpless little sound that nearly did him in. "I want to drop to my knees and worship you for..." *The rest of my life.*

"Kiss me, Mike."

"But..." He wanted to think about this, discuss it.

"Kiss." As if she'd read his thoughts and had been equally terrified, she hauled him close. "Just shut up and kiss me." Making sure he complied, she glued her mouth to his, making love to it with her tongue, sliding in and out in a motion he didn't even try to resist, and within moments they were clinging to each other. He couldn't touch enough of her, and when he tried harder, she lifted a leg to his hip, pressing the heat of her to him, gliding over him until his eyes crossed.

"Okay, we've got to get horizontal," he decided breathlessly. "Before we kill each other." Tipping her to the bed, he crawled up her body, spreading her legs to make a place for himself between them.

Corrine pushed her hips up, meeting his erection more than halfway. Somehow her skirt had gotten shoved up to her waist, leaving only the silky barrier of her panties between them, but the friction of that, along with the helpless but insistent thrust of her hips, nearly did him in.

Nearly. Because while she took his breath, she'd also somehow taken his heart. He wanted to talk, wanted to know what was happening, wanted to know why he suddenly felt as though maybe it was far more than simple, unquenchable heat they were generating right here on this bed. Only she grabbed his ears and pulled his mouth back to hers, keeping it busy while she pumped and rocked her hips against the biggest hard-on he'd ever sported.

"Now," she demanded, panting. If she could have heard herself, she'd have been horrified, but she couldn't hear, couldn't do anything but feel. Sensation after sensation rocked through her, and she found herself holding on by a thread as his greedy, talented mouth ravaged hers. When they broke apart for air, he slid down her body, opening his lips wide around her nipple, using his tongue and his teeth to exact more dark, needy sounds from her. She watched helplessly as he drove her further toward the edge with just that tongue. Then his big, rough hand worked its way down her belly, beneath the edging of her panties. Lifting his head, he gauged her reaction closely as his finger unerringly located the exact spot designed to drive her to the brink.

She made some unintelligible sound, which turned into a moan when he lightly feathered it with the pad of his thumb. Her every nerve ending throbbed and pulsed and begged for more, but the fact was, she was out of her league. She had no clue, no road map and no guidance. She was parachuting without a damn parachute. "Wait!"

"I don't think so, not now." He touched and stroked and mastered her, whipping her into a desperate frenzy. Staring down at her, his eyes were dark with desire. "You wanted this." With the finger that had become the center of her universe, he circled her opening, once, twice, making her cry out and move convulsively against his hand. "Didn't you?"

"Yes," she gasped, thrashing on the bed. "Yes, I wanted this!"

Galvanized into action, he stripped off his jeans, then made her clothes vanish as well. He ripped open a condom, his gaze devouring her as he put it on. Shamelessly needy, she pulled her knees back, opening herself to him in a way that was utterly foreign to her, but felt so right at the moment.

His eyes all but gobbled her up. "You are so beautiful. And so mine." He pushed into her, just a little, just an inch, dragging a whimper of need out of her.

"More." She thrust up to meet him.

"Oh, yeah. More." He pulled his hips back slightly, and another little whimper shuddered in her throat, but then he thrust again, deeper this time. And then deeper still. And again, until he was so far seated inside her that she couldn't tell where she ended and he began.

He held himself still, then, looking down at her as a parade of emotions crossed his face: dazed wonder, harsh need.

"Mike," she whispered, feeling all those emotions right back, and he thrust into her harder, deeper, over and over again. Her head fell back. She arched up into him. She was dying. *"Mike."*

"Right here, baby. Come." He delved a thumb into the wet tangle of curls above where they were joined, stroking as she writhed beneath him. "Come for me."

He was watching her. Waiting. Egging on all that sensation inside her until it came to a roaring explosion. She'd never been watched before. It should have stopped her cold, should have left her unable to fall apart, screaming, panting, making an unholy fool of herself as she shuddered and jerked under the assault of ecstasy, but it didn't.

And when she could breathe again, she realized she hadn't been the only one to completely lose herself. He'd collapsed against her, having banded his arms tight around her, holding her to him in a bone-crushing grip.

Amazingly enough, they fell asleep like that.

MIKE WOKE WITH a wide, canary-eating grin and yet another erection. Turning toward Corrine, already thinking about exactly what he intended to do to her, he stopped, shocked into immobility.

She was gone.

Again.

Damn her! And damn him for allowing it. He should have handcuffed her to the headboard. Should have never fallen asleep.

Should have…should have…should have. The truth was, there was nothing he could do to keep her, nothing at all.

Unless she wanted to be kept.

Which she didn't.

9

MIKE WALKED INTO the conference room and Corrine's heart took off like a rocket. "Good morning," she said coolly. No one had to know she was on the verge of death by mortification, or that her palms were damp with nerves, just from seeing him again.

She'd left him blissfully, gloriously naked, fully sated and fast asleep. He'd accuse her of being a chicken, but it hadn't been fear that made her run; it had simply been time to put aside all personal stuff and get to work.

Here at work, she couldn't afford to be thinking of someone else, grieving over what could never be. Concentration was required. Time to put everything else aside and get on with her scheduled team meeting.

No problem. Putting everything else aside had always come easy for Corrine.

Until now.

Mike didn't answer or return her greeting, didn't even acknowledge it. He looked tall, dark and royally pissed off, not to mention so beautiful he took her breath away.

"Um...coffee?" she asked, gesturing toward the pot. The few sips she'd already taken were making her jittery.

Or maybe that was Mike.

"No, thanks."

She busied herself adding sugar and cream to her coffee, though she preferred it black. But she needed in the worst way to not look at him.

"Corrine."

He was going to want to talk about it. She should have known.

"Corrine." His eyes glittered with attitude and knowledge, knowledge that she'd run from him. Which really was proof positive that he could never understand her. His dark hair was still wet from what must have been a very recent shower, one in which he hadn't shaved, as witnessed by the dark, day-old stubble on his jaw.

She knew that stubble, knew it intimately, knew how it felt gliding over her skin, the raspy sound it made when he lingered, and the citrusy scent of it.

"Don't," he said in a gruff, almost harsh voice, and she was thankful they were the only ones in the room, because that voice made her blood start singing.

"Don't what?" she asked as lightly as she could.

"Don't look at me as if you can't take your eyes off me, because we both know that's not true."

It *was* true, but she wasn't about to admit that. "I'm only looking at you because you're early. I'm surprised, is all."

"I'm early," he said, stalking toward her with his long-gaited, very confident stride. "Because I woke up early. With a raging hard-on, as a matter of fact."

She bit her lip and held her ground, forcing her chin up so she would look fearless. Which she absolutely was. Fearless. Nothing got to her, nothing…except for maybe, just maybe, this man. "I thought all men woke up that way."

"Yes, but I woke up expecting to be wrapped around a warm, sleepy woman." He was nearly upon her now. "One whom I could slowly caress and kiss and taste until she was wide-awake and writhing beneath me, making those soft, desperate sounds, which, by the way, are the sexiest I've ever heard."

"Mike—"

"And then when I had her that way," he continued in a soft, silky voice, "I was going to slowly sink inside her, one inch at a time, until—"

"Stop," she whispered desperately, weakly, glancing at the open doorway. But no one else had arrived yet. She was shaking, damp from perspiration, just at his words!

Did she really sound soft and desperate when he was buried deep inside her?

And did he really think she was sexy? No one had ever told her such things. No one had ever even thought them of her, she was quite certain. "We can't do this here."

"Oh, yes, we can." His eyes were flashing, and despite his unbearably sensuous words and soft tone, his mouth was grim. "We can do this here, because you're not going to let me do it anywhere else. I might be a little slow on the uptake, Corrine, but I'm not stupid."

No, no he wasn't. And he really was furious. She supposed he had a right, but she had a right, too. And damn it, hadn't she told him nothing could come of this…this *thing* between them? It wasn't as if she'd led him on, or purposely set out to hurt anyone's feelings. Besides, if anyone was going to get hurt here, it was going to be her. Because she couldn't fool herself any longer; he was magnificent. And he wouldn't stay single for long. Some other woman would come along and snag him.

But she…she would forever pine over what might have been. "I realize you're upset—"

"Upset," he repeated in a quiet, reasonable voice. He even nodded. But he didn't stop coming toward her. "Yes, you're right about that, Corrine. I'm upset."

"I know." Not allowing herself to back up, she reached behind her and gripped the conference table for support. "I do know. But—"

"No, I don't think you do." He stopped a breath away from her, so close she had to tip her head back to see into his face, but no way was she going to retreat.

She retreated for no one.

"I'm beginning to realize you know nothing about me or my feelings," he said. "Nothing at all. In fact…" He tipped his head and studied her for a long, squirmy moment. "Maybe you really are the Ice Queen everyone says you are."

She couldn't even open her mouth, his words cut such a deep wound. Her hand came up to rub at the sudden ache in her chest and she was half surprised to find no sign of blood. "You…you think I'm an Ice Queen."

"Look me in the eyes and tell me you're not. Tell me you're not frozen to the emotions running wild within me. Do it," he begged softly, reaching out, trying to make her look at him. But she was done. Done with this, and done with him, because damn it, he didn't understand at all, and she wasn't about to try to make him.

Not when all her life she'd had to explain herself, except with her family. They'd always accepted her just as she was, and she'd always believed that someday, somewhere, she'd find that same acceptance elsewhere. And when she did, she'd always promised herself, that would be the man she'd marry.

It had never happened, not yet anyway, and she was beginning to believe it never would. Another bitter disappointment, knowing love, true love, always eluded her.

"Corrine."

His voice was so soft, so urgent, so utterly gripping. She

lifted her head, but Stephen entered the room just then, followed by Frank.

"Ready to rock and roll?" Frank asked, rubbing his hands together with glee. Nothing made Frank happier than a SIM, which was what they were going to be doing directly after their team meeting.

"Let's get to it," Stephen said, the two of them oblivious to the tension in the room.

Jimmy came in next, his eyes suddenly measured and assessing as he looked back and forth between the commander and pilot. "What's going on?"

"Nothing," Corrine said quickly. Too quickly, damn it. She felt herself starting to crumble. They could see something, some crack in her control, and she knew it would be beyond awful if she didn't get it together right here, right now. "We're just getting ready for the meeting, going over some notes."

Jimmy's eyebrows came together as he studied her. And now Frank and Stephen were more closely assessing her as well.

"Did we miss something?"

"Yeah. The doughnuts," Mike said, shocking Corrine with his rescue, especially since she'd jumped all over him the last time he'd done that.

"There were doughnuts and you ate them all?" Stephen sighed. "You owe me, Wright."

"Two kinds of people on this team," Mike said, still looking at Corrine. "The quick and the hungry."

Frank laughed. "Well, color me hungry then."

"Damn," Jimmy said, pulling out a chair.

Stephen waggled a finger beneath Mike's nose. "You're buying lunch, pal. With dessert."

Corrine managed a smile as she grabbed her clipboard.

"Lunch is on me. We'll be needing to calorie up for this afternoon's SIM."

Among the pretend groans and eye rolling, she dared a glance at Mike. He looked back at her steadily, and utterly without expression.

Not once since they'd first met had the heat and even basic affection been gone from his gaze. Not once.

It was gone now. Good. Just as she'd wanted.

But her throat burned and her chest felt tight as a drum. And for the first time, she had to wonder what she'd sacrificed in the name of success and her job.

For the next month Corrine didn't have time to so much as breathe, nor did anyone else associated with the mission.

Still, Mike was everywhere—in her SIM, in her meetings, at her side…and in her dreams.

At work they did nothing but simulation after simulation. Everything from this point on would be a run-through of the upcoming mission, only a month away now. Everything they did, they did as a team.

So she was constantly with Mike.

Her frozen heart, along with all its complicated, newly defrosted emotions, left her with no defenses. During one particularly grueling afternoon, when things weren't going right, her first instinct was to bark out orders and get the team back on track. But two words stopped her.

Ice Queen.

Walking the length of the hangar, consulting her clipboard and trying to smooth out a dozen things at once, she happened to catch sight of herself, reflected in a shiny control panel.

Her hair was clipped back, not a strand out of place. She wore little makeup and no smile, making her appear… stern.

The Ice Queen.

Around her was controlled chaos as her team prepared for yet another simulated flight, but she went stock-still. Was she really as stern as she looked? She didn't want to think so. She was as fun-loving and full of joy as anyone else.

So why did she look so hard? Pulling her lips back, she attempted a smile, but it didn't reach her eyes. Standing there, she tried to think of something funny, something that would evoke a genuine smile. Leaning closer to her reflection, she racked her brain and—

"Need a mirror, Commander?"

The half-ass smile froze in place. Moving her eyes from her reflection to the one that had appeared right next to her, she groaned.

Mike, of course.

"What are you doing?" She straightened up as if she hadn't just been practicing ridiculous smiles at herself in the reflective panel of a space shuttle.

"Watching you watch yourself." He leaned back, making himself comfortable. He was always comfortable, damn him. "That's some smile you've got there, Commander."

"Why do you keep calling me that?"

"Because that's what you are, remember? My commander. Nothing more, nothing less."

Well. Her own doing, that, so there was no reason to get her feelings hurt.

"You ought to try using it more." For just a moment, his eyes roamed over her face like a sweet touch, before he caught himself and looked away. "The smile, that is."

She'd used her smile plenty with him, mostly in bed. At that thought, she bent down, pretending to study a panel, but it was merely an excuse to gather herself. Yet the facade she wore like a coat wouldn't work this time, because it would only prove his point.

Oh hell, why did she even care? She didn't. She'd just have to be the woman she always was, and if he chose to misunderstand, then so much the better. It would remind her of her own foolishness.

While she was hunkered down, contemplating all this, a hand appeared in front of her face. Mike's hand. She stared at those reaching fingers. With any other man, she'd have taken the gesture as an insult, because she could get up herself and always had. But with Mike, she knew it had nothing at all to do with her capabilities, or his perception of them. He was simply being a gentleman.

Which meant she was a lady, at least in his eyes. Well, she'd been a lady and more with him, hadn't she?

Silently she took his hand and rose. Together they joined the team on the other side of the hangar, and all moved into place for their SIM.

For this particular exercise—simulating the landing at the space station, the "parking" and the subsequent unloading—Mike and she had to sit side by side in a relatively small space, with little natural light, mostly just the blue-green glare from the glowing controls. Even the air felt constricted, creating an intimate ambience that was almost too much to take.

With every passing second, as Corrine worked the controls, she became more and more aware of him. She couldn't even breathe without his scent filling her lungs. Did he mean to be so overwhelming with his presence? Did he know that his dark eyes drew her, that every time he swallowed, his Adam's apple danced and she felt the insane urge to put her mouth to that very spot? Did he know that his rolled-up sleeves, so carelessly shoved up his strong arms, made her want to reach out and touch?

That when she leaned to the right, her shoulder brushed his broader, stronger one? And that she kept doing it on purpose for the small thrill of it?

He didn't look at her, but had dropped into the "zone" where he was utterly calm and totally focused, ready for anything.

As she should have been.

She'd nearly managed it when their fingers tangled as they both reached for the same control.

Her eye caught his, and though he was completely into his work, something flickered there, warmed.

It should be against the code of space travel to be so sexy, she thought, and turned away to focus on unloading the cargo.

And when, two minutes later, one of the solar panels malfunctioned during the unfurling, it took her a moment to understand it wasn't her fault, that it had nothing to do with what she was feeling for her pilot.

The broken equipment was only a prototype for the *real* component, one of three that had been built for exactly these practice missions, but that made it no less of a problem. It required sending hordes of engineers back to the drawing board, soothing freaked-out NASA officials and dealing with the press, who were dying to put a negative spin on the price of the space program.

Hours and hours later, when Corrine finally took a moment to draw a deep breath, she escaped to the staff kitchen.

Mike had gotten there first.

He said nothing, just lifted the milk carton he held as if in a silent toast.

A job well done? Is that what he meant? "Thanks for your hard work today," she said.

He took a long swig, then licked his upper lip. "You worked harder than any of us. Did anyone thank *you?*"

"No."

"They should have." He stayed where he was, which was unlike him, but then again, she'd made it pretty clear that's what she wanted. A lot of space between them. "Then thank you," he said simply. "You've done a great job."

"For an Ice Queen."

"What?"

"I've done a good job, for an Ice Queen. Isn't that what you meant?"

He actually looked surprised, then slowly shook his head. "You still stewing over that?"

Apparently so. How terribly revealing.

"I would have apologized. *Should* have apologized." He looked at her for a long second, then let out a hard breath. "I was mad at you, Corrine. I wanted to break through and see, if only for a moment, the woman beneath the tough veneer, the woman I've laughed with, talked to, made love with. I was frustrated and hot and full of temper, a bad combo on any day."

"You're saying that was just temper talking?"

"As in do I really think of you as an Ice Queen?" He stepped closer, touched her hair. "I don't want to. God, I don't want to."

But he *did,* she thought.

His voice lowered. Softened. Became irresistible. "I hurt you. I'm sorry for that, Corrine. So sorry."

He was sorry, which left her floundering, because without her anger, everything else pushed and shoved its way to the surface. It was that everything else she couldn't handle.

As usual, she slept alone, haunted by dreams of warm, loving arms holding her, pressing her against a long, hard, muscled body that knew exactly how to give and what to take.

She woke up hot, damp and frustrated, and wrapped around her pillow.

A bad start, to say the least, and the day didn't improve from there. A critical communications program, brand-new for this mission, crashed. Another catastrophe, and another rush for the drawing board.

By the end of the day she was tense, tired and maybe more than a tad irritable. Grumbling to herself, she went to the staff room for scalding, black coffee...and ran into Mike.

He wasn't drinking milk this time, wasn't doing anything but standing near the coffeepot. She wondered if maybe he'd been waiting there for her.

"You going to thank me again for a job well done?" she asked, more than a little caustically. She couldn't help it. If ever she'd deserved her Ice Queen title, it had been today. "After all, I've worked pretty damn hard these past hours, yelling at computer programmers, scaring engineers, terrorizing rogue reporters, etcetera."

"Yeah, I'm going to thank you." He smiled at her dare, deflating her anger with nothing more than his presence. "You saved our butts today. You saved our butts yesterday, too, and you know what? I think you're magnificent."

"I..." How did he do that, render her speechless? "I don't know what to say to you."

His mouth curved. "You never do, when it comes to a compliment."

The way he looked at her made her suddenly long for the simplicity of what they shared only when they were in bed.

His eyes darkened. "I'd give anything to hear your thought, the one that made your cheeks flush hot."

"Not a chance."

"Damn."

"I figured you were still mad at me."

"Mad?" He slowly shook his head. "I've been a lot of things when it comes to you, most of which you don't want to hear, so think good and hard, Corrine, before you open up this can of worms."

She might have done just that, if her beeper hadn't suddenly gone off. An emergency page, she discovered, which didn't bode well.

What else can go wrong? she wondered, rushing through the maze of hallways.

"Anything," Mike said grimly, startling her, because she hadn't realized he'd come along or that she'd spoken out loud.

It was the robotic arm, they discovered a few moments later, which was now malfunctioning after Stephen's weight had been on it, while he was working on a relaying function.

"Defunct," Stephen called down in disgust.

The arm, too, was just a prototype, but a malfunction was a malfunction. Corrine didn't hesitate to climb up, pushing aside all the technicians to get there. Then dug right in, barking suggestions and orders, and more suggestions.

Two hours later, they'd solved the problem. By the time Corrine climbed down, she was exhausted, had a headache and could eat a horse.

Mike wasn't in the kitchen this time as she finally grabbed her things and prepared to go home, but he was in the parking lot, getting into his rental car.

When he saw her, he went still, carefully studying her face for a long moment.

Always uncomfortable with scrutiny, she shifted. "What? Why are you looking at me like that?"

"Nothing. Forget it." But he pocketed his keys and moved toward her with that long-legged stride of his. He'd worked all day, too, right by her side, but he didn't look as rumpled as she felt, not at all. His sleeves were still shoved back, and maybe his shirt was a little wrinkled from where he'd been crawling around on the robotic arm alongside her, but he looked…well, unbearably familiar, and unbearably sexy.

Reaching out, he tucked a stray strand of hair behind her ear. "You look beat."

His voice was low, soft. Gentle. His fingers on her cheek, where they lingered, were tender.

Damn him for all the inconsistencies! And damn him for still, after all this time, being able to melt her with nothing more than a half smile and the touch of a finger on her skin.

"You're an amazing woman, Corrine," he said quietly, with a different light in his gaze than she'd ever seen before. Was that…respect she saw there now? Respect and— oh God, he was leaning down to kiss her. Just once, and ever so softly.

It took everything she had not to cling to that soft, yet firm mouth.

Yes, it *was* respect in his gaze; she could see that now as he pulled back. And even more irresistible, there was heart, too.

Terrifying, that heart and its emotions, because she'd never received that from anyone other than her family before. She couldn't resist. "Mike."

Slipping his fingers along her jaw, he skimmed the pad of his thumb over her lips, holding her words in. "Night, Corrine."

As she watched him drive away, standing there alone

in the NASA parking lot, she had to face an uncomfortable realization.

Her life wasn't nearly as complete as she thought it was, not now that she understood some of what she was missing.

10

THEY WERE IN the final stages, coming into the home stretch before the launch. With a month left to go, Mike's days were wild, chaotic and nerve-racking. They were the most exciting days of his life.

Exhausting, too. He couldn't remember the last time he'd had a full night's sleep and a decent meal, but he wouldn't have changed his life at the moment for anything.

Well, actually, he amended, looking across the large hangar to where he could see Corrine pointing and directing several crew members, there was one thing he would change if he could.

His relationship with Corrine.

It had started out on a whim, that night three months ago. A thrilling sexual adventure, and it had flamed hot and bright. *Still* flamed hot and bright, only now she pretended it didn't exist, and he'd let her.

He'd been willing to let her pretend forever, thinking no woman, no matter how great in bed, was worth the upheaval that the demanding, incorrigible, unforgiving, passionate, determined Corrine Atkinson would cause in his life.

But that had been when he'd considered only the sexual

nature of their relationship. Now, after working with her day in and day out, for weeks and weeks, he felt differently. He knew what it took to make her smile, even laugh. Knew how to make her entire face light up with the thrill of what they were doing. Knew how she thought, and what she wanted out of her day.

And incredibly, he could no longer remember what it was to want her only physically, because that want had deepened. Grown. Hell, it had *skyrocketed,* if the truth was told.

He wanted it all.

Their day was done now, and it was actually early enough that if he wanted, he could go home and have a life until bedtime. But he didn't want to go home—not alone, anyway.

He wanted the company of a woman. Not just any woman, but one he knew, and who knew him. One who could simply look at him and know that he needed her body close to his, her arms around his neck and her mouth curved in a smile just for him.

Corrine. He wanted Corrine.

Slowly, he walked toward her, watching as everyone called out their good-nights to her. For most she had parting words, advice, comments, commands, and it made him smile.

He couldn't believe it, but along the way, he'd actually come to enjoy the fact that she was higher ranked than him. He liked her demanding ways. In fact, at this moment, he ached for her to look at him, with her will of steel, and demand something special of him. Of course, he doubted she'd think his thoughts appropriate—or his erection, for that matter. *Tough luck.*

She and Stephen were high above him now, on a platform. They were studying the west bay of the shuttle prototype. Corrine was pointing, using her hands as she talked. As always, she was oblivious to the height, to the danger, to how absolutely appealing she looked. Any other woman would be…but she *wasn't* any other woman.

After another few minutes, Stephen came down, looking beat. When he saw Mike, he shook his head. "I need sleep, even if she doesn't," he grumbled, and left.

When Corrine came down, he could see she was lost in thought, probably calculating something in her head, or formulating some new way to torture her team tomorrow. Whatever it was, it gave him the advantage, as she clearly believed herself alone.

She hopped off the last rung of the ladder, turned and plowed right into him. Stiffening, she gasped.

Mike used the opportunity to put his hands on her arms in the pretext of holding her steady, though there was no one steadier than Corrine Atkinson.

"Mike."

"In the flesh." His fingers brushed the bare skin of her forearms, then slid up beneath her short sleeves to skim over her shoulders.

She shivered. "What are you doing?"

"Working for a woman is very satisfying, did you know that?"

"Mike."

"Know what else? I've been unfair to both of us, letting us get away with ignoring each other."

"Don't be silly, we—" She broke off with a harsh intake of breath when his thumbs brushed the sides of her breasts. "Stop that."

"Think how good an orgasm would be for your stress level right now."

"Mike!"

Because she smelled so good, and looked so annoyed,

yet bewildered, he rubbed his jaw against hers. He'd meant
only to soothe, but like a cat, she stretched against him,
and the thought of soothing fled from his mind, replaced
by something far deeper. And hotter.

Concentrate, he told himself. *Screw this up now and
you won't get another chance.* "I don't want you to ignore
me anymore."

"We haven't been ignoring each other. As you've mentioned, we work together, every single day."

"You know what I mean. You think you can't let anyone in your life, that you have to be one big, bad, tough
woman to make it in this world." Beneath his hands, she
stiffened, and he touched her face lightly, lifting her chin
up to look into her eyes. "Any response to that?"

"I'm considering several."

Because her eyes were flashing and her body was tense,
he held her tight, knowing, now, that she held black belts
in several different martial arts. "Okay, let's skip to me,"
he said quickly. "I believed I didn't need anyone in my life
because it was so full already. Women had a place there,
but it wasn't a very big one. But you know what, Corrine?"

"I can't imagine."

"I was wrong." He laughed in delight at her one raised
brow. "I know, can you believe it? *Wrong.* Dead wrong.
And guess what, baby? You were wrong, too."

"I don't know what you're talking about."

"Oh, yes, you do." He smiled, feeling some sympathy
because he understood the fear that he knew was cours-
ing through her veins. He understood it well. "This has
been a long time coming," he murmured, wondering just
how alone they were, and whether, if he kissed her now,
he'd ever be able to stop. But he cupped her face, tilted
it to suit him, and bent. She slapped a hand to his chest.
"Someone will see!"

"Everyone has left." He touched her mouth with his.

She gasped and he simply used that to his advantage, deepening the kiss. When she met his tongue with her own, his knees nearly buckled. "Corrine," he whispered, pulling back to gaze into her eyes. "I know this looks impossible."

"It *is* impossible."

He set a finger to her lips. "So we work together. Lots of couples do, and—"

"Couples?" she choked out. "My God, Mike. We're not a couple!"

"I know, that word's hard to wrap your tongue around, much less your brain. But I can't imagine my life without you in it." He let out a harsh laugh and shook his head. "Can you believe it? Me saying those words? But it's the utter, terrifying truth. I have no idea what's happened to me—wait, I do know. It's you. *You've* happened to me. I want you, control freak or not—"

"Now, wait a minute—"

"In fact, I like that about you. You know what you want, you're not afraid to go get it, with the exception being, of course…me."

She just stared at him. "I think you inhaled too much oxygen on that last SIM."

"And you know what else?" he asked her cheerfully. "I even like that you're higher ranked than me."

"You're a sick man, Mike."

"Look, if you're worried about the people here, and what they think, this mission will be over soon enough, and then we'll both be reassigned for other missions."

"What are you saying?" she cried, wide-eyed. "My God, Mike, what are you saying?"

"That we should give in to what we feel for each other."

She shook her head, so sidetracked she'd forgotten he still held her. "But I don't *know* what I feel."

"Then let's explore that." Nibbling at one corner of her mouth, then the other, he slowly pulled back. Her eyes were half-closed, sleepy and sexy. Her mouth, wet from his, pulled into a pout when he didn't kiss her again, making him let out a laugh that turned into a groan when he looked down and saw her hardened nipples pressing against the fabric of her blouse. "Cold, Corrine?"

"No." Her voice was low. Almost harsh. "Damn you, I'd almost stopped dreaming about you, almost stopped waking up hot and bothered."

"Really?"

"No," she said miserably.

Now he did grin, and when she saw it, she pushed him back, walking away. "I need...air," she said over her shoulder.

Needing some himself, he followed, but she stopped in the hallway in front of her office.

She stared at the door and he stared at her slim back, wondering if she could possibly be feeling half of what he was.

Turning only her head, she looked at him, and there was no mistaking her need, her hunger. Slowly she opened the door. Flicked off the light. Stepped inside the darkened room and turned to face him. "I've obviously lost my head, but... would you care to come in?"

He moved so fast, coming in, shutting and then locking the door, fumbling with his jacket, that she let out a low laugh that was unbearably erotic in its sudden confidence. "We're really going to do this?"

"Yes." He came forward in the dim light shining through her slated blinds, to haul her close. "Now kiss me like you did in my dreams last night."

"It will help, right?" she asked. "If we appease this... this heat now? Then maybe we won't implode on our mission, when we're locked in space together for ten long days."

He didn't know how to tell her that he was beginning to suspect they'd always be this desperate for each other.

Always.

That word was a doozy. It went along with others, like *forever.*

And *love.*

Oh God. He needed to sit down.

"Mike?" Corrine nervously licked her lips in an innocent, artless way that went straight to his gut. And then his heart. And suddenly he felt strong, so very, very strong.

"Is this crazy?" she whispered, covering her face. "What are we doing?"

"What we were born to do." He took her hands and pinned them behind her, which left her body thrust against his. His voice was far thicker than it had been. "Let's make love."

"And get it out of our system."

"Hmm," he murmured noncommittally.

Corrine was beginning to wonder if that was even possible, but she couldn't think effectively with her attention so drawn to his wonderful, firm, masculine mouth. "We really shouldn't. You know that."

He drew her closer, but didn't kiss her, just held her until her entire body was throbbing with need.

"Love that," he murmured. "The connection. Can you feel it?"

"What is *it,* exactly?" she asked, needing to know. But instead of answering, he unbuttoned her blouse, unhooked her bra, pulling the material away from her body. Then he just looked at her for a long, long moment before slowly shaking his head in wonder. Touching a nipple with his finger, he watched intently as it puckered and darkened for him. "So pretty."

Silly, really, how just a few words from him could make her lose her head. "Here, Mike?"

He smiled against her throat. "Oh yeah, here. And everywhere."

"What if someone comes?"

"Everyone is gone."

Turning, she swept everything on her desk to the floor with one swipe, watching as the piles of paper hit with a thunk. "I've always wanted to do that."

Laughing, Mike helped her up, then stepped between her thighs. He undid her slacks and slipped his hands inside her panties, holding her bottom, pulling her close to a most impressive erection.

Wrapping her arms around his neck, she pressed her face into his neck and breathed deeply of the masculine scent that had haunted her for months. With his big, warm hands he squeezed her bottom, then cupped her breasts, plumping them up, dipping his mouth down to taste, using his tongue and then his teeth until her hips jerked in reaction. "Mike."

"I know."

"Hurry."

"Take everything off, then," he said in a rough whisper, and lent his own hands to the cause. In two seconds flat they were both stripped. Corrine had barely straightened up before Mike slipped his hands between her thighs, opening them wide. "Mmm, you're wet."

Yes. Wet and hot, and she'd made his fingers that way, too, the fingers that were softly stroking, over and over again, until she was arching up into him, helplessly thrusting against that hand. "Mike!"

"Tell me."

"Don't stop." To make sure he wouldn't, that he couldn't, she closed her legs around him and that hand, shamelessly rubbing and writhing, desperate for more, for the touch that would send her reeling. "I need to—"

"Then do it," he urged, leaning down and drawing one nipple into his mouth, sucking it as he slid a finger inside her.

She would have fallen backward if he hadn't brought one hand to her waist to support her. Now that finger withdrew slowly—so slowly she thought she'd scream—only to dance over and over her with infinite, thorough patience. At every pass she cried out his name.

"Come for me," he coaxed, his mouth full of breast, his fingers diving back into her. "Come for me, baby."

And she did. She exploded. Imploded. Burst out of herself. All of that and more, and when she could hear again, see again, she realized she had him in a death grip and was still chanting his name.

Mike was breathing every bit as harshly as she. Lifting his head, he looked at her, his eyes hot and dark, so very dark.

Cupping his face, she kissed him. "We're not done."

He smiled and sighed reverently, pulling a little packet out of his wallet.

Boldly she took the condom and put it on, not as easy a feat as she'd have imagined. By the time she was done, he was trembling and she couldn't get him inside her fast enough.

"No," he said when she tried to pull him onto the desk with her. "It won't hold us."

The desk was old and rickety, and making loud, creaking, protesting noises, but with Mike stroking her halfway back to bliss, she couldn't think. He craned his neck and looked toward the shelving unit, making her laugh breathlessly. "Not the shelves."

Scooping her up, he started toward them anyway, and she wasn't so far gone that she couldn't imagine them collapsing to the floor in a loud heap that would bring the custodian running. "Mike, no."

He turned abruptly, and before she could say another word, he had her against the office door. She'd barely spread her thighs when he buried himself deeply inside her. At the feel of him filling her beyond full, her eyes fluttered closed, her heart raged. Her senses soared. *"Yes."*

Another powerful stroke pounded both her and the door, and she cried out again, completely lost, as always with him. She might have been terrified, even furious, at his mastery over her, but if his hoarse groan and quivering limbs were any indication, he was just as lost as she.

And then he lifted his head, his eyes dark with passion, need and a hunger so fierce it took her breath. Holding her gaze captive within his, he started to take them both right over the edge. "Look at me," he all but growled.

"I am. Mike, I am."

"Don't stop. Don't ever stop seeing me, even after—" He broke off when she tossed her head back and arched against him, already shuddering with another orgasm.

He followed.

They were still damp and trembling, and still quite breathless, when the knock came at the door.

"Corrine?" It was Stephen, and he sounded worried. And wary.

"We heard some banging," he called out. "Just wanted to make sure you were okay. Corrine?"

Horrified, stunned and still wrapped around Mike as if she'd been trying to climb his body—which of course she had!—she went utterly still, staring at Mike. Mike, who'd promised her they were alone.

"Corrine? Is that Mike in there with you?"

"I'll be right with you," she somehow managed to reply.

Which was worse? Being caught in this compromising position, with Mike still buried deep inside her, or the look on his face? A look that didn't hold surprise so much as acceptance. "How did this happen?" she whispered. "My God, Mike, you said they were gone. You didn't do this on purpose, did you?"

He didn't so much as blink, but let go of her thighs so she could slide down his still hard, still hot body.

She stood there, naked and shaking, as fury mounted, along with humiliation. "You did."

Turning away, he reached for his pants, the long, leanly muscled lines of his sleek back drawing her even now. "Is that what you think?" he asked. "That I would? That I could?"

Where were her panties? Oh perfect, they were hanging off the filing cabinet. "I don't know. Why don't you just answer the question?"

He left his pants unfastened as he turned to face her. "Because you should know better."

11

He felt guilty, no doubt. But not for the reason Corrine seemed to think he should. No matter what she believed, he had not made love to her at work so that they would get caught.

He'd done it because he could no more stop breathing than not take her. That they'd been in her office *should* have been enough to stop him, to bring him to his senses, but that was just another sign of how far gone he was.

He'd taken her, hard, against the door, for crying out loud, and while he was furious at himself, one look at Corrine's dark face told him she was even more furious.

But damn it, she'd had an equal part in this.

In less than sixty seconds, she put herself together, looking like the commander once more. Mike watched, fascinated in spite of himself by the transformation. When she'd smoothed her hair back, straightened her shoulders and was reaching for the door, he whistled low and long. "That's amazing," he said, sounding a little bitter in spite of himself. "How you do that—go from a warm, hot, loving woman to cold, hard and centered, all in the blink of an eye."

It was a direct hit—he knew it had to be—and yet it

didn't faze her. She glared daggers at him. "We weren't going to tell anyone."

"News flash. I think it's too late."

"I'm not going to forgive you for this."

He nodded, as if she hadn't just stabbed him right in the heart. "Because you think I did this to you on purpose." That she could even think it made him sick, but before they could have that particular battle, she pulled open the door and faced what he knew was her greatest fear—exposure.

Stephen was standing there, waiting.

"Good news," Corrine said briskly. "We've been working our butts off for months now, and given that we're in stall mode until the arrival of the new equipment, not to mention the computer programming glitch, we're all entitled to take a long weekend." She checked her watch, studied the date, cool as a cucumber, miles from the woman who'd been shuddering in orgasm only moments ago. "It's Thursday now. I don't want to see either of you again until Monday. I'll call the others."

Normally this dictate would be greeted with whoops and hollers, and the backs of quickly retreating astronauts as they hightailed it out of the space center, and maybe even Texas.

But no matter how good Corrine was, she couldn't sidetrack Stephen so easily.

"Damn," he whispered, looking over his shoulder to make sure they were alone. "Do you guys have any idea how noisy you were?"

Corrine blanched, but otherwise showed no outward sign of emotion. "Did you hear what I just said?"

"Yeah, time off, whatever. But—"

"What is it you need?" Corrine asked with that famed chilly voice.

"Need?" Blankly, Stephen looked at them. "Um…"

"Okay, then. See you on Monday." Corrine went to close her office door, then seemed to remember Mike was still standing behind her. Turning, she sent him a get-out-of-here look.

He wasn't going anywhere, damn it, not until they talked this out.

"I need a moment," she said.

He just bet she did. But no matter what she wanted, this moment was not going to go away with a flick of her wrist. Knowing that, he turned to Stephen. "Look, I'm not sure what you heard, but—"

"You don't want to know."

Corrine closed her eyes.

"But if you twist my arm," Stephen said, watching them both with growing amusement as his shock faded, "I heard the banging first." He slapped his hand on the wall with a rhythmic sound that could have come from a set of drums…or two adults having wild, unbridled, out-of-control sex against the door. "Just like that."

"Okay," Corrine said quickly. "Bottom line. I'm human, okay? But it's after hours, and I refuse to apologize for what amounts to my own personal business." She grabbed Mike's elbow and pulled him out of her office.

Then, before he could so much as blink, she went back in and slammed the door, shutting them out.

The lock clicked into place.

Stephen looked at Mike speculatively. "I guess that's that, huh?"

"Yes," Mike said, relieved he wasn't going to press or tease him. "That's that."

"Don't worry. It wasn't really all that obvious, anyway."

"Okay." Mike sighed. "Good."

"I mean, really, you could have been doing anything in there. Copying. Faxing. Computer stuff. Anything."

That's right, Mike told himself. They could have been doing anything, anything at all.

"Except for the 'Don't stop, Mike, oh, please don't stop' part," Stephen said. "That sorta gave you away, big guy."

"Hey, we *could* have been working! She really likes her work!"

Stephen just snorted, then looked at Mike for a long moment.

"What? You have something to say, say it."

"Well, I could tell you how incredibly stupid this is."

"Yeah."

"Or I could ask for details."

Mike frowned. "You're going to make me hurt you, Stephen."

"Oh, boy. Tell me you're not in love, man. Tell me you're not *that* stupid."

"Why would falling in love be stupid?" Mike asked, far too defensively.

"That's not the stupid part. Unless you're falling in love with the Ice Queen."

"Her name is Corrine."

Stephen let out a moan at that. "Oh man. You are. Damn, Mike. You're in deep."

Yeah. *Damn, Mike.*

And then finally he was alone, staring at the shut office door, wondering at the three things that had just happened to him.

One, he'd lost control and made love to Corrine at work, putting them in an incredibly compromising position.

Two, she was never going to forgive him for it.

And three, he'd just realized Stephen might have stumbled onto something, in which case Mike was in a far bigger mess than even he could get out of. Fact was, he still wanted her, and there was nothing physical about it.

That's not the stupid part. Unless you're falling in love with the Ice Queen.

Which he was. Lord, wouldn't his brothers get a kick out of this? He, the man who was afraid of nothing except for maybe commitment, now suddenly wanted with all his heart to be committed to a woman who was not only his commander, but who didn't believe in any weakness. And he was certain she would consider this need of his a biggie.

He wanted a commitment, with Corrine.

Mike actually staggered at that, and wished for a chair. There wasn't one, so he sank to the floor and stared at her still-closed office door.

What was happening to him? To his satisfyingly single, devil-may-care, wild existence?

He wished he knew. Ah, hell, forget that. He did know. He knew exactly.

Corrine paced her office but no matter how long she walked, the images wouldn't go away. Her, with her back to the wall, legs shrink-wrapped around Mike, head thrown back as she let him take her hard and fast.

Let him take her.

She'd never *let* anyone take her in her entire life. No, she'd demanded it, and the memory of that now burned.

And everyone knew.

Well, whatever. It was done and she was not going to sit around and cry over spilled milk. So her team knew. She'd deal with that. What she couldn't deal with was having it happen again. Ever.

Grabbing the phone, she pounded out a number. "Mom," she said with relief when her mother picked up. "I miss you." An understatement. Nowhere on earth did she ever feel so good, so comfortable, so happy in her own skin, as she did with her family. "I have three days off, and I'm coming home."

When she'd dealt with her mother's joy, she picked up her purse, ignored her briefcase and hauled open her office door.

Tripping over Mike, she fell right into his lap.

His arms came around her and, wrapped in his warm strength, she forgot to hate him.

"You okay?" he murmured, and that voice, God, that sexy voice, reminded her.

Scrambling to her knees, she pointed at him. *"You."*

He was sitting crosslegged, right there on the floor, looking, to her satisfaction, every bit as miserable as she'd felt before she'd called home. "Me," he agreed.

"Why are you sitting on the floor?"

"I'm not sure you'd believe it. I don't hardly believe it myself," he muttered. "And anyway, it occurred to me, leaving you this mad might be a really bad idea."

With as much dignity as she could, she stood, then sent him a withering glance when he reached out and stopped her from leaving. "Now's not a good time to take me on, Mike."

"I realize that." He held her anyway. "I want you to look me in the eyes, Corrine, and tell me you really believe I did this to hurt you. That I took you against the door of your office for the sole purpose of letting everyone around us know what's going on."

Of course she couldn't look him in the eyes and tell him that. "Now is a bad time."

"Look at me, damn it—" He grappled with her when she fought him. "Tell me."

He was fierce and hurt and full of bad temper. Well, so was she, so she shrugged him off and reached for the purse she'd dropped. "Goodbye, Mike."

She headed for the bathroom to clean up. When she came out he was still there, waiting. Not acknowledging him she turned to leave.

She was halfway down the hall before she realized he was right behind her. Silent. Brooding. She ignored him all the way to her car, even though she wanted to grab him, wanted to hold on to him, lay her head on his shoulder and forget the rest of the world existed.

What a weakness. It terrified her. "Don't even think about following me." She got in her car, started it and pictured the next three days of peace and quiet.

No Mike.

And in the not-too-distant future, after their mission was complete, he'd be out of her life for more than just three days. He'd be gone for good.

Things would be great, she'd be fine and her life would get back to normal. But the truth was, she wasn't fine and nothing would ever be normal again. Not without Mike.

Starting the car, she looked straight ahead and resisted putting her head on the steering wheel to have a good, and very rare, pity party. Mike would be watching, she knew.

IN HIS DUMBEST move since decorating his high-school math teacher's house with toilet paper after a particularly rough test, Mike followed Corrine.

Not that he easily kept up with her on the freeway; the woman was a holy terror, dodging through traffic left and right, making him wince.

She wasn't going to her condo.

It took less than thirty minutes to arrive in a lovely, quiet little suburb where there were white picket fences and pretty yards with flowers and SUVs and children playing—a world away from the military childhood he'd had.

Having spent the past ten years in Russia, in the teeming, overcrowded cities there, he was experiencing quite a culture shock.

Corrine got out of her car, ran up the walk of one exceptionally pretty house and embraced an older couple. There was a beaming smile across her usually solemn face.

And he understood.

She'd come home. Interesting, as he'd never thought of her as the family type. But then again, he'd never thought he'd find himself chasing down a woman he couldn't get out of his head.

Well, meeting her family ought to do it, really. That should bring on both hives *and* the need to run far and fast.

He was counting on it, anyway.

He parked and got out, not sure of his next move, or even what he really wanted. Maybe for Corrine to acknowledge she'd been unfair to him back there in her office. Or maybe for her to tell him what the hell they had, because he'd feel better if he could somehow label this whole thing.

He knew the exact moment she sensed him; she stiffened and turned, then frowned. He imagined she growled as well, but he was, thankfully, far enough away that he could only hear the birds chirping and the light breeze rustling the trees in the yard.

Oh, and his own nerves. He could hear those loud and clear.

A glutton for punishment, he moved closer.

"From work," she muttered over her shoulder, obviously in response to her mother's question. "He's my pilot. No, don't look at him, maybe he'll go away."

"Corrine Anne!" Her mother looked shocked and horrified. "That is no way to greet a guest!"

Now Corrine looked directly into Mike's eyes, her own gaze filled with dread, resignation. Fear. Everything he was feeling.

There! he thought. *We're in this together, baby.*

"Hello," said the man who he assumed was Corrine's father. He thrust out his hand. "Donald Atkinson."

"*Dr.* Donald Atkinson," Corrine corrected. "My father." She gestured to the petite, dark-haired woman next to her, who was watching Mike closely, brimming with curiosity. "And this is my mother. Dr. Louisa Atkinson." She smiled sweetly. "And now you can go."

This was going to require finesse. "We need to talk, Corrine."

"Actually, Mike, we don't."

"I know you're mad at me, but—"

"Not here. I'm... busy. Really busy."

"Why do you keep running?"

"Running?" She nearly gaped, then seemed to remember their audience and slammed her mouth shut. "I never run. Now go away, Mike."

"Of course he can't go away, darling," her mother said, stepping forward and reaching out a hand to Mike. "He hasn't even come inside yet."

He took her hand immediately, expecting a handshake, but found himself pulled into her warm arms for a welcoming hug. "Well," he said, at an utter loss. Held tight in her embrace, he finally settled for patting her back uncertainly. "Uh...nice to meet you, Dr. Atkinson."

"Oh, just Louisa."

"Mom." Corrine didn't look like a commander at the moment, nor the lover who'd rocked his world; she looked like a peeved daughter. "He doesn't belong here."

Louisa shot her daughter a long look. "I raised you better than that." She smiled at Mike. "We don't stand on formality here. Come in." She slipped an arm through his and led him toward the front door. "So you work with my daughter? All the things you people are doing up there in space, it just blows my mind. Did you get the solar panels to work properly? And what about that complicated computer communications system? What a shame, the troubles, this close to launch. Well, let's not think about that now, hmm? Donald, honey, get the door, will you? And Corrine, put on a pot of water, please. Now, Mike." She squeezed his hand. "Tell me all about yourself. Where are you from? I find that all of you astronauts have such fascinating backgrounds. Corrine's included," she said with a delighted little laugh.

Somehow Mike found himself up the steps, through the front door and sitting in a charming, warm, open living room with a cup of hot tea in his hands.

Corrine paced the length of the room, pausing every five seconds or so to give him a glare that he would have sworn amused her mother all the more.

It should have been awkward, showing up here unannounced and uninvited, but it felt right. And as he opened up for the first time in a long time, he decided Corrine was just going to have to get used to it.

"Oh my goodness," Louisa said, shaking her head after he'd told her a little about himself. "All those years in Russia. What a wonderful experience! I went there for a conference, several years ago now, and I found it to be one of the most beautiful yet haunting places on earth. How lucky you are, to receive that heritage from your mother."

And just that simply, Mike fell in love. He couldn't help it; he had no defenses against a mother, any mother. His had been gone for so long, and his world had always been lacking in any maternal presence or influence whatsoever. But Louisa crossed all barriers and entered his heart.

He looked up and caught Corrine's eye. She'd gone still, and now she was looking at him with something new, something he couldn't place. "What?" he asked softly, but she only shook her head.

And yet her irritation at having him there seemed to diminish. When her parents left the room, ostensibly for cookies, Mike knew it was to give them some privacy.

"You like them," Corrine said with a sigh. "I couldn't have imagined you here, holding a teacup, making nice. But here you are."

"I couldn't have imagined you here, either. But here you are."

"And here *we* are."

"Yeah." He reached out and touched her hand, wanting, needing, yearning for so much it hurt, and yet he didn't have the words. "What now, Corrine?"

"That depends."

"On?"

"On why you're here. Why are you really here, Mike?"

He opened his mouth, but as he didn't have a clear answer for that, or at least one he understood enough to explain, he closed it again.

Looking oddly deflated, she pulled back.

"What did you want me to say?" he asked in turn.

"That's just it," she whispered with a heartbreaking sigh. "I don't know, either."

12

No doubt about it, Mike's presence in her family home scared Corrine, really scared her.

He looked good here, comfortable. Confused, she took a walk. Unsatisfied, she ended up in her parents' garden, where she found her father showing off his prize roses to Mike.

Both of them were hunkered down in the dirt, their backs to her, admiring the growth of a flower.

It was a contradiction in terms, these so very masculine men surrounded by such sweet, feminine beauty, and yet that was one of the things she loved so much about her dad.

He didn't fit into a type. She stood there, rooted by a sudden realization.

That was why she liked Mike as well.

Oh, God, it was true. He was an astronaut, which meant by definition he should have been cocky, arrogant and in possession of a certain recklessness. A wild adventurer.

He *was* those things, but he was also so much more. And watching as he reached out now and touched the tip of a blooming rose with such joy, with his entire face lit up, made her heart tighten.

The reason for being one half of a couple had always

escaped Corrine, mostly because she'd never wanted to be half of anything. She'd certainly never wanted anyone able to veto her decisions, or God forbid, make them for her.

And yet her parents were a couple, a solid one, and for years they'd managed to work things out with an ease that Corrine always admired but never understood. They were both well-educated overachievers, stubborn as hell, and single-minded, so really, their success was one big mystery.

A mystery Corrine suddenly, urgently needed to solve.

SHE WAITED UNTIL dinner time, when she found both her parents together in the kitchen. Her father was chopping vegetables. Her mother was standing over him, shaking her head. "You're not cutting diagonally, dear. You need to—"

"I think I know how to cut a tomato, Louisa."

"No, obviously you don't. You have to—"

"Louisa, honey? Either let me be or order take-out."

"Take-out sounds wonderful."

"Don't you dare," Donald said, smiling when his teasing wife laughed at him.

"How do you do that?" Corrine asked, baffled by the mix of temper and affection. "How do you fight over a tomato and still love each other?"

"Forty years of practice." Her father grinned. "You going to marry Mike and learn how?"

"No!"

Louisa sighed. "Well, darn."

"Mom, I didn't invite him here."

"But he followed you." Her mother sent her a dreamy look. "He loves you, you know."

"What?"

"He's head over heels. Ga-ga. Fallen off the cliff."

Corrine felt the color drain from her face, but managed a perfectly good laugh. "You've been dipping into the cooking sherry."

"No, really. He—" At the elbow in her ribs, Louisa glared at her husband, who gave her a wordless glance. Whatever unspoken communication they'd shared, Louisa went quiet on the matter. But she did manage to get the knife from him and push him toward the door.

"I can tell when I'm not wanted," he said, kissing his wife on the cheek before he went.

"Why did you argue with him over the knife, Mom? He was just trying to help."

"Oh, I know."

"But you kicked him out."

"Kicked him out… Oh, honey." Louisa laughed. "You think I hurt his feelings. Trust me, I didn't. It's just that he always cooks, and he's worked an eighty-hour week already. The poor man is dead on his feet, but he didn't want to leave me alone to do the work. It's just a little game we play, that's all."

Corrine glanced at the swinging double doors where her father had vanished, and knew the mysteries of cohabiting were still escaping her. "A game."

"Yes." Louisa set down the knife and smiled easily. "Of love."

Mike poked his head in the kitchen. "Can I help?" He moved to the cutting board and picked up the knife Corrine's mother had just set down. "I'm good at slicing veggies," he said, following Louisa's diagonal cuts.

Corrine's mother positively beamed. "What a handy man you are." She shot Corrine a telling look, pointing at Mike's back and mouthing the words, *Loves you.*

Corrine rolled her eyes and turned away, but that lasted

no more than a second before she had to crane her neck and stare at him. He was the same person he'd always been: the same dark hair and darker eyes; the same long, leanly muscled body that made her mouth water; the same here-I-am attitude that both drew and annoyed her at the same.

So why was she looking at him in such a different light here in the house where she'd been raised?

"Louisa." Donald stuck his head back in the kitchen and waved a checkbook. "Babe, this thing is a mess. I can't figure out how much money is in here."

"Look at the bottom line, hon," Louisa said, pulling more salad makings out of the fridge.

"Which bottom line? You have three of them here."

"Oh." Louisa straightened, lettuce in one hand, a beet in the other. "Well, the first is in case the check I lost clears the bank. If I lost it *before* I wrote it, which is entirely likely, then that wouldn't be necessary. Hence the second number."

Donald sighed. "And the third?"

"Why, that's what we'll have when my automatic deposit comes in tomorrow."

"Tomorrow."

"That's right."

"But what do we have *today?*"

"I just told you, it's either—"

"Never mind!" He withdrew his head and vanished.

Louisa grinned. "Perfect."

"Why is annoying him to distraction perfect?" Corrine asked, confused beyond belief.

"I just bought his birthday present." Louisa grinned. "And if he wasn't so annoyed, he'd have found the check entry. He would talk me into giving him that present early, no doubt about it. Now he'll toss the checkbook aside and give up." She laughed. "Secret kept."

"Louisa!" Donald bellowed from the other room. "I'm going out to chop wood!"

"Good Lord," Louisa murmured. "I meant to have that nice young man down the street do that before your father tried it himself. Last year he nearly lost his fingers."

Mike set down the knife. "I'll go help him."

"Bless you," Corrine's mother said fervently, giving him a quick hug.

Corrine watched pleasure dance across Mike's face as he hugged her back, far more easily this time.

Why was he still here, damn him?

"He's a wonderful man," her mother said when he was gone. "Shame on you for keeping your feelings to yourself."

Out the kitchen window Mike reappeared, walking toward her father.

Corrine forced herself to turn away. "He's a pest."

Louisa laughed. "Okay, hon. If that's how you want to play this thing. Just tell me he's not an adventurous, intelligent, gorgeous man and I'll believe you."

"I hadn't noticed."

"Uh-huh."

"Okay, he's adventurous."

"And intelligent."

"Yes."

"And gorgeous."

"Mom, please."

"And gorgeous," Louisa repeated.

"Okay, fine." Corrine sighed. "And gorgeous."

"He's a keeper, Corrine."

A keeper. Her heart tugged. "Yeah, about that. Keepers. I don't understand something." She drew a deep breath. "You and Dad. What keeps you together? You should have killed each other by now."

"Why? Because we're two strong-minded, strong-willed people?"

"Well…yeah."

"That doesn't mean we can't make peace over such simple things as making dinner and paying the bills."

"It just seems…" Corrine once again glanced out the window. Watched Mike's muscles bunch and flex as he raised the ax over his head and brought it down, perfectly splitting a log in two.

Every hormone in her body reacted, but that was physical. Would she still want in him in forty years? "Hard," she said, no pun intended. "It seems hard."

Louisa looked shocked and more than a little annoyed. "I can't believe we didn't show you better than that, after all these years."

"You're telling me this is easy?"

"Of course not! But it's beautiful anyway, and worth all the work."

"You work at it?" she asked doubtfully. What she'd seen so far didn't seem like work so much as…good luck.

"Goodness, darling." Louisa let out a little laugh. "I think I'm insulted that you have to ask. Yes, we work hard. You can't believe such a loving relationship comes naturally."

"It does in the romance novels," Corrine muttered, taking another quick peek at Mike. He straightened and pulled off his shirt, tossing it aside before once again lifting the ax.

Oh. My. God.

Muscles. Skin shining with sweat. She purposely looked away. And this time, she wasn't going to take another sneak peek!

"Phooey," Louisa was saying. "Nothing this good comes easy. It takes compromise." She picked up the paring knife again. "Give and take. And after so many years, it just keeps getting better and better."

"It does?" What was this silly hope that sprang through Corrine at that? What did it matter if marriage was wonderful? She wasn't planning on trying.

Was she?

Oh God. She was. She was planning on exactly that. Putting a hand to her suddenly damp forehead, she sank to a chair.

"Corrine? Corrine, honey, what's the matter?" Her mother dropped the paring knife and rushed over. "You look terribly pale."

"Oh, Mom. It's…it's…"

"What? It's what?" She knelt down and gripped Corrine's knees. "Are you going to be sick? Do you need a bucket?"

"Yes, I think I do." Corrine gulped, but then managed a hysterical laugh when her mother turned to leave. Grabbing Louisa's wrist, she shook her head. "No, it's not that kind of sickness. It's my heart, you see." And she rubbed the ache that had settled there the day she'd met Mike and had never, not once in all these months, gone away.

"Oh, dear Lord. You've got heart problems? You didn't tell me! We'll get a second opinion. Your father—"

"Mom, it's…" She took a big gulp of air. "It's love. I think I'm in love with Mike. I just realized it, just now, and it's making me sick."

"Oh, darling!"

"Don't look so excited," Corrine warned, pointing a finger at the joy scrambling across her mother's face. "This is a terrible thing. I actually—" she pressed both hands to her heart now "—I actually want forever with him."

Louisa's eyes filled. "Oh, baby."

"Don't you dare cry."

Louisa sniffed and wiped a tear from her cheek. "I'm not." Then a sob escaped and she slapped a hand over her mouth. "Really, I'm not."

"Mom!"

"I can't help it," Louisa cried. "It's just that I'm so thrilled for me. He's just what I always wanted in a son-in-law."

"No! Mike can't know!"

"What? Why not?"

"Don't you see? This can't happen. It just can't. It's an impossible situation, for a million different reasons." Though all of them were crowding her head, she couldn't put words to any of them.

"Name one," her mother commanded.

"There's...well..."

Louisa cocked a brow. "Why, Corrine?"

"Yes," Mike said from the doorway, with a perfectly indescribable look on his face. "Why?"

Corrine's stomach dropped to her toes. So did her heart, and all her other vital organs.

How much had he heard?

There was no telling from the look on his face. "I—I thought you were chopping wood."

"I was. Until I got the strange feeling there was something far more interesting going on in here." He leaned back against the doorjamb, casual as you please. "I was right."

"Yes, well." Corrine leaped to her feet and became a whirlwind of activity, busying herself by straightening up an already tidy kitchen. "We were just—"

"Talking about me," he said, taking her shoulders, turning her to face him.

How had he moved so fast? Reluctantly she looked into those dark eyes, thinking *Please don't have heard me, oh please don't have heard.*

But those eyes were filled with knowing, and she swallowed hard. "You caught it all, didn't you?" she whispered. "Every word."

13

SHE LOVED HIM.

Mike hadn't imagined it, had never dared give thought to the possibility. But now his heart was racing, his entire body humming. He could think of nothing else. "Say it again," he demanded.

"I don't think so."

"Please?"

That surprised her, and he realized he hadn't often shown her his polite, gentle, tender side, not unless they were in bed.

That would change, because he intended to make her the happiest woman on earth.

"I think you should go," she said calmly, her eyes alone showing her panic.

"Nope, that wasn't what you said." He cocked his head and smiled, though he was so nervous he could hardly draw a breath. "Try again."

"No, I mean I think you should leave. Now."

He looked at Louisa, who gave a sympathetic shrug. "You have things to discuss," she said. "I'm going to give you some privacy."

"We don't need it," Corrine said quickly, but her mother only put a finger to her lips.

"Listen to him, honey. For once, slow down and listen."

Louisa left, and Corrine stood there looking cornered. When cornered, Mike knew, she came out fighting.

But fight or discuss, calm or agitated, they were doing this. "We can make it," he said softly. "We can make this work, no matter what our jobs are, no matter how different we are, no matter what. Are you getting this?" She studied her shoes. "If we try hard enough, nothing can stop us," he insisted.

"I can think of lots of things to stop us."

"Such as?" He smiled in the face of her fear, even as his heart constricted. "I know it's terrifying." Close enough to touch now, he took her hands in his. "Truth is, I've been terrified since the day I met you, and I didn't realize why until just a moment ago, when I heard you say you love me."

She made a sound of misery and fury, and tried to tug her hands free.

He held on.

She tugged again, but he was quicker and stronger. "I love you back, Corrine. I always have and I always will."

She hadn't so much as blinked. "What did you say?"

"I said I love you back." He waited while that sank in, while her eyes went from heated to glassy with shock. "I want this to work."

"Work."

"Between us. And I want forever. As in the white dress, the minivan, kids…"

"Kids."

"Or not." He shrugged. "I can go either way, unless we're talking about us. Because that's one thing I'm pretty set on, Corrine. *You.*"

"You're set."

He had to smile. "You're sounding like a parrot. Tell me this is good news. Tell me you meant what you said to your mom. That you know we can do this."

She only stared at him.

"Tell me something. *Anything.*"

"You love me."

"Yes."

"You want to get married."

"Yes. Wait, I didn't do that right at all." He dropped to one knee, then reached for her hand. "Corrine." His heart was in his throat. "You waltzed into my life and changed it forever with your incredible smile and fierce passion. You—"

"My, God. Are you...*proposing?*"

"I'm trying."

"You'd better hurry, then." A half laugh escaped her. "I don't think my legs are going to hold me."

"Did I mention your bossy ways?"

"Mike—"

"Yes," he said with a laugh, even as his throat burned. "I'm proposing. I love you, Corrine. I want to love you forever. Will you marry me?"

"If it's just passion and a smile you're attached to, I give those to you freely. You don't have to marry me for them."

"I know." He tugged her down to her knees in front of him. "But I *want* to marry you."

"I'm still ranked higher at work," she warned.

He had to laugh again. "This is not a trick. I actually *want* to wake up next to you every morning for the rest of my life."

"You've seen me first thing in the morning, right?" she asked with suspicion.

"No, actually I haven't."

"This is not a joke."

"Nope, it's not. The answer is yes or no."

"How can it be that easy?" she cried. "My God, you're looking at me with a straight face proposing m-m—"

"Marriage. The word is *marriage*."

"We have no business doing this."

He cupped her face, waited until her wild eyes settled on his. "Do you love me?"

"This is ridiculous."

"Do you?"

Her hands came up to cover his. "Yes," she said simply. "It's crazy, but I do. I love you, Mike."

"Then everything else is a piece of cake," he said, the fist around his heart loosening for the first time since he'd met her. He could have flown to Mars without a spacecraft. "Be my commander, be my lover, my best friend, my spouse. Be my life, Corrine."

"For better, for worse, and maybe lots of worse?"

"Bring it on. All of it. Marry me."

"I will, Mike. Yes, I will."

Epilogue

One Year Later

"THE SPACE SHUTTLE LANDED without a hitch today," the television anchor announced. "Thanks to the hard and amazing work of a select few, we're one step closer to completing the International Space Station."

Corrine sighed with pleasure, both because the mission had been successful, and because her husband had come up behind her, slipped his big hands around her and was rubbing her stomach.

"Nice?" he murmured, dipping down to kiss her neck.

"Any nicer and you'll send me into labor." His hands stroked her nine-month-pregnant belly until she wanted to melt with bliss. "Just saw the news," she told him. "They're back. The landing was perfect."

"Not as perfect as ours last year."

"I know." She sighed again, remembering just how wonderfully successful their own mission had been. "I'm ready to go back up."

Mike laughed and turned her in his arms. "Can you wait until you give birth, do you think?"

"What do you think he'll be when he grows up?" she

wondered, feeling the baby within her kick with the velocity of a rocket.

"*She'll* be anything she wants, though I imagine stubborn as hell, poor baby. Just like her mommy."

"I'm not stubborn."

"Uh-huh. And I'm not the luckiest man on the planet."

"You're the luckiest man on the planet?"

He smiled that just-for-her smile he had, the one that made her feel like the most special, precious woman alive. Even after all this time, her heart went pitter-patter. Her mother had been right, as always. Love was worth the work.

"What?" he asked with a little smile, his thumb gliding over her lower lip, his eyes full of so much warmth and love her throat tightened.

Her stomach contracted.

It wasn't the first contraction, or the second, and she knew the time had come. "I love you, Mike."

"You say that as though you just realized it," he said with a little laugh.

"No." She hid her wince as the contraction stole her breath. "I've always known," she managed to say, watching his eyes mist. "Oh, and Mike?" Unable to keep it in, she gasped as the contraction ended. "It's time."

"Baby, we can't. You're too far along for lovemaking now."

"No, I mean it's *time*."

He blinked, then his jaw dropped. "Oh my God."

The look of pure terror on his face made her laugh in spite of her pain. "You've flown every aircraft known to man. You've traveled off this planet. And yet the thought of having a baby terrifies you?"

He scooped her up into his arms. "Sit down," he demanded.

"I already am," she said, as he paced the room with her.

"We need to get organized!"

"We are." She pointed to the packed bag by their front door.

"We need a doctor!"

"Maybe," she conceded, pulling him down for a quick kiss. "But honestly, Mike, everything I need, or will need, is right here. He's holding me."

"God, Corrine." He rubbed his cheek to hers. "You've given me everything I could ever need, too."

And five hours later, she gave him even more. A beautiful baby girl with dark, dark eyes and wild hair and a fierce, demanding cry that reminded him of his amazing, accomplished, beautiful wife.

* * * * *